THE TWO DESTINIES

WILKIE COLLINS

THE TWO DESTINIES

SUTTON PUBLISHING

First published in 1876

First published in this edition in the United Kingdom in 1995 by
Alan Sutton Publishing Limited, an imprint of Sutton Publishing Limited
Phoenix Mill · Thrupp · Stroud · Gloucestershire · GL5 2BU

Reprinted 1998

British Library Cataloguing in Publication Data

A catalogue record for this book is available from the British Library

ISBN 0 7509 1046 1

Cover picture: detail from The Windmiller's Guest, 1898 *by Frederic Leighton (photograph Fine Art Photographic Library Ltd)*

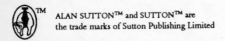

Typeset in 10/11 Bembo.
Typesetting and origination by
Sutton Publishing Limited.
Printed in Great Britain by
The Guernsey Press Company Limted,
Guernsey, Channel Islands.

CONTENTS

BIOGRAPHICAL INTRODUCTION

WILLIAM WILKIE COLLINS was born in Marylebone on 8 January 1824. He died sixty-five years later in Wimpole Street, little more than three blocks away, and lived most of his life in that central part of London. Yet from that narrow base he managed to live as colourful a life as any other Victorian and wrote some of the most gripping novels of the nineteenth century. He is still regarded as 'the father of the detective story' and 'the novelist who invented sensation'. He himself put it more modestly. He was, he said, just a simple story teller.

Such stories, however, included *The Moonstone* and *The Woman in White*. His first published novel, *Antonina*, appeared in 1851, and his last, *Blind Love*, had to be finished by an old friend, Walter Besant, in 1889. In the intervening years Collins wrote over thirty novels and collections of stories, as well as a biography of his father William Collins. The manuscript of the first novel he actually wrote, though it was turned down by every publisher he approached and vanished for nearly 150 years, finally surfaced in New York in 1990. Entitled *Iolani; Or Tahiti as it Was*, its somewhat belated publication is now planned. Collins himself was remarkably frank about that early failure. 'My youthful imagination ran riot among the noble savages, in scenes which caused the respectable British publisher [actually Chapman and Hall] to declare that it was impossible to put his name on the title page of such a novel'.

It was during the writing of that first, unsuccessful, novel that Collins' parents first became fully aware that all their assumptions about 'Willy's future' (as he was known in the family) were quite wrong. His father, William Collins, already an RA, with a string of wealthy clients, including the late George IV, was a leading landscape artist and had readily assumed that both sons (Charles Allston Collins was two years younger than Wilkie) would also take up painting. William's own father, another William, was a picture dealer and Harriet, Wilkie Collins' mother, came from a family of painters. Both Constable and Linnell were close friends of the family as the boys grew up in Hampstead, and sketching became second nature to them both.

Yet it was the written word and a good story well told that tugged at Wilkie Collins. He later described how at his second school at Highbury, where he was a boarder, he was regularly bullied at night by the head boy.

'You will go to sleep, Collins', he was apparently told, 'when you have told me a story'. Quite an incentive. 'It was this brute who first awakened in me, his poor little victim, a power of which but for him I might never have been aware. . . . When I left school I continued story telling for my own pleasure'.

The occasions when he could do so were varied indeed. His school days were remarkably interrupted by his father's decision to take the family to Italy for two years, an extended visit that gave Collins not only visual stimuli but provided the background for what would be his first published novel, *Antonina*. It was also in Italy that, according to Dickens, Collins experienced his 'first love adventure'. As Dickens explained the affair to his sister-in-law later, it 'had proceeded, if I may be allowed the expression, to the utmost extremities'. Collins was thirteen at the time. Perhaps more important, for his writing if not his character, it was probably in Italy that his attraction to the visual began to seek an alternative outlet to painting, and where the embryo writer began to emerge from the family of artists.

When, a few years later, his father was considering whether Wilkie should be entered at art school, prior to applying to the Royal Academy, it was already clear that his interests lay elsewhere. One idea was that he should go to Oxford, before entering the Church. But William was eventually persuaded that a spell in a tea merchant's office would at least provide Wilkie with a more secure income than the desultory writing that seemed to attract him. It did not last, though since the office in the Strand was near all the publishers it at least allowed him to trail round them with his articles in spare moments. He had his first short story, *The Last Stage Coachman*, published under his name in *The Illuminated Magazine* at this time. His father's next initiative was to arrange for Wilkie to enter Lincoln's Inn and to read for the Bar, again on the assumption that it might provide a better source of income than writing. It was to be one of William's last family concerns, for he died the following year, in 1847.

Collins managed to sustain his legal studies, or at least his necessary attendances, sufficiently over the next few years to be finally called to the Bar in 1851. It may not have been a particularly attractive calling, in his eyes, but it was later to serve its purpose. Eight of his novels have lawyers as prominent characters and the drawing up of wills was crucial to several of his later plots, including *The Woman in White*. When his father died, Collins, though still ostensibly studying for the Bar, had reached the third chapter of the second volume of *Antonina*, and had already read the bulk of the first volume to his father. Thereafter he immediately laid the novel aside and took up the preparations for a memoir of his father. It was thus a biographical work, *The Life of William Collins*, and not a novel that in

1848 became his first published work and established his name in the publishing world.

With the death of William Collins his family, though saddened by his suffering, were soon showing a new kind of independence. His love for them had never been in doubt, but William had early acquired a streak of moral rectitude which over the years irritated his friends and restricted his family. Wilkie had probably felt the heavy hand more than his brother Charles, but had chosen to ride the storms when they occurred, while pursuing his personal inclinations as best he could. Once the memoirs were completed, Harriet and her two sons settled down in an imposing house overlooking Regents Park, where she was happy to play host to her sons' younger friends from the artistic and literary worlds. It was here that Wilkie came under the wing of Charles Dickens and his brother befriended John Millais, William Holman-Hunt and other Pre-Raphaelites.

It was in this period that Wilkie Collins extended the range of his writing, providing leading articles for *The Leader*, short stories and essays for *Bentley's Miscellany*, a travel book about Cornwall entitled *Rambles Beyond Railways*, as well as dramatic criticisms and a short play. Charles Dickens had already enticed him to participate in the private theatricals he was developing and within eighteen months Wilkie had performed, in a small part, at a Dickens-directed charity performance in the presence of Queen Victoria. It was a short step from this to a joint production of Wilkie's first play, *The Lighthouse,* and a later commercial production at the Olympic Theatre. Soon they were co-operating on Dickens' journal *Household Words* and, with Wilkie in the lead, nicely egged on by Dickens, sharing colourful entertainments and distractions together in London and Paris.

It was a time when Collins began to write the kind of novels that were always to be identified with him, combining well-constructed plots with strong characters, beginning with *Basil* in the early fifties, followed by *Hide and Seek*, *After Dark* (short stories) and *The Dead Secret*, and culminating in *The Woman in White* in 1860. It was also the time when he met the two women – Caroline Graves and Martha Rudd – who were to weave in and out of his life for the next thirty years.

Caroline Graves appeared first, dramatically if Collins himself is to be believed, in much the same way as the mysterious lady in St John's Wood at the outset of *The Woman in White*. The story goes that the woman in distress gave a piercing scream one moonlit night as Wilkie and his brother were accompanying John Millais back to his lodgings. Millais simply exclaimed 'What a lovely woman'. Wilkie followed her into the darkness and later told them that she was a lady of good birth who had fallen into the clutches of a man who was threatening her life.

An element of truth perhaps, but it was tinged with Collins' undoubted storytelling ability. We now know that Caroline came from a humble family in the west country, had been married young, had a child and had been left a widow. It was not long before Collins was sharing lodgings with her, even answering letters openly from the various addresses they occupied in and around Marylebone. He even put her down as his wife, quite inaccurately, in the Census of 1861. He shared his triumphs with her, from *The Woman in White* onwards, but in spite of her obvious wishes, he was determined not to marry her.

These were the years of Collins' best-known novels. *The Woman in White* was followed by *Armadale* (for which he received the then record sum of £5,000 before a word had been written), *No Name* and *The Moonstone*. It was the preparation of *Armadale* and the writing of *The Moonstone*, however, that were to produce such dramatic upheavals in his private life and, to some extent, account for what many critics have detected as a relative falling off in his narrative power as a novelist.

His search for background for *Armadale* took him to the Norfolk Broads and to the small coastal village of Winterton. There, or nearby, he met Martha Rudd, the nineteen-year-old daughter of a large, though poor, family. Her parents and relations have been traced (their graves are still in the local churchyard), but the timing of Martha's move to be closer to Collins in London remains obscure. What we do know is that only a few years later, when Collins was writing instalments of *The Moonstone*, already laid low by an acute attack of rheumatic gout and grieving over the death of his mother, Caroline decided to leave him and to marry a much younger man. Dickens felt that she had tried to bluff Collins into marriage and had failed. It could also have been Martha's appearance in London that proved to be the last straw.

Collins was devastated and finished *The Moonstone* in a haze of pain and with increasing doses of laudanum. It was a habit he was to follow for the rest of his life, his intake of opium eventually reaching remarkable levels, with inevitable repercussions on his writing ability. The domestic drama, however, was not yet over. Within nine months of Caroline's marriage, Martha, living in lodgings in Bolsover Street, was to bear Collins his first child and within another two years Caroline had left her husband and returned to Collins in Gloucester Place and Martha was pregnant with his second child.

And so it continued for the rest of his life, with Caroline once more established in Gloucester Place, though probably as housekeeper and hostess rather than mistress, and Martha and his 'morganatic' family (eventually two girls and a boy: Marian, Harriet and William Charles) not far away. When he visited Martha he became William Dawson, Barrister-at-Law, and she was known as Mrs Dawson. His male friends readily accepted these arrangements, though their wives were rarely, if ever, invited to Gloucester Place or, later, Wimpole Street.

His two families, basically Caroline's grandchildren and Martha's children, happily mingled together on holiday in Ramsgate and even occasionally in Gloucester Place, but Martha and Caroline never met. It was against this domestic background, with a host of literary and theatrical friends, that he pursued the last decade and a half of his life, completing some of his more socially conscious novels, such as *Heart and Science*, as well as his more recognizable suspense novels, like *Poor Miss Finch, The Haunted Hotel, The New Magdalen, The Black Robe*, and *Jezebel's Daughter*.

He died in Wimpole Street in September 1889, and was buried at Kensal Green Cemetery. Caroline was eventually buried with him and Martha continued to tend the grave until she left London. She died in Southend in 1919. The gold locket Wilkie gave Martha in 1868, marking the death of his mother, is still in the possession of my wife, Faith, their great-granddaughter.

WILLIAM M. CLARKE

Further Reading

Ashley, R., *Wilkie Collins*, London, 1952.
Clarke, William M., *The Secret Life of Wilkie Collins*, London, 1988.
Peters, Catherine, *The King of Inventors: A Life of Wilkie Collins*, London, 1991.
Robinson, Kenneth, *Wilkie Collins*, London, 1951 & 1974.

THE PRELUDE

IN TWO NARRATIVES

I. THE GUEST WRITES THE HISTORY OF THE DINNER-PARTY

Many years have passed since my wife and I left the United States to pay our first visit to England.

We were provided with letters of introduction, as a matter of course. Among them there was a letter which had been written for us by my wife's brother. It presented us to an English gentleman who held a high rank on the list of his friends.

'You will become acquainted with Mr George Germaine,' my brother-in-law said when we took leave of him, 'at a very interesting period of his life. My last news of him tells me that he is just married. I know nothing of the lady, or of the circumstances under which my friend first met with her. But of this I am certain: married or single, George Germaine will give you and your wife a hearty welcome to England, for my sake.'

The day after our arrival in London, we left our letter of introduction at the house of Mr Germaine.

The next morning we went to see a favourite object of American interest, in the metropolis of England – the Tower of London. The citizens of the United States find this relic of the good old times of great use in raising their national estimate of the value of Republican Institutions. On getting back to the hotel, the cards of Mr and Mrs Germaine told us that they had already returned our visit. The same evening we received an invitation to dine with the newly-married couple. It was enclosed in a little note from Mrs Germaine to my wife, warning us that we were not to expect to meet a large party. 'It is the first dinner we give, on our return from our wedding-tour' (the lady wrote); 'and you will only be introduced to a few of my husband's old friends.'

In America, and (as I hear) on the continent of Europe also, when your host invites you to dine at a given hour, you pay him the compliment of arriving punctually at his house. In England alone, the incomprehensible and discourteous custom prevails of keeping the host and the dinner

1

waiting for half an hour or more – without any assignable reason, and without any better excuse than the purely formal apology that is implied in the words, 'Sorry to be late.'

Arriving at the appointed time at the house of Mr and Mrs Germaine, we had every reason to congratulate ourselves on the ignorant punctuality which had brought us into the drawing-room half an hour in advance of the other guests.

In the first place, there was so much heartiness, and so little ceremony, in the welcome accorded to us that we almost fancied ourselves back in our own country. In the second place, both husband and wife interested us, the moment we set eyes on them. The lady, especially, although she was not, strictly speaking, a beautiful woman, quite fascinated us. There was an artless charm in her face and manner, a simple grace in all her movements, a low delicious melody in her voice, which we Americans felt to be simply irresistible. And then, it was so plain (and so pleasant) to see that here at least was a happy marriage! Here were two people who had all their dearest hopes, wishes and sympathies in common – who looked, if I may risk the expression, born to be man and wife. By the time when the fashionable delay of the half-hour had expired, we were talking together as familiarly and as confidentially as if we had been, all four of us, old friends.

Eight o'clock struck; and the first of the English guests appeared.

Having forgotten this gentleman's name, I must beg leave to distinguish him by a letter of the alphabet. Let me call him Mr A. When he entered the room alone, our host and hostess both started, and both looked surprised. Apparently, they expected him to be accompanied by some other person. Mr Germaine put a curious question to his friend.

'Where is your wife?' he asked.

Mr A. answered for the absent lady by a neat little apology, expressed in these words:

'She has got a bad cold. She is very sorry. She begs me to make her excuses.'

He had just time to deliver his message before another unaccompanied gentleman appeared. Reverting to the letters of the alphabet, let me call him Mr B. Once more I noticed that our host and hostess started when they saw him enter the room, alone. And, rather to my surprise, I heard Mr Germaine put his curious question again to the new guest.

'Where is your wife?'

The answer – with slight variations – was Mr A.'s neat little apology, repeated by Mr B.

'I am sorry. Mrs B. has got a bad headache. She is subject to bad headaches. She begs me to make her excuses.'

Mr and Mrs Germaine glanced at one another. The husband's face plainly expressed the suspicion which this second apology had roused in his mind. The wife was steady and calm. An interval passed – a silent interval. Mr A. and Mr B. retired together guiltily into a corner. My wife and I looked at the pictures.

Mrs Germaine was the first to relieve us from our own intolerable silence. Two more guests, it appeared, were still wanting to complete the party.

'Shall we have dinner at once, George?' she said to her husband. 'Or shall we wait for Mr and Mrs C.?'

'We will wait five minutes,' he answered shortly – with his eye on Mr A. and Mr B., guiltily secluded in their corner.

The drawing-room door opened. We all knew that a third married lady was expected; we all looked towards the door in unutterable anticipation. Our unexpressed hopes rested silently on the possible appearance of Mrs C. Would that admirable, but unknown woman at once charm and relieve us by her presence? I shudder as I write it. Mr C. walked into the room – and walked in, *alone*.

Mr Germaine suddenly varied his formal enquiry, in receiving the new guest.

'Is your wife ill?' he asked.

Mr C. was an elderly man; Mr C. had lived (judging by appearances) in the days when the old-fashioned laws of politeness were still in force. He discovered his two married brethren in their corner, unaccompanied by *their* wives; and he delivered his apology for *his* wife, with the air of a man who felt unaffectedly ashamed of it.

'Mrs C. is so sorry. She has got such a bad cold. She does so regret not being able to accompany me.'

At this third apology Mr Germaine's indignation forced its way outwards into expression in words.

'Two bad colds, and one bad headache,' he said, with ironical politeness. 'I don't know how your wives agree, gentlemen, when they are well. But, when they are ill, their unanimity is wonderful!'

The dinner was announced as that sharp saying passed his lips.

I had the honour of taking Mrs Germaine to the dining-room. Her sense of the implied insult offered to her by the wives of her husband's friends only showed itself in a trembling, a very slight trembling, of the hand that rested on my arm. My interest in her increased tenfold. Only a woman who had been accustomed to suffer, who had been broken and disciplined to self-restraint, could have endured the moral martyrdom inflicted on her as *this* woman endured it, from the beginning of the evening to the end.

Am I using the language of exaggeration, when I write of my hostess in these terms? Look at the circumstances, as they struck two strangers like my wife and myself.

Here was the first dinner-party which Mr and Mrs Germaine had given since their marriage. Three of Mr Germaine's friends, all married men, had been invited with their wives, to meet Mr Germaine's wife, and had (evidently) accepted the invitation without reserve. What discoveries had taken place, between the giving of the invitation and the giving of the dinner, it was impossible to say. The one thing plainly discernible was that, in the interval, the three wives had agreed in the resolution to leave their husbands to represent them at Mrs Germaine's table; and, more amazing still, the husbands had so far approved of the grossly discourteous conduct of the wives, as to consent to make the most insultingly trivial excuses for their absence. Could any crueller slur than this have been cast on a woman, at the outset of her married life, before the face of her husband, and in the presence of two strangers from another country? Is 'martyrdom' too big a word to use in describing what a sensitive person must have suffered, subjected to such treatment as this? Well, I think not.

We took our places at the dinner-table. Don't ask me to describe that most miserable of mortal meetings, that weariest and dreariest of human festivals. It is quite bad enough to remember that evening – it is indeed!

My wife and I did our best to keep the conversation moving as easily and as harmlessly as might be. I may say that we really worked hard. Nevertheless, our success was not very encouraging. Try as we might to overlook them, there were the three empty places of the three absent women, speaking in their own dismal language for themselves. Try as we might to resist it, we all felt the one sad conclusion which those empty places persisted in forcing on our minds. It was surely too plain that some terrible report, affecting the character of the unhappy woman at the head of the table, had unexpectedly come to light, and had at one blow destroyed her position in the estimation of her husband's friends. In the face of the excuses in the drawing-room, in the face of the empty places at the dinner-table, what could the friendliest guests do, to any good purpose, to help the husband and wife in their sore and sudden need? They could say good-night at the earliest possible opportunity, and mercifully leave the married pair to themselves.

Let it at least be recorded to the credit of the three gentlemen designated in these pages as A., B. and C., that they were sufficiently ashamed of themselves and their wives to be the first members of the dinner-party who left the house. In a few minutes more, we rose to follow their example. Mrs Germaine earnestly requested that we would delay our departure.

'Wait a few minutes,' she whispered, with a glance to her husband. 'I have something to say to you before you go.'

She left us; and, taking Mr Germaine by the arm, led him away to the opposite side of the room. The two held a little colloquy together in low voices. The husband closed the consultation by lifting his wife's hand to his lips.

'Do as you please, my love,' he said to her. 'I leave it entirely to you.'

He sat down sorrowfully, lost in his thoughts. Mrs Germaine unlocked a cabinet at the farther end of the room, and returned to us alone, carrying a small portfolio in her hand.

'No words of mine can tell how gratefully I feel your kindness,' she said, with perfect simplicity and with perfect dignity at the same time. 'Under very trying circumstances, you have treated me with the tenderness and the sympathy which you might have shown to an old friend. The one return I can make for all that I owe you, is to admit you to my fullest confidence, and leave you to judge for yourselves whether I deserve the treatment which I have received to-night.'

Her eyes filled with tears. She paused to control herself. We both begged her to say no more. Her husband, joining us, added his entreaties to ours. She thanked us, but she persisted. Like most sensitively-organised persons, she could be resolute when she believed that the occasion called for it.

'I have a few words more to say,' she resumed, addressing my wife. 'You are the only married woman who has come to our little dinner-party. The marked absence of the other wives explains itself. It is not for me to say whether they are right or wrong in refusing to sit at our table. My dear husband – who knows my whole life as well as I know it myself – expressed the wish that we should invite these ladies. He wrongly supposed that *his* estimate of me would be the estimate accepted by his friends; and neither he nor I anticipated that the misfortunes of my past life would be revealed by some person acquainted with them, whose treachery we have yet to discover. The least I can do, by way of acknowledging your kindness, is to place you in the same position towards me which the other ladies now occupy. The circumstances under which I have become the wife of Mr Germaine are, in some respects, very remarkable. They are related, without suppression or reserve, in a little narrative which my husband wrote, at the time of our marriage, for the satisfaction of one of his old friends whose good opinion he was unwilling to forfeit. The manuscript is in this portfolio. After what has happened, I ask you to read it as a personal favour to me. It is for you to decide, when you know all, whether I am a fit person for an honest woman to associate with, or not.'

She held out her hand with a sweet sad smile, and bade us good-night. My wife, in her impulsive way, forgot the formalities proper to the occasion, and kissed her at parting. At that one little act of sisterly sympathy, the fortitude which the poor creature had preserved all through the evening gave way in an instant. She burst into tears.

I felt as fond of her and as sorry for her as my wife. But (unfortunately) I could not take my wife's privilege of kissing her. On our way down stairs, I found the opportunity of saying a cheering word to her husband as he accompanied us to the door.

'Before I open this,' I remarked, pointing to the portfolio under my arm, 'my mind is made up, sir, about one thing. If I wasn't married already, I tell you this – I should envy you your wife.'

He pointed to the portfolio, in his turn.

'Read what I have written there,' he said; 'and you will understand what those false friends of mine have made me suffer to-night.'

The next morning my wife and I opened the portfolio. It contained two manuscripts, which we here present in their order as we read them.

II. GEORGE GERMAINE WRITES THE HISTORY OF HIS FIRST LOVE

I

Look back, my memory, through the dim labyrinth of the past, through the mingling joys and sorrows of twenty years. Rise again, my boyhood's days by the winding green shores of the little lake. Come to me once more, my child-love, in the innocent beauty of your first ten years of life. Let us live again, my angel, as we lived in our first Paradise, before sin and sorrow lifted their flaming swords, and drove us out into the world.

The month was March. The last wildfowl of the season were floating on the waters of the lake which, in our Suffolk tongue, we called Greenwater Broad.

Wind where it might, the grassy banks and the overhanging trees tinged the lake with the soft green reflections from which it took its name. In a creek at the south end the boats were kept – my own pretty sailing-boat having a tiny natural harbour all to itself. In a creek at the north end stood the great trap (called a 'Decoy'), used for snaring the wild-fowl who flocked every winter, by thousands and thousands, to Greenwater Broad.

My little Mary and I went out together, hand in hand, to see the last birds of the season lured into the Decoy.

The outer part of the strange bird-trap rose from the waters of the lake in a series of circular arches, formed of elastic branches bent to the needed shape, and covered with folds of fine network making the roof. Little by little diminishing in size, the arches and their network followed the secret windings of the creek inland to its end. Built back round the arches, on their landward side, ran a wooden paling, high enough to hide a man kneeling behind it from the view of the birds on the lake. At certain intervals, a hole was broken in the paling, just large enough to allow of the passage through it of a dog of the terrier or the spaniel breed. And there began and ended the simple yet sufficient mechanism of the Decoy.

In those days, I was thirteen, and Mary was ten years old. Walking our way to the lake, we had Mary's father with us, for guide and companion. The good man served as bailiff on my father's estate. He was, besides, a skilled master in the art of decoying ducks. The dog who helped him (we used no tame ducks as decoys in Suffolk) was a little black terrier: a skilled master also in his way; a creature who possessed, in equal proportions, the enviable advantages of perfect good-humour and perfect commonsense.

The dog followed the bailiff, and we followed the dog.

Arrived at the paling which surrounded the Decoy, the dog sat down to wait until he was wanted. The bailiff and the children crouched behind the paling, and peeped through the outermost doghole, which commanded a full view of the lake. It was a day without wind; not a ripple stirred the surface of the water; the soft grey clouds filled all the sky, and hid the sun from view.

We peeped through the hole in the paling. There were the wild ducks – collected within easy reach of the Decoy – placidly dressing their features on the placid surface of the lake.

The bailiff looked at the dog, and made a sign. The dog looked at the bailiff, and, stepping forward quietly, passed through the hole, so as to show himself on the narrow strip of ground shelving down from the outer side of the paling to the lake.

First one duck, then another, then half a dozen together, discovered the dog.

A new object showing itself on the solitary scene, instantly became an object of all-devouring curiosity to the ducks. The outermost of them began to swim slowly towards the strange four-footed creature, planted motionless on the bank. By twos and threes the main body of the waterfowl gradually followed the advanced guard. Swimming nearer and nearer to the dog, the wary ducks suddenly came to a halt, and, poised on the water, viewed from a safe distance the phenomenon on the land.

The bailiff, kneeling behind the paling, whispered, 'Trim!'

Hearing his name, the terrier turned about, and retiring through the hole, became lost to the view of the ducks. Motionless on the water, the wildfowl wondered and waited. In a minute more, the dog had trotted round, and had shown himself through the next hole in the paling;

pierced farther inward, where the lake ran up into the outermost of the windings of the creek.

The second appearance of the terrier instantly produced a second fit of curiosity among the ducks. With one accord, they swam forward again, to get another and a nearer view of the dog; then, judging their safe distance once more, they stopped for the second time, under the outermost arch of the Decoy. Again, the dog vanished, and the puzzled ducks waited. An interval passed – and the third appearance of Trim took place, through a third hole in the paling, pierced farther inland, up the creek. For the third time, irresistible curiosity urged the ducks to advance, farther and farther inward under the fatal arches of the Decoy. A fourth and a fifth time the game went on, until the dog had lured the waterfowl, from point to point, into the inner recesses of the Decoy. There, a last appearance of Trim took place. A last advance, a last cautious pause was made by the ducks. The bailiff touched the strings. The weighted network fell vertically into the water, and closed the Decoy. There, by dozens on dozens, were the ducks, caught by means of their own curiosity – with nothing but a little dog for a bait! In a few hours afterwards, they were all dead ducks, on their way to the London market.

As the last act in the curious comedy of the Decoy came to its end, little Mary laid her hand on my shoulder, and, raising herself on tiptoe, whispered in my ear:

'George! come home with me. I have got something to show you that is better worth seeing than the ducks.'

'What is it?'

'It's a surprise. I won't tell you.'

'Will you give me a kiss?'

The charming little creature put her slim sunburnt arms round my neck, and answered:

'As many kisses as you like, George.'

It was innocently said on her side. It was innocently done on mine. The good easy bailiff, looking aside at the moment from his ducks, discovered us pursuing our boy and girl courtship in each other's arms. He shook his big forefinger at us, with something of a sad and doubting smile.

'Ah, master George! master George!' he said. 'When your father comes home, do you think he will approve of his son and heir kissing his bailiff's daughter?'

'When my father comes home,' I answered with great dignity, 'I shall tell him the truth. I shall say I am going to marry your daughter.'

The bailiff burst out laughing, and looked back again at his ducks.

'Well! well!' we heard him say to himself. 'They're only children. There's no call, poor things, to part them yet awhile.'

Mary and I had a great dislike to be called children. Properly understood, one of us was a lady aged ten, and the other was a gentleman aged thirteen. We left the good bailiff indignantly, and went away together, hand in hand, to the cottage.

II

'He is growing too fast,' said the doctor to my mother; 'and he is getting a great deal too clever for a boy at his age. Remove him from school, ma'am, for six months; let him run about in the open air at home; and, if you find him with a book in his hand, take it away directly. There is my prescription!'

Those words decided my fate in life.

In obedience to the doctor's advice, I was left, an idle boy – without brothers, sisters, or companions of my own age – to roam about the grounds of our lonely country house. The bailiff's daughter, like me, was an only child; and, like me, she had no playfellows. We met in our wanderings on the solitary shores of the lake. Beginning by being inseparable companions, we ripened and developed into true lovers. Our preliminary courtship concluded, we next proposed (before I returned to school) to burst into complete maturity by becoming man and wife.

I am not writing in jest. Absurd as it may appear to 'sensible people,' we two children were lovers – if ever there were lovers yet.

We had no pleasures apart from the one all-sufficient pleasure which we found in each other's society. We objected to the night, because it parted us. We entreated our parents, on either side, to let us sleep in the same room. I was angry with my mother, and Mary was disappointed in her father, when they laughed at us, and wondered what we should want next. Looking onward, from those days to the days of my manhood, I can vividly recall such hours of happiness as have fallen to my share. But I remember no delights of that later time comparable to the exquisite and enduring pleasure that filled my young being when I walked with Mary in the woods; when I sailed with Mary in my boat on the lake; when I met Mary, after the cruel separation of the night, and flew into her open arms as if we had been parted for months and months together.

What was the attraction that drew us so closely one to the other, at an age when the sexual sympathies lay dormant in her and in me?

We neither knew nor sought to know. We obeyed the impulse to love one another as a bird obeys the impulse to fly.

Let it not be supposed that we possessed any natural gifts or advantages which singled us out as differing in a marked way from other children at our time of life. We possessed nothing of the sort. I had been called a clever boy at school; but there were thousands of other boys at thousands of other schools, who headed their classes and won their prizes like me. Personally speaking, I was in no way remarkable – except for being, in the ordinary phrase, 'tall for my age.' On her side, Mary displayed no striking attractions. She was a fragile child, with mild grey eyes and a pale complexion; singularly undemonstrative, singularly shy and silent, except when she was alone with me. Such beauty as she had, in those early days, lay in a certain artless purity and tenderness of expression, and in the charming reddish-brown colour of her hair, varying quaintly and prettily in different lights. To all outward appearance two perfectly commonplace children, we were mysteriously united by some kindred association of the spirit in her and the spirit in me, which not only defied discovery by our young selves, but which lay too deep for investigation by far older and far wiser heads than ours.

You will naturally wonder whether anything was done by our elders to check our precocious attachment, while it was still an innocent love-union between a boy and a girl.

Nothing was done by my father – for the simple reason that he was away from home.

He was a man of a restless and speculative turn of mind. Inheriting his estate burdened with debt, his grand ambition was to increase his small available income by his own exertions; to set up an establishment in London; and to climb to political distinction by the ladder of Parliament. An old friend who had emigrated to America had proposed to him a speculation in agriculture in one of the Western States, which was to make both their fortunes. My father's eccentric fancy was struck by the idea. For more than a year past he had been away from us in the United States; and all we knew of him (instructed by his letters) was, that he might be shortly expected to return to us in the enviable character of one of the richest men in England.

As for my poor mother – the sweetest and softest-hearted of women – to see me happy was all she desired.

The quaint little love-romance of the two children amused and interested her. She jested with Mary's father about the coming union between the two families, without one serious thought of the future – without even a foreboding of what might happen when my father returned. 'Sufficient for the day is the evil (or the good) thereof,' had been my mother's motto all her life. She agreed with the easy philosophy of the bailiff, already recorded in these pages: 'They're only children; there's no call, poor things, to part them yet awhile!'

There was one member of the family, however, who took a sensible and serious view of the matter.

My father's brother paid us a visit in our solitude – discovered what was going on between Mary and me – and was at first, naturally enough, inclined to laugh at us. Closer investigation altered his way of thinking. He became convinced that my mother was acting like a fool; that the bailiff (a faithful servant, if ever there was one yet) was cunningly advancing his own interests by means of his daughter; and that I was a young idiot, who had developed his native reserves of imbecility at an unusually early period of life. Speaking to my mother, under the influence of these strong impressions, my uncle offered to take me back with him to London, and keep me there until I had been brought to my senses by association with his own children, and by careful superintendence under his own roof.

My mother hesitated about accepting this proposal; she had the advantage over my uncle of understanding my disposition. While she was still doubting, while my uncle was still impatiently waiting for her decision, I settled the question for my elders by running away.

I left a letter to represent me in my absence; declaring that no mortal power should part me from Mary, and promising to return and ask my mother's pardon as soon as my uncle had left the house. The strictest search was made for me, without discovering a trace of my place of refuge. My uncle departed for London; predicting that I should live to be a disgrace to the family, and announcing that he should transmit his opinion of me to my father in America, by the next mail.

The secret of the hiding-place in which I contrived to defy discovery is soon told.

I was hidden (without the bailiff's knowledge) in the bedroom of the bailiff's mother. And did the bailiff's mother know it? you will ask. To which I answer: the bailiff's mother did it. And what is more, gloried in doing it – not, observe, as an act of hostility to my relatives, but simply as a duty that lay on her conscience.

What sort of old woman, in the name of all that is wonderful, was this? Let her appear and speak for herself – the wild and weird grandmother of gentle little Mary; the Sibyl of modern times, known far and wide, in our part of Suffolk, as Dame Dermody.

I see her again, as I write, sitting in her son's pretty cottage parlour, hard by the window, so that the light fell over her shoulder while she knitted or read. A little lean wiry old woman was Dame Dermody – with fierce black eyes, surmounted by bushy white eyebrows, by a high wrinkled forehead and by thick white hair gathered neatly under her old-fashioned 'mob-cap.' Report whispered (and whispered truly) that she had been a lady by birth and breeding, and that she had deliberately closed her prospects in life by marrying a man greatly her inferior in social rank. Whatever her family might think of the marriage, she herself never regretted it. In her estimation, her husband's memory was a sacred memory; his spirit was a guardian spirit watching over her, waking or sleeping, morning or night.

Holding this faith, she was in no respect influenced by those grossly material ideas of modern growth, which associate the presence of spiritual beings with clumsy conjuring tricks and monkey-antics performed on tables and chairs. Dame Dermody's nobler superstition formed an integral part of her religious convictions – convictions which had long since found their chosen resting-place in the mystic doctrines of Emanuel Swedenborg. The only books which she read were the works of the Swedish Seer. She mixed up Swedenborg's teachings on angels and departed spirits, on love to one's neighbour and purity of life, with wild fancies and kindred beliefs of her own, and preached the visionary religious doctrines thus derived – not only in the bailiff's household, but also on proselytising expeditions to the households of her humble neighbours, far and near.

Under her son's roof – after the death of his wife – she reigned a supreme power; priding herself alike on her close attention to her domestic duties, and on her privileged communications with angels and spirits. She would hold her long colloquies with the spirit of her dead husband, before anybody who happened to be present – colloquies which struck the simple spectators mute with terror. To her mystic view, the love-union between Mary and me was something too sacred and too beautiful to be tried by the mean and matter-of-fact tests set up by society. She wrote for us little formulas of prayer and praise, which we were to use when we met and when we parted, day by day. She solemnly warned her son to look upon us as two young consecrated creatures, walking unconsciously on a heavenly path of their own, whose beginning was on earth, but whose bright end was among the angels in a better state of being. Imagine my appearing before such a woman as this, and telling her with tears of despair that I was determined to die rather than let my uncle part me from little Mary – and you will no longer be astonished at the hospitality which threw open to me the sanctuary of Dame Dermody's own room.

When the safe time came for my leaving my hiding-place, I committed a serious mistake. In thanking the old woman at parting I said to her (with a boy's sense of honour), 'I won't tell upon you, Dame; my mother shan't know that you hid me in your bedroom.'

The Sibyl laid her dry fleshless hand on my shoulder, and forced me roughly back into the chair from which I had just risen.

'Boy!' she said, looking through and through me with her fierce black eyes, 'do you dare suppose that I ever did anything that I was ashamed of? Do you think I am ashamed of what I have done now? Wait there. Your mother may mistake me too. I shall write to your mother.'

She put on her great round spectacles with tortoiseshell rims, and sat down to her letter. Whenever her thoughts flagged, whenever she was at a loss for an expression, she looked over her shoulder, as if some visible creature was stationed behind her, watching what she wrote — consulted the spirit of her husband, exactly as she might have consulted a living man — smiled softly to herself — and went on with her writing.

'There!' she said, handing me the completed letter with an imperial gesture of indulgence. '*His* mind and *my* mind are written there. Go, boy. I pardon you. Give my letter to your mother.'

So she always spoke, with the same formal and measured dignity of manner and language.

I gave the letter to my mother. We read it, and marvelled over it, together. Thus, counselled by the ever-present spirit of her husband, Dame Dermody wrote:

'Madam, — I have taken, what you may be inclined to think, a great liberty. I have assisted your son George in setting his uncle's authority at defiance. I have encouraged your son George in his resolution to be true, in time and in eternity, to my grandchild, Mary Dermody.

'It is due to you, and to me, that I should tell you with what motive I have acted in doing these things.

'I hold the belief that all love that is true, is fore-ordained and consecrated in Heaven. Spirits destined to be united in the better world, are divinely commissioned to discover each other, and to begin their union in this world. The only happy marriages are those in which the two destined spirits have succeeded in meeting one another in this sphere of life.

'When the kindred spirits have once met, no human power can really part them. Sooner or later, they must, by divine law, find each other again, and become united spirits once more. Worldly wisdom may force them into widely different ways of life; worldly wisdom may delude them, or may make them delude themselves, into contracting an earthly and a fallible union. It matters nothing. The time will certainly come, when that union will manifest itself as earthly and fallible; and the two disunited spirits, finding each other again, will become united here, for the world beyond this — united, I tell you, in defiance of all human laws, and of all human notions of right and wrong.

'This is my belief. I have proved it by my own life. Maid, wife, and widow, I have held to it, and I have found it good.

'I was born, madam, in the rank of society to which you belong. I received the mean material teaching which fulfils the worldly notion of education. Thanks be to God, my kindred spirit met *my* spirit while I was still young. I knew true love and true union before I was twenty years of age. I married, madam, in the rank from which Christ chose his apostles – I married a labouring man. No human language can tell my happiness while we lived united here. His death has not parted us. He helps me to write this letter. In my last hours, I shall see him standing among the angels, waiting for me on the banks of the shining river.

'You will now understand the view I take of the tie which unites the young spirits of our children, at the bright outset of their lives.

'Believe me, the thing which your husband's brother has proposed to you to do, is a sacrilege and a profanation. I own to you freely that I look on what I have done towards thwarting your relative in this matter, as an act of virtue. You cannot expect *me* to think it a serious obstacle to an union predestined in Heaven, that your son is the Squire's heir, and that my grandchild is only the bailiff's daughter. Dismiss from your mind, I implore you, the unworthy and unchristian prejudices of rank. Are we not all equal before God? Are we not all equal (even in this world) before disease and death? Not your son's happiness only, but your own peace of mind is concerned, in taking heed to my words. I warn you, madam, you cannot hinder the destined union of these two child-spirits, in after years, as man and wife. Part them now – and YOU will be responsible for the sacrifices, degradations, and distresses through which your George and my Mary may be condemned to pass, on their way back to each other in later life.

'Now, my mind is unburdened. Now, I have said all.

'If I have spoken too freely, or have in any other way unwittingly offended, I ask your pardon, and remain, madam, your faithful servant and well-wisher,

'HELEN DERMODY'

So the letter ended.

To me, it is something more than a mere curiosity of epistolary composition. I see in it the prophecy – strangely fulfilled in later years – of events in Mary's life and in mine which future pages are now to tell.

My mother decided on leaving the letter unanswered. Like many of her poorer neighbours, she was a little afraid of Dame Dermody; and she was, besides, habitually averse to all discussions which turned on the mysteries of spiritual life. I was reproved, admonished, and forgiven – and there was the end of it.

For some happy weeks, Mary and I returned, without hindrance or interruption, to our old intimate companionship. The end was coming, however, when we least expected it. My mother was startled one morning by a letter from my father which informed her that he had been unexpectedly obliged to sail for England at a moment's notice; that he had arrived in London, and that he was detained there by business which would admit of no delay. We were to wait for him at home, in daily expectation of seeing him – the moment he was free.

This news filled my mother's mind with foreboding doubts about the stability of her husband's grand speculation in America. The sudden departure from the United States, and the mysterious delay in London, were ominous of misfortune to come. I am now writing of those dark days in the past, when the railway and the electric telegraph were still visions in the minds of inventors. Rapid communication with my father (even if he would have consented to take us into his confidence) was impossible. We had no choice but to wait and hope.

The weary days passed – and still my father's brief letters described him as detained by his business. The morning came, when Mary and I went out with Dermody the bailiff, to see the last wild-fowl of the season lured into the Decoy – and still the welcome home waited for the master, and waited in vain.

III

The narrative may now follow my little sweetheart and myself, on our way to Dermody's cottage.

As we approached the garden gate, I saw a servant from the house waiting there. He carried a message from my mother – a message for me.

'My mistress wishes you to go home, Master George, as soon as you can. A letter has come by the coach. My master means to take a post-chaise from London, and sends word that we may expect him in the course of the day.'

Mary's attentive face saddened when she heard those words.

'Must you really go away, George,' she whispered, 'before you see what I have got waiting for you at home?'

I remembered Mary's promised 'surprise,' the secret of which was only to be revealed to me when we got to the cottage. How could I disappoint her? My poor little lady-love looked ready to cry at the bare prospect of it.

I dismissed the servant with a message of the temporising sort. My love to my mother – and I would be back at the house in half an hour.

We entered the cottage.

Dame Dermody was sitting in the light of the window as usual, with one of the mystic books of Emanuel Swedenborg open on her lap. She solemnly lifted her hand on our appearance; signing to us to occupy our customary corner, without speaking to her. It was an act of domestic high treason to interrupt the Sibyl at her books. We crept quietly into our places. Mary waited until she saw her grandmother's grey head bend down, and her grandmother's bushy eyebrows contract attentively, over her reading. Then, and then only, the discreet child rose on tiptoe; disappeared noiselessly in the direction of her bedchamber; and came back to me, carrying something carefully wrapped up in her best cambric handkerchief.

'Is that the surprise?' I whispered.

Mary whispered back, 'Guess what it is!'

'Something for me?'

'Yes. Go on guessing. What is it?'

I guessed three times – and each guess was wrong. Mary decided on helping me by a hint.

'Say your letters,' she suggested; 'and go on till I stop you.'

I began: 'A, B, C, D, E, F ——' There she stopped me.

'It's the name of a Thing,' she said. 'And it begins with F.'

I guessed 'Fern,' 'Feather,' 'Fife –' and there my resources failed me.

Mary sighed and shook her head. 'You don't take pains,' she said. 'You are three whole years older than I am. After all the trouble I have taken to please you, you may be too big to care for my present when you see it. Guess again.'

'I can't guess.'

'You must!'

'I give it up.'

Mary refused to let me give it up. She helped me by another hint.

'What did you once say you wished you had in your boat?' she asked.

'Was it long ago?' I enquired, at a loss for an answer.

'Long, long ago! Before the winter. When the autumn leaves were falling – and you took me out one evening for a sail. Ah, George, *you* have forgotten!'

Too true, of me and of my brethren, old and young alike! It is always *his* love that forgets, and *her* love that remembers. We were only two children – and we were types of the man and the woman already!

Mary lost patience with me. Forgetting the terrible presence of her grandmother, she jumped up, and snatched the concealed object out of the handkerchief.

'There!' she cried briskly, '*now* do you know what it is?'

I remembered at last. The thing I had wished for in my boat, all those months ago, was a new flag. And here was the flag made for me in secret by Mary's own hand! The ground was green silk, with a dove embroidered on it in white, carrying in its beak the typical olive-branch, wrought in gold thread. The work was the tremulous uncertain work of a child's fingers. But how faithfully my little darling had remembered my wish – how patiently she had plied the needle over the traced lines of the pattern – how industriously she had laboured through the dreary winter days; and all for my sake! What words could tell my pride, my gratitude, my happiness? I too forgot the presence of the Sibyl bending over her book – I took the little workwoman in my arms, and kissed her till I was fairly out of breath and could kiss no longer.

'Mary!' I burst out, in the first heat of my enthusiasm – 'my father is coming home to-day. I will speak to him to-night; and I will marry you to-morrow.'

'Boy!' said the awful voice at the other end of the room. 'Come here.'

Dame Dermody's mystic book was closed; Dame Dermody's weird black eyes were watching us in our corner. I approached her, and Mary followed me timidly, by a footstep at a time.

The Sibyl took me by the hand, with a caressing gentleness which was new in my experience of her.

'Do you prize that toy?' she enquired, looking at the flag. 'Hide it,' she cried before I could answer. 'Hide it, or it may be taken from you.'

'Why should I hide it?' I asked. 'I want to fly it at the mast of my boat.'

'You will never fly it at the mast of your boat!' With that answer she took the flag from me, and thrust it impatiently into the breast-pocket of my jacket.

'Don't crumple it, grandmother!' said Mary piteously.

I put another question.

'Why shall I never fly it at the mast of my boat?'

Dame Dermody laid her hand on the closed volume of Swedenborg lying in her lap.

'Three times I have opened this book since the morning,' she said. 'Three times the words of the prophet warn me that there is trouble coming. Children! it is trouble that is coming to You. I look there,' she went on, pointing to the place where a ray of sunlight poured slanting into the room; 'and I see my husband in the heavenly light. He bows his head in grief, and he points his unerring hand at You. George and Mary, you are consecrated to each other! Be always worthy of your consecration; be always worthy of yourselves.' She paused. Her voice faltered. She looked at us with softening eyes, as those look who know sadly that there is a parting at hand. 'Kneel!' she said, in low tones of awe and grief. 'It may be the last time I bless you; it may be the last time I pray over you in this house. Kneel!'

We knelt close together at her feet. I could feel Mary's heart throbbing, as she pressed nearer and nearer to my side. I could feel my own heart quickening its beat, with a fear that was a mystery to me.

'God bless and keep George and Mary, here and hereafter. God prosper, in future days, the union which God's wisdom has willed. Amen. So be it. Amen.'

As the last words fell from her lips, the cottage door was thrust open. My father — followed by the bailiff — entered the room.

Dame Dermody got slowly on her feet, and looked at him with a stern scrutiny.

'It has come,' she said to herself. 'It looks with the eyes — it will speak with the voice — of that man.'

My father broke the silence that followed, addressing himself to the bailiff.

'You see, Dermody,' he said, 'here is my son in your cottage, when he ought to be in my house.' He turned, and looked at me as I stood with my arm round little Mary, patiently waiting for my opportunity to speak.

'George,' he said, with the hard smile which was peculiar to him, when he was angry and was trying to hide it, 'you are making a fool of yourself there. Leave that child, and come to me.'

Now or never was my time to declare myself. Judging by appearances, I was still a boy. Judging by my own sensations, I had developed into a man at a moment's notice.

'Papa,' I said, 'I am glad to see you home again. This is Mary Dermody. I am in love with her, and she is in love with me. I wish to marry her as soon as it is convenient to my mother and you.'

My father burst out laughing. Before I could speak again, his humour changed. He had observed that Dermody too presumed to be amused. He seemed to become mad with anger all in a moment.

'I have been told of this infernal tomfoolery,' he said; 'but I didn't believe it till now. Who has turned the boy's weak head? Who has encouraged him to stand there hugging that girl? If it's you, Dermody, it shall be the worst day's work you ever did in your life.' He turned to me again, before the bailiff could defend himself. 'Do you hear what I say? I tell you to leave Dermody's girl, and come home with me.'

'Yes, papa,' I answered. 'But I must go back to Mary, if you please, after I have been with you.'

Angry as he was, my father was positively staggered by my audacity.

'You young idiot, your insolence exceeds belief,' he burst out. 'I tell you this — you will never darken these doors again! You have been taught to disobey me here. You have had things put into your head here, which no boy of your age ought to know; I'll say more, which no decent people would have let you know.'

'I beg your pardon, sir,' Dermody interposed, very respectfully and very firmly at the same time. 'There are many things which a master, in a hot temper, is privileged to say to the man who serves him. But you have gone beyond your privilege. You have shamed me, sir, in the presence of my mother, in the hearing of my child.'

My father checked him there.

'You may spare the rest of it,' he said. 'We are master and servant no longer. When my son came hanging about your cottage, and playing at sweethearts with your girl there, your duty was to close the door on him. You have failed in your duty. I trust you no longer. Take a month's notice, Dermody. You leave my service.'

The bailiff steadily met my father on his own ground. He was no longer the easy, sweet-tempered, modest man, who was the man of my remembrance.

'I beg to decline taking your month's notice, sir,' he answered. 'You shall have no opportunity of repeating what you have just said to me. I will send in my accounts to-night; and I will leave your service to-morrow.'

'We agree for once,' retorted my father. 'The sooner you go the better.'

He stepped across the room, and put his hand on my shoulder.

'Listen to me,' he said, making a last effort to control himself. 'I don't want to quarrel with you before a discarded servant. There must be an end to this nonsense. Leave these people to pack up and go, and come back to the house with me.'

His heavy hand, pressing on my shoulder, seemed to press the spirit of resistance out of me. I so far gave way as to try to melt him by entreaties.

'Oh, papa! papa!' I cried, 'don't part me from Mary! See how pretty and good she is! She has made me a flag for my boat. Let me come here and see her sometimes. I can't live without her.'

I could say no more. My poor little Mary burst out crying. Her tears and my entreaties were alike wasted on my father.

'Take your choice,' he said, 'between coming away of your own accord, or obliging me to take you away by force. I mean to part you and Dermody's girl.'

'Neither you nor any man can part them,' interposed a voice, speaking behind us. 'Rid your mind of that notion, master, before it is too late.'

My father looked round quickly, and discovered Dame Dermody facing him in the full light of the window. She had stepped back at the outset of the dispute, into the corner behind the fireplace. There she had remained, biding her time to speak, until my father's last threat brought her out of her place of retirement.

They looked at each other for a moment. My father seemed to think it beneath his dignity to answer her. He went on with what he had to say to me.

'I shall count three slowly,' he resumed. 'Before I get to the last number, make up your mind to do what I tell you, or submit to the disgrace of being taken away by force.'

'Take him where you may,' said Dame Dermody, 'he will still be on his way to his marriage with my grandchild.'

'And where shall I be, if you please?' asked my father, stung into speaking to her this time.

The answer followed instantly, in these startling words:—

'*You* will be on your way to your ruin and your death.'

My father turned his back on the prophetess, with a smile of contempt.

'One!' he said, beginning to count.

I set my teeth, and clasped both arms round Mary, as he spoke. I had inherited some of his temper, and he was now to know it.

'Two!' proceeded my father, after waiting a little.

Mary put her trembling lips to my ear, and whispered, 'Let me go, George! I can't bear to see it. Oh, look how he frowns! I know he'll hurt you!'

My father lifted his forefinger, as a preliminary warning before he counted Three.

'Stop!' cried Dame Dermody.

My father looked round at her again, with sardonic astonishment.

'I beg your pardon, ma'am – have you anything particular to say to me?' he asked.

'Man!' returned the Sibyl, 'you speak lightly. Have I spoken lightly to you? I warn you to bow your wicked will before a Will that is mightier than yours. The spirits of these children are kindred spirits. For time and for eternity they are united one to the other. Put land and sea between them – they will still be together; they will communicate in visions, they will be revealed to each other in dreams. Bind them by worldly ties; wed your son, in the time to come, to another woman, and my granddaughter to another man. In vain! I tell you, in vain! You may doom them to misery, you may drive them to sin – the day of their union on earth is still a day predestined in Heaven. It will come! It will come! Submit, while the time for submission is yours. You are a doomed man. I see the shadow of disaster, I see the seal of death, on your face. Go; and leave these consecrated ones to walk the dark ways of the world together, in the strength of their innocence, in the light of their love. Go – and God forgive you.'

In spite of himself, my father was struck by the irresistible strength of conviction which inspired those words. The bailiff's mother had impressed him as a tragic actress might have impressed him on the stage. She had checked the mocking answer on his lips; but she had not shaken his iron will. His face was as hard as ever, when he turned my way once more.

'The last chance, George,' he said – and counted the last number: 'Three!'

I neither moved nor answered him.

'You *will* have it?' he said, as he fastened his hold on my arm.

I fastened *my* hold on Mary; I whispered to her, 'I won't leave you!' She seemed not to hear me. She trembled from head to foot, in my arms. A faint cry of terror fluttered from her lips. Dermody instantly stepped forward. Before my father could wrench me away from her, he had said in my ear, 'You can give her to *me*, Master George,' and had released his child from my embrace. She stretched her little frail hands out yearningly to me, as she lay in Dermody's arms. 'Goodbye, dear,' she said faintly. I saw her head sink on her father's bosom, as I was dragged to the door. In my helpless rage and misery, I struggled against the cruel hands that had got me, with all the strength I had left. I cried out to her, 'I love you, Mary! I will come back to you, Mary! I will never marry anyone but you!' Step by step, I was forced farther and farther away. The last I saw of her, my darling's head was still resting on Dermody's breast. Her grandmother stood near – and shook her withered hands at my father – and shrieked her terrible prophecy, in the hysteric frenzy that possessed her when she saw the separation accomplished. 'Go! – you go to your ruin! you go to your death!' While her voice still rang in my ears, the cottage door was opened and closed again. It was all over. The modest world of my boyish love and my boyish joy, disappeared like the vision of a dream. The empty outer wilderness which was my father's world, opened before me void of love and void of joy. God forgive me – how I hated him at that moment!

IV

For the rest of the day, and throughout the night, I was kept a close prisoner in my room – watched by a man, on whose fidelity my father could depend.

The next morning, I made an effort to escape, and was discovered before I had got free of the house. Confined again to my room, I contrived to write to Mary, and to slip my note into the willing hand of the housemaid who attended on me. Useless! The vigilance of my guardian was not to be evaded. The woman was suspected and followed, and the letter was taken from her. My father tore it up with his own hands.

Later in the day, my mother was permitted to see me.

She was quite unfit, poor soul, to intercede for me, or to serve my interests in any way. My father had completely overwhelmed her by announcing that his wife and his son were to accompany him when he returned to America.

'Every farthing he has in the world,' said my mother, 'is to be thrown away in that hateful speculation. He has raised money in London; he has found some rich tradesman to take the house on a long lease; he has sold the plate, and the jewels that came to me from his mother. The land in America swallows it all up. We have no home, George, and no choice but to go with him.'

An hour afterwards, the post-chaise was at the door.

My father himself took me to the carriage. I broke away from him with a desperation which not even his resolution could resist. I ran, I flew, along that path that led to Dermody's cottage. The door stood open; the parlour was empty. I went into the kitchen; I went into the upper rooms. Solitude everywhere. The bailiff had left his place; and his mother and his daughter had gone with him. No friend or neighbour lingered near with a message; no letter lay waiting for me; no hint was left to tell me in what direction they had taken their departure. After the insulting words which his master had spoken to him, Dermody's pride was concerned in leaving no trace of his whereabouts; my father might consider it as a trace purposely left, with the object of reuniting Mary and me. I had no keepsake to speak to me of my lost darling, but the flag which she had embroidered with her own hand. The furniture still remained in the cottage. I sat down in our customary corner, by Mary's empty chair, and looked again at the pretty green flag, and burst out crying.

A light touch roused me. My father had so far yielded, as to leave to my mother the responsibility of bringing me back to the travelling carriage.

'We shall not find Mary here, George,' she said, gently. 'And we *may* hear of her in London. Come with me.'

I rose, and silently gave her my hand. Something low down on the clean white doorpost caught my eye as we passed it. I stopped, and discovered some writing in pencil. I looked closer, it was writing in Mary's hand. The unformed childish characters traced these last words of farewell:

'Goodbye, dear. Don't forget Mary.'

I knelt down and kissed the writing. It comforted me – it was like a farewell touch from Mary's hand. I followed my mother quietly to the carriage.

Late that night we were in London.

My good mother did all that the most compassionate kindness could do (in her position) to comfort me. She privately wrote to the solicitors employed by her family, inclosing a description of Dermody and his mother and daughter, and directing enquiries to be made at the various coach offices in London. She also referred the lawyers to Dermody's relatives, who lived in the city, and who might know something of his movements after he left my father's service. When she had done this, she had done all that lay in her power. We neither of us possessed money enough to advertise in the newspapers.

A week afterwards we sailed for the United States. Twice in that interval I communicated with the lawyers; and twice I was informed that the enquiries had led to nothing.

With this, the love-story of my boyhood comes to an end. I still kept the green flag, with the dove worked on it. For the rest, the waters of oblivion had closed over the golden days at Greenwater Broad.

THE STORY

FROM THE MANUSCRIPT OF GEORGE GERMAINE

CHAPTER I

TEN YEARS OF MY LIFE

When you last saw me, I was a boy of thirteen. You now see me a man of twenty-three.

The story of my life, in the interval between these two ages, is a story that can be soon told.

Speaking of my father first, I have to record that the end of his career did indeed come as Dame Dermody had foretold it. Before we had been a year in America, the total collapse of his land speculation was followed by his death. The catastrophe was complete. But for my mother's little income (settled on her at her marriage) we should both have been left helpless at the mercy of the world.

We made some kind friends among the hearty and hospitable people of the United States, whom we were unaffectedly sorry to leave. But there were reasons which inclined us to return to our country, after my father's death – and we did return accordingly.

Besides her brother-in-law (already mentioned in the earlier pages of my narrative) my mother had another relative – a cousin, named Germaine – on whose assistance she mainly relied for starting me, when the time came, in a professional career. I remember it, as a family rumour, that Mr Germaine had been an unsuccessful suitor for my mother's hand, in the days when they were young people together. He was still a bachelor, at the later period when his eldest brother's death without issue placed him in possession of a handsome fortune. The accession of wealth made no difference in his habits of life; he was a lonely old man, estranged from his other relatives, when my mother and I returned to England. If I could only succeed in pleasing Mr Germaine, I might consider my prospects (in some degree at least) as being prospects assured.

This was one consideration that influenced us in leaving America. There was another – in which I was especially interested – that drew me back to the lonely shores of Greenwater Broad.

My only hope of recovering a trace of Mary was to make enquiries among the cottagers in the neighbourhood of my old home. The good bailiff had been heartily liked and respected in his little sphere. It seemed at least possible that some among his many friends in Suffolk might have discovered traces of him, in the year that had passed since I had left England. In my dreams of Mary – and I dreamed of her constantly – the lake and its woody banks formed a frequent background in the visionary picture of my lost companion. To the lake-shores I looked, with a natural superstition, as to my way back to the one life that had its promise of happiness for *me* – my life with Mary.

On our arrival in London, I started alone for Suffolk, at my mother's request. At her age she naturally shrank from revisiting the home-scenes now occupied by the strangers to whom our house had been let.

Ah, how my heart ached (young as I was), when I saw the familiar green waters of the lake once more! It was evening. The first object that caught my eye was the gaily-painted boat, once mine, in which Mary and I had so often sailed together. The people in possession of our house were sailing now. The sound of their laughter floated towards me merrily over the still water. *Their* flag flew at the little mast-head, from which Mary's flag had never fluttered in the pleasant breeze. I turned my eyes from the boat; it hurt me to look at it. A few steps onward brought me to a promontory on the shore, and revealed the brown archways of the Decoy on the opposite bank. There was the paling behind which we had knelt to watch the snaring of the ducks; there was the hole through which 'Trim,' the terrier, had shown himself to rouse the stupid curiosity of the waterfowl; there, seen at intervals through the trees, was the winding woodland path along which Mary and I had traced our way to Dermody's cottage, on the day when my father's cruel hand had torn us from each other. How wisely my good mother had shrunk from looking again at the dear old scenes! I turned my back on the lake, to think with calmer thoughts in the shadowy solitude of the woods.

Half an hour's walk along the winding banks brought me round to the cottage which had once been Mary's home.

The door was opened by a woman who was a stranger to me. She civilly asked me to enter the parlour. I had suffered enough already: I made my enquiries standing on the doorstep. They were soon at an end. The woman was a stranger in our part of Suffolk; neither she nor her husband had ever heard of Dermody's name.

I pursued my investigations among the peasantry, passing from cottage to cottage. The twilight came; the moon rose; the lights began to vanish from the lattice windows – and still I continued my weary pilgrimage; and still, go where I might, the answer to my questions was the same. Nobody knew anything of Dermody: everybody asked if I had not brought news of him myself. It pains me even now to recall the cruelly-complete defeat of every effort which I made on that disastrous evening. I passed the night in one of the cottages; and I returned to London the next day, broken by disappointment, careless what I did, or where I went, next.

Still we were not wholly parted. I saw Mary – as Dame Dermody said I should see her – in dreams.

Sometimes she came to me with the green flag in her hand, and repeated her farewell words: 'Don't forget Mary.' Sometimes she led me to our well-remembered corner in the cottage-parlour, and opened the paper on which her grandmother had written our prayers for us: we prayed together again, and sang hymns together again, as if the old times had come back. Once she appeared to me with tears in her eyes, and said, 'We must wait, dear; our time has not come yet.' Twice I saw her looking at me, like one disturbed by anxious thoughts; and twice I heard her say, 'Live patiently, live innocently, George, for my sake.'

We settled in London, where my education was undertaken by a private tutor. Before we had been long in our new abode, an unexpected change in our prospects took place. To my mother's astonishment, she received an offer of marriage (addressed to her in a letter) from Mr Germaine.

'I entreat you not to be startled by my proposal' (the old gentleman wrote); 'you can hardly have forgotten that I was once fond of you, in the days when we were both young and both poor? No return to the feelings associated with that time is possible now. At my age, all I ask of you is to be the companion of the closing years of my life, and to give me something of a father's interest in promoting the future welfare of your son. Consider this, my dear, and tell me whether you will take the empty chair at an old man's lonely fireside.'

My mother (looking almost as confused, poor soul, as if she had become a young girl again) left the whole responsibility of decision on the shoulders of her son! I was not long in making up my mind. If she said Yes, she would accept the hand of a man of worth and honour, who had been throughout his whole life devoted to her; and she would recover the comfort, the luxury, the social prosperity and position, of which my father's reckless course of life had deprived her. Add to this, that I liked Mr Germaine, and that Mr Germaine liked me. Under these circumstances, why should my mother say No? She could produce no satisfactory answer to that question, when I put it. As the necessary consequence, she became in due course of time, Mrs Germaine. I have only to add that, to the end of her life, my good mother congratulated herself (in this case at least) on having taken her son's advice.

The years went on – and still Mary and I were parted, except in our dreams. The years went on, until the perilous time which comes in every man's life, came in mine. I reached the age when the strongest of all the passions seizes on the senses, and asserts its mastery over mind and body alike.

I had hitherto passively endured the wreck of my earliest and dearest hopes; I had lived patiently, I had lived innocently, for Mary's sake. Now, my patience left me; my innocence was numbered among the lost things of the past. My days, it is true, were still devoted to the tasks set me by my tutor. But my nights were given, in secret, to a reckless profligacy, which (in my present frame of mind) I look back on with disgust and dismay. I profaned my remembrances of Mary in the company of women who had reached the lowest depths of degradation. I impiously said to myself, 'I have hoped for her long enough; I have waited for her long enough: the one thing now to do is to enjoy my youth, and to forget her.'

From the moment when I dropped into this degradation, I might sometimes think regretfully of Mary – at the morning time, when penitent thoughts mostly came to us – but I ceased absolutely to see her in my dreams. We were now, in the completest sense of the word, parted. Mary's pure spirit could hold no communion with mine – Mary's pure spirit had left me.

It is needless to say that I failed to keep the secret of my depravity from the knowledge of my mother. The sight of her grief was the first influence that sobered me. In some degree at least, I restrained myself – I made the effort to return to purer ways of life. Mr Germaine, though I had disappointed him, was too just a man to give me up as lost. He advised me, as a means of self-reform, to make my choice of a profession, and to absorb myself in closer studies than any that I had yet pursued.

I made my peace with this good friend and second father, not only by following his advice, but by adopting the profession to which he had himself been attached, before he had inherited his fortune – the profession of medicine. Mr Germaine had been a surgeon: I resolved on being a surgeon too.

Having entered, at rather an earlier age than usual, on my new way of life, I may at least say for myself that I worked hard. I won, and kept, the interest of the Professors under whom I studied. On the other hand, it is not to be denied that my reformation was, morally speaking, far from being complete. I worked – but what I did was done selfishly, bitterly, with a hard heart. In religion and morals I adopted the views of a materialist companion of my studies – a worn-out man of more than double my age. I believed in nothing but what I could see, or taste, or feel. I lost all faith in humanity. With the one exception of my mother, I had no respect for women. My remembrances of Mary deteriorated until they became little more than a lost link of association with the past. I still preserved the green flag, as a matter of habit – but it was no longer kept about me; it was left undisturbed in a drawer of my writing-desk. Now and then a wholesome doubt whether my life was not utterly unworthy of me, would rise in my mind. But it held no long possession of my thoughts. Despising others, it was in the logical order of things that I should follow my conclusions to their bitter end, and consistently despise myself.

The term of my majority arrived. I was twenty-one years old – and of the illusions of my youth not a vestige remained!

Neither my mother nor Mr Germaine could make any positive complaint of my conduct. But they were both thoroughly uneasy about me. After anxious consideration, my step-father arrived at a conclusion. He decided that the once chance of restoring me to my better and brighter self, was to try the stimulant of a life among new people and new scenes.

At the period of which I am now writing, the home government had decided on sending a special diplomatic mission to one of the native princes ruling over a remote province of our Indian empire. In the disturbed state of the province at that time, the mission, on its arrival in India, was to be accompanied to the prince's court by an escort, including the military as well as the civil servants of the Crown. The surgeon appointed to sail with the expedition from England was an old friend of Mr Germaine's, and was in want of an assistant on whose capacity he could rely. Through my step-father's interest the post was offered to me. I accepted it, without hesitation. My only pride left was the miserable pride of indifference. So long as I pursued my profession, the place in which I pursued it was a matter of no importance to my mind.

It was long before we could persuade my mother even to contemplate the new prospect now set before me. When she did at length give way, she yielded most unwillingly. I confess I left her with the tears in my eyes – the first I had shed for many a long year past.

The history of our expedition is part of the history of British India: it has no place in this narrative.

Speaking personally, I have to record that I was rendered incapable of performing my professional duties in less than a week from the time when the mission reached its destination. We were encamped outside the city; and an attack was made on us, under cover of darkness, by the fanatical natives. The attempt was defeated with little difficulty, and with only a trifling loss on our side. I was among the wounded – having been struck by a javelin, or spear, while I was passing from one tent to another.

Inflicted by an European weapon, my injury would have been of no serious consequence. But the tip of the Indian spear had been poisoned. I escaped the mortal danger of 'lock-jaw;' but, through some peculiarity in the action of the poison on my constitution (which I am quite unable to explain), my wound obstinately refused to heal.

I was invalided, and sent to Calcutta, where the best surgical help was at my disposal. To all appearance, the wound healed here – then broke out again. Twice this happened; and the medical men agreed that the best course to take would be to send me home. They calculated on the invigorating effect of the sea voyage, and, failing this, on the salutary influence of my native air. In the Indian climate, I was pronounced incurable.

Two days before the ship sailed, a letter from my mother brought me startling news. My life to come – if I *had* a life to come – had been turned into a new channel. Mr Germaine had died suddenly of heart disease. His will, bearing date at the time when I left England, bequeathed an income for life to my mother, and left the bulk of his property to me; on the one condition that I adopted his name. I accepted the condition, of course – and became George Germaine.

Four months later, my mother and I were restored to each other.

Except that I still had some trouble with my wound, behold me now to all appearance one of the most enviable of existing mortals: promoted to the position of a wealthy gentleman; possessor of a house in London, and of a country seat in Perthshire – and nevertheless, at twenty-three years of age, one of the most miserable men living!

And Mary?

In the ten years that had now passed, what had become of Mary?

You have heard my story. Read the few pages that follow, and you will hear hers.

CHAPTER II

TEN YEARS OF HER LIFE

What I have now to tell you of Mary, is derived from information obtained at a date in my life later by many years than any date of which I have written yet. Be pleased to remember this.

Dermody the bailiff possessed relatives in London of whom he occasionally spoke; and relatives in Scotland whom he never mentioned. My father had a strong prejudice against the Scotch nation. Dermody knew his master well enough to be aware that the prejudice might extend to *him*, if he spoke of his Scotch kindred. He was a discreet man, and he never mentioned them.

On leaving my father's service, he had made his way, partly by land and partly by sea, to Glasgow – in which city his friends resided. With his character and his experience, Dermody was a man in a thousand, to any master who was lucky enough to discover him. His friends bestirred themselves. In six weeks' time, he was placed in charge of a gentleman's estate on the eastern coast of Scotland, and was comfortably established with his mother and his daughter in a new home.

The insulting language which my father had addressed to him had sunk deep in Dermody's mind. He wrote privately to his relatives in London, telling them that he had found a new situation which suited him, and that he had his reasons for not at present mentioning his address. In this way, he baffled the enquiries which my mother's lawyers (failing to discover a trace of him in other directions) addressed to his London friends. Stung by his old master's reproaches, he sacrificed his daughter and he sacrificed me – partly to his own sense of self-respect; partly to his conviction that the difference between us in rank made it his duty to check all further intercourse before it was too late.

Buried in their retirement in a remote part of Scotland, the little household lived, lost to me, and lost to the world.

In dreams, I had seen and heard Mary. In dreams, Mary saw and heard me. The innocent longings and wishes that filled my heart while I was still a boy, were revealed to her in the mystery of sleep. Her grandmother, holding firmly to her faith in the predestined union between us, sustained the girl's courage and cheered her heart. She could hear her father say (as *my* father had said) that we were parted to meet no more, and could privately think of her happy dreams as the sufficient promise of another future than the future which Dermody contemplated. So she still lived with me in the spirit – and lived in hope.

The first affliction that befell the little household was the death of the grandmother, by the exhaustion of extreme old age. In her last conscious moments, she said to Mary, 'Never forget that you and George are spirits consecrated to each other. Wait – in the certain knowledge that no human power can hinder your union in the time to come.'

While those words were still vividly present to Mary's mind, our visionary union by dreams was abruptly broken on her side, as it had been abruptly broken on mine. In the first few days of my self-degradation I had ceased to see Mary. Exactly at the same period, Mary had ceased to see me.

The girl's sensitive nature sank under the shock. She had now no elder woman to comfort and advise her; she lived alone with her father, who invariably changed the subject whenever she spoke of the old times. The secret sorrow that preys on body and mind alike, preyed on *her*. A cold, caught at the inclement season, turned to fever. For weeks she was in danger of death. When she recovered, her head had been stripped of its beautiful hair by the doctor's order. The sacrifice had been necessary to save her life. It proved to be, in one respect, a cruel sacrifice – her hair never grew plentifully again. When it did reappear, it had completely lost its charming mingled hues of deep red and brown; it was now of one monotonous light brown colour throughout. At first sight, Mary's Scotch friends hardly knew her again.

But Nature made amends for what the head had lost, by what the face and figure gained.

In a year from the date of her illness, the frail little child of the old days at Greenwater Broad, had ripened, in the bracing Scotch air and the healthy mode of life, into a comely young woman. Her features were still, as in her early years, not regularly beautiful; but the change in her was not the less marked on that account. The wan face had filled out, and the pale complexion had found its colour. As to her figure, its remarkable development was perceived even by the rough people about her. Promising nothing when she was a child, it had now sprung into womanly fulness, symmetry, and grace – it was a strikingly beautiful figure, in the strictest sense of the word.

Morally as well as physically, there were moments, at this period of their lives, when even her own father hardly recognised his daughter of former days. She had lost her childish vivacity – her sweet equable flow of goodhumour. Silent and self-absorbed, she went through the daily routine of her duties enduringly. The hope of meeting me again had sunk to a dead hope in her by this time. She made no complaint. The bodily strength that she had gained in these later days had its sympathetic influence in steadying her mind. When her father once or twice ventured to ask if she was still thinking of me, she answered quietly that she had brought herself to share his opinions. She could not doubt that I had long since ceased to think of her. Even if I had remained faithful to her, she was old enough now to know, that the difference between us in rank made our union by marriage an impossibility. It would be best (she thought) not to refer any more to the past – best to forget me, as I had forgotten her. So she spoke now. So, tried by the test of appearances, Dame Dermody's confident forecast of our destinies had failed to justify itself, and had taken its place among the predictions that are never fulfilled.

The next notable event in the family annals which followed Mary's illness happened when she had attained the age of nineteen years. Even at this distance of time, my heart sinks, my courage fails me, at the critical stage in my narrative which I have now reached.

A storm of unusual severity burst over the eastern coast of Scotland. Among the ships that were lost in the tempest was a vessel bound from Holland, which was wrecked on the rocky shore near Dermody's place of abode. Leading the way in all good actions, the bailiff led the way in rescuing the passengers and crew of the lost ship. He had brought one man alive to land, and was on his way back to the vessel – when two heavy seas following in quick succession, dashed him against the rocks. He was rescued at the risk of their own lives, by his neighbours. The medical examination disclosed a broken bone, and severe bruises and lacerations. So far, Dermody's sufferings were easy of relief. But, after a lapse of time, symptoms appeared in the patient which revealed to his medical attendant the presence of a serious internal injury. In the doctor's opinion, he could never hope to resume the active habits of his life. He would be an invalided and a crippled man for the rest of his days.

Under these melancholy circumstances the bailiff's employer did all that could be strictly expected of him. He hired an assistant to undertake the supervision of the farmwork; and he permitted Dermody to occupy his cottage for the next three months. This concession gave the poor man time to recover such relics of strength as were left to him, and to consult his friends in Glasgow on the doubtful question of his life to come.

The prospect was a serious one. Dermody was quite unfit for any sedentary employment; and the little money that he had saved was not enough to support his daughter and himself. The Scotch friends were willing and kind; but they had domestic claims on them, and they had no money to spare.

In this emergency, one of the passengers in the wrecked vessel (whose life Dermody had saved) came forward with a proposal which took father and daughter alike by surprise. He made Mary an offer of marriage; on the express understanding (if she accepted him) that her home was to be her father's home also, to the end of his life.

The person who thus associated himself with the Dermodys in the time of their trouble was a Dutch gentleman, named Ernest Van Brandt. He possessed a share in a fishing establishment on the shores of the Zuyder Zee; and he was on his way to establish a correspondence with the fisheries in the North of Scotland, when the vessel was wrecked. Mary had produced a strong impression on him, when they first met. He had lingered in the neighbourhood, in the hope of gaining her favourable regard with time to help him. Personally, he was a handsome man, in the prime of life; and he was possessed of a sufficient income to marry on. In making his proposal he produced references to persons of high social position in Holland, who could answer for him, so far as the questions of character and position were concerned.

Mary was long in considering which course it would be best for her helpless father, and best for herself, to adopt.

The hope of marriage with me had been a hope abandoned by her years since. No woman looks forward willingly to a life of cheerless celibacy. In thinking of her future, Mary naturally thought of herself in the character of a wife. Could she fairly expect, in the time to come, to receive any more attractive proposal than the proposal now addressed to her? Mr Van Brandt had every personal advantage that a woman could desire; he was devotedly in love with her; and he felt a grateful affection for her father, as the man to whom he owed his life. With no other hope in her heart – with no other prospect in view – what could she do better than marry Mr Van Brandt?

Influenced by these considerations, she decided on speaking the fatal word. She said, Yes.

At the same time she spoke plainly to Mr Van Brandt; unreservedly acknowledging that she had contemplated another future than the future now set before her. She did not conceal that there had been an old love in her heart, and that a new love was more than she could command. Esteem, gratitude, and regard she could honestly offer – and, with time, love might come. For the rest, she had, long since, disassociated herself from the past, and had definitely given up all the hopes and wishes once connected with it. Repose for her father, and tranquil happiness for herself, were the only favours that she asked of fortune now. These she might find under the roof of an honourable man who loved and respected her. She could promise, on her side, to make him a good and faithful wife, if she could promise no more. It rested with Mr Van Brandt to say whether he really believed he would be consulting his own happiness in marrying her on these terms.

Mr Van Brandt accepted the terms without a moment's hesitation.

They would have been married immediately, but for an alarming change for the worse in the condition of Dermody's health. Symptoms showed themselves which the doctor confessed that he had not anticipated, when he had given his opinion on the case. He warned Mary that the end might be near. A physician was summoned from Edinburgh, at Mr Van Brandt's expense. He confirmed the opinion entertained by the country doctor. For some days longer the good bailiff lingered. On the last morning, he put his daughter's hand in Van Brandt's hand. 'Make her happy, sir,' he said, in his simple way; 'and you will be even with me for saving your life.' The same day, he died quietly in his daughter's arms.

Mary's future was now entirely in her lover's hands. The relatives in Glasgow had daughters of their own to provide for. The relatives in London resented Dermody's neglect of them. Van Brandt waited delicately and considerately, until the first violence of the girl's grief had worn itself out – and then he pleaded irresistibly for a husband's claim to console her.

The time at which they were married in Scotland was also the time at which I was on my way home from India. Mary had then reached the age of twenty years.

The story of our ten years' separation is now told; the narrative leaves us at the outset of our new lives.

I am with my mother, beginning my career as a country gentleman on the estate in Perthshire which I have inherited from Mr Germaine. Mary is with her husband, enjoying her new privileges, learning her new duties, as a wife. She too is living in Scotland – living, by a strange fatality, not very far distant from my country house. I have no suspicion that she is so near to me: the name of Mrs Van Brandt (even if I had heard it) appeals to no familiar associations in my mind. Still, the kindred spirits are parted. Still, there is no idea on her side, and no idea on mine, that we shall ever meet again.

CHAPTER III

THE WOMAN ON THE BRIDGE

My mother looked in at the library door, and disturbed me over my books.

'I have been hanging a little picture in my room,' she said. 'Come upstairs, my dear, and give me your opinion of it.'

I rose and followed her. She pointed to a miniature portrait, hanging above the mantelpiece.

'Do you know whose likeness that is?' she asked half sadly, half playfully: 'George! do you really not recognise yourself at thirteen years old?'

How should I recognise myself? Worn by sickness and sorrow; browned by the sun, on my long homeward voyage; my hair already growing thin over my forehead, my eyes already habituated to their one sad and weary look – what had I in common with the fair, plump, curly-headed, bright-eyed boy who confronted me in the miniature? The mere sight of the portrait produced the most extraordinary effect on my mind. It struck me with an overwhelming melancholy; it filled me with a despair of myself too dreadful to be endured. Making the best excuse I could to my mother, I left the room. In another minute, I was out of the house.

I crossed the park, and left my own possessions behind me. Following a bye-road I came to our well-known river – so beautiful in itself, so famous among trout-fishers throughout Scotland. It was not then the fishing season. No human being was in sight as I took my seat on the bank. The old stone bridge which spanned the stream was within a hundred yards of me; the setting sun still tinged the swift-flowing water under the arches with its red and dying light.

Still the boy's face in the miniature pursued me. Still the portrait seemed to reproach me, in a merciless language of its own: 'Look at what you were once – think of what you are now!'

I hid my face in the soft fragrant grass. I thought of the wasted years of my life between thirteen and twenty-three.

How was it to end? If I lived to the ordinary life of man, what prospect had I before me?

Love? Marriage? I burst out laughing as the idea crossed my mind. Since the innocently-happy days of my boyhood, I had known no more of love than the insect that now crept over my hand as it lay on the grass. My money to be sure would buy me a wife; but would my money make her dear to me? – dear as Mary had once been, in the golden time when my portrait was first painted?

Mary! Was she still living? Was she married? Should I know her again, if I saw her? Absurd! I had not seen her since she was ten years old: she was now a woman, as I was a man. Would she know *me*, if we met? The portrait, still pursuing me, answered the question: 'Look at what you were once – think of what you are now.'

I rose, and walked backwards and forwards, and tried to turn the current of my thoughts in some new direction.

It was not to be done. After a banishment of years, Mary had got back again into my mind. I sat down once more on the river-bank. The sun was sinking fast. Black shadows hovered under the arches of the old stone bridge. The red light had faded from the swift-flowing water, and had left it overspread with one monotonous hue of steely grey. The first stars looked down peacefully from the cloudless sky. The first shiverings of the night-breeze were audible among the trees, and visible here and there in the shallow places of the stream. And still, the darker it grew, the more persistently my portrait led me back to the past – the more vividly the long-lost image of the child Mary showed itself to me in my thoughts.

Was this the prelude to her coming back to me in dreams – in her pefect womanhood, in the young prime of her life?

It might be so.

I was no longer unworthy of her, as I had once been. The effect produced on me by the sight of my portrait was in itself due to moral and mental changes in me for the better, which had been steadily proceeding since the time when my wound had laid me helpless among strangers in a strange land. Sickness, which has made itself teacher and friend to many a man, had made itself teacher and friend to me. I looked back with horror at the vices of my youth – at the fruitless after-days when I had impiously doubted all that is most noble, all that is most consoling in human life. Consecrated by sorrow, purified by repentance, was it vain in me to hope that her spirit and my spirit might yet be united again? Who could tell?

I rose once more. It could serve no good purpose to linger until night by the banks of the river. I had left the house, feeling the impulse which drives us, in certain excited conditions of the mind, to take refuge in movement and change. The remedy had failed: my mind was as strangely disturbed as ever. My wisest course would be to go home, and keep my good mother company over her favourite game of piquet.

I turned to take the road back – and stopped, struck by the tranquil beauty of the last faint light in the western sky, shining behind the black line formed by the parapet of the bridge.

In the grand gathering of the night shadows, in the deep stillness of the dying day, I stood alone, and watched the sinking light.

As I looked, there came a change over the scene. Suddenly and softly, a living figure glided into view on the bridge. It passed behind the black line of the parapet, in the last long rays of the western light. It crossed the bridge. It paused, and crossed back again half way. Then it stopped. The minutes passed – and there the figure stood, a motionless black object, behind the black parapet of the bridge.

I advanced a little, moving near enough to obtain a closer view of the dress in which the figure was attired. The dress showed me that the solitary stranger was a woman.

She did not notice me, in the shadow which the trees cast on the bank. She stood with her arms folded in her cloak, looking down at the darkening river.

Why was she waiting there, at the close of evening, alone?

As the question occurred to me, I saw her head move. She looked along the bridge, first on one side of her, then on the other. Was she waiting for some person who was to meet her? Or was she suspicious of observation, and anxious to make sure that she was alone?

A sudden doubt of her purpose in seeking that solitary place – a sudden distrust of the lonely bridge and the swift-flowing river – set my heart beating quickly, and roused me to instant action. I hurried up the rising ground which led from the river bank to the bridge; determined on speaking to her, while the opportunity was still mine.

She neither saw nor heard me until I was close to her. I approached with an irrepressible feeling of agitation; not knowing how she might receive me when I spoke to her. The moment she turned and faced me, my composure came back. It was as if, expecting to see a stranger, I had unexpectedly encountered a friend.

And yet she *was* a stranger. I had never before looked on that grave and noble face, on that grand figure whose exquisite grace and symmetry even her long cloak could not wholly hide. She was not perhaps a strictly beautiful woman. There were defects in her which were sufficiently marked to show themselves in the fading light. Her hair, for example, seen under the large garden hat that she wore, looked almost as short as the hair of a man; and the colour of it was that dull lustreless brown hue which is so commonly seen in Englishwomen of the ordinary type. Still, in spite of these drawbacks, there was a latent charm in her expression, there was an inbred fascination in her manner, which instantly found its way to my sympathies, and its hold on my admiration. She won me, in the moment when I first looked at her.

'May I enquire if you have lost your way?' I asked.

Her eyes rested on my face with a strange look of enquiry in them. She did not appear to be surprised or confused at my venturing to address her.

'I know this part of the country well,' I went on. 'Can I be of any use to you?'

She still looked at me with steady enquiring eyes. For a moment, stranger as I was, my face seemed to trouble her as if it had been a face that she had seen and forgotten again. If she really had this idea, she at once dismissed it with a little toss of her head, and looked away at the river, as if she felt no further interest in me.

'Thank you. I have not lost my way. I am accustomed to walking alone. Good evening.'

She spoke coldly, but courteously. Her voice was delicious; her bow as she left me was the perfection of unaffected grace. She left the bridge on the side by which I had first seen her approach it, and walked slowly away along the darkening track of the high road.

Still I was not quite satisfied. There was something underlying the charming expression, and the fascinating manner, which my instinct felt to be something wrong. As I walked away towards the opposite end of the bridge, the doubt began to grow on me whether she had spoken the truth. In leaving the neighbourhood of the river, was she simply trying to get rid of me?

I resolved to put this suspicion of her to the test. Leaving the bridge I had only to cross the road beyond, and to enter a plantation on the bank of the river. Here, concealed behind the first tree which was large enough to hide me, I could command a view of the bridge, and I could fairly count on detecting her, if she returned to the river, while there was a ray of light to see her by. It was not easy walking in the obscurity of the plantation; I had almost to grope my way to the nearest tree that suited my purpose.

I had just steadied my foothold on the uneven ground behind the tree, when the stillness of the twilight hour was suddenly broken by the distant sound of a voice.

The voice was a woman's. It was not raised to any high pitch; its accent was the accent of prayer – and the words it uttered were these: –

'Christ have mercy on me!'

There was silence again. A nameless fear crept over me as I looked out on the bridge.

She was standing on the parapet. Before I could move, before I could cry out, before I could even breathe again freely, she leapt into the river.

The current ran my way. I could see her, as she rose to the surface, floating by in the light on the mid-stream. I ran headlong down the bank. She sank again in the moment when I stopped to throw aside my hat and coat, and to kick off my shoes. I was a practised swimmer. The instant I was in the water my composure came back to me – I felt like myself again.

The current swept me out into the mid-stream, and greatly increased the speed at which I swam. I was close behind her when she rose for the second time – a shadowy thing just visible a few inches below the surface of the river. One more stroke – and my left arm was round her; I had her face out of the water. She was insensible. I could hold her in the right way to leave me master of all my movements; I could devote myself, without flurry or fatigue, to the exertion of taking her back to the shore.

My first attempt satisfied me that there was no reasonable hope, burdened as I now was, of breasting the strong current running towards the mid-river from either bank. I tried it on one side, and tried it on the other – and gave it up. The one choice left was to let myself drift with her down the stream. Some fifty yards lower, the river took a turn round a promontory of land, on which stood a little inn, much frequented by anglers in the season. As we approached the place, I made another attempt (again an attempt in vain) to reach the shore. Our last chance now was to be heard by the people of the inn. I shouted at the full pitch of my voice, as we drifted past. The cry was answered. A man put off in a boat. In five minutes more, I had her safe on the bank again; and the man and I were carrying her to the inn by the river side.

The landlady and her servant-girl were equally willing to be of service, and equally ignorant of what they were to do. Fortunately, my medical education made me competent to direct them. A good fire, warm blankets, hot water in bottles, were all at my disposal. I showed the women myself how to ply the work of revival. They persevered, and I persevered; and still, there she lay, in her perfect beauty of form, without a sign of life perceptible – there she lay, to all outward appearance, dead by drowning.

A last hope was left – the hope of restoring her (if I could construct the apparatus in time), by the process called 'artificial respiration.' I was just endeavouring to tell the landlady what I wanted, and was just conscious of a strange difficulty in expressing myself – when the good woman started back and looked at me with a scream of terror.

'Good God, sir, you're bleeding!' she cried. 'What's the matter? where are you hurt?'

In the moment when she spoke to me, I knew what had happened. The old Indian wound (irritated, doubtless, by the violent exertion that I had imposed upon myself) had opened again. I struggled against the sudden sense of faintness that seized on me; I tried to tell the people of the inn what to do. It was useless. I dropped to my knees; my head sank on the bosom of the woman stretched senseless upon the low couch beneath me. The death-in-life that had got *her* had got *me*. Lost to the world about us, we lay, with my blood flowing on her, united in our deathly trance!

Where were our spirits, at that moment? Were they together, and conscious of each other? United by a spiritual bond, undiscovered and unsuspected by us in the flesh, did we two, who had met as strangers on the fatal bridge, know each other again in the trance? You who have loved and lost – you whose one consolation it has been to believe in other worlds than this – can you turn from my questions in contempt? can you honestly say that they have never been *your* questions, too?

CHAPTER IV

THE KINDRED SPIRITS

The morning sunlight, shining in at a badly curtained window; a clumsy wooden bed, with big twisted posts that reached to the ceiling; on one side of the bed my mother's welcome face; on the other side, an elderly gentleman, unremembered by me at that moment – such were the objects that presented themselves to my view, when I first consciously returned to the world that we live in.

'Look, doctor, look! he has come to his senses at last.'

'Open your mouth, sir, and take a sup of this.'

My mother was rejoicing over me on one side of the bed; and the unknown gentleman, addressed as 'doctor,' was offering me a spoonful of whisky and water, on the other. He called it the 'elixir of life;' and he bade me remark (speaking in a strong Scotch accent) that he tasted it himself to show he was in earnest.

The stimulant did its good work. My head felt less giddy; my mind became clearer. I could speak collectedly to my mother; I could vaguely recall the more marked events of the previous evening. A minute or two more – and the image of the person in whom those events had all centred became a living image in my memory. I tried to raise myself in the bed; I asked impatiently, 'Where is she?'

The doctor produced another spoonful of the elixir of life, and gravely repeated his first address to me:

'Open your mouth, sir, and take a sup of this.'

I persisted in repeating my question:

'Where is she?'

The doctor persisted in repeating his formula:

'Take a sup of this.'

I was too weak to contest the matter – I obeyed. My medical attendant nodded across the bed to my mother, and said, 'Now he'll do.' My mother had some compassion on me: she relieved my anxiety in these plain words:

'The lady has quite recovered, George; thanks to the doctor here.'

I looked at my professional colleague with a new interest. He was the legitimate fountain-head of the information that I was dying to have poured into my mind.

'How did he revive her?' I asked. 'Where is she now?'

The doctor held up his hand; warning me to stop.

'We shall do well, sir, if we proceed systematically,' he began, in a very positive manner. 'You will understand that every time you open your mouth it will be to take a sup of this – and not to speak. I shall tell you in due course, and the good lady your mother will tell you, all that you have any need to know. As I happen to have been first on what you may call the scene of action, it stands in the fit order of things that I should speak first. You will just permit me to mix a little more of the elixir of life – and then, as the poet says, my plain unvarnished tale I shall deliver.'

So he spoke, pronouncing, in a strong Scotch accent, the most carefully selected English I had ever heard. A hard-headed, square-shouldered, pertinaciously-self-willed man – it was plainly useless to contend with him. I turned to my mother's gentle face for encouragement, and I let my doctor have his own way.

'My name,' he proceeded, 'is MacGlue. I had the honour of presenting my respects at your house yonder, when you first came to live in this neighbourhood. You don't remember me at present, which is natural enough in the unbalanced condition of your mind; consequent, you will understand (as a professional person yourself), on copious loss of blood.'

There my patience gave way.

'Never mind me,' I interposed. 'Tell me about the lady.'

'You have opened your mouth, sir!' cried Mr MacGlue severely. 'You know the penalty – take a sup of this. I told you we should proceed systematically,' he went on, after he had forced me to submit to the penalty. 'Everything in its place, Mr Germaine; everything in its place. I was speaking of your bodily condition. Well, sir, and how did I discover your bodily condition? Providentially for *you*, I was driving home, yesterday evening, by the lower road (which is the road by the river-bank); and, drawing near to the inn here (they call it an hotel: it's nothing but an inn), I heard the screeching of the landlady half a mile off. A good woman enough, you will understand, as times go; but a poor creature in an emergency. Keep still; I'm coming to it now. Well, I went in to see if the screeching related to anything wanted in the medical way; and there I found you and the stranger lady – in a position which I may truthfully describe as standing in some need of improvement on the score of propriety. Tut! tut! I speak jocosely – you were both in a dead swoon. Having heard what the landlady had to tell me, and having to the best of my ability separated history from hysterics, in the course of the woman's narrative, I found myself, as it were, placed between two laws. The law of gallantry, you see, pointed to the lady as the first object of my professional services – while the law of humanity (seeing that you were still bleeding) pointed no less imperatively to you. I am no longer a young man – I left the lady to wait. My word! it was no light matter, Mr Germaine, to deal with your case, and get you carried up here out of the way. That old wound of yours, sir, is not to be trifled with. I bid you beware how you open it again. The next time you go out for an evening walk, and you see a lady in the water – you will do well for your own health to leave her there. What's that I see? Are you opening your mouth again? Do you want another sup already?'

'He wants to hear more about the lady,' said my mother, interpreting my wishes for me.

'Oh, the lady,' resumed Mr MacGlue, with the air of a man who found no great attraction in the subject proposed to him. 'There's not much that I know of to be said about the lady. A fine woman no doubt. If you could strip the flesh off her bones, you would find a splendid skeleton underneath. For, mind this! there's no such thing as a finely-made woman, without a good bony scaffolding to build her on at starting. I don't think much of this lady – morally speaking, you will understand. If I may be permitted to say so, in your presence, ma'am, there's a man in the background of that dramatic scene of hers on the bridge. However – not being the man myself – I have nothing to do with that. My business with the lady was just to set her vital machinery going again. And, heaven knows, she proved a heavy handful! It was even a more obstinate case to deal with, sir, than yours. I never, in all my experience, met with two people more unwilling to come back to this world and its troubles than you two were. And when I had done the business at last, when I was well-nigh swooning myself with the work and the worry of it, guess – I give you leave to speak for this once – guess what were the first words the lady said to me, when she came to herself again.'

I was too much excited to be able to exercise my ingenuity. 'I give it up!' I said impatiently.

'You may well give it up,' remarked Mr McGlue. 'The first words she addressed, sir, to the man who had dragged her out of the very jaws of death were these: "How dare you meddle with me? Why didn't you leave me to die?" Her exact language – I'll take my Bible oath of it. I was so provoked that I gave her the change back (as the saying is) in her own coin. "There's the river handy, ma'am," I said. "Do it again. I, for one, won't stir a hand to save you; I promise you that." She looked up sharply. "Are you the man who took me out of the river?" she said. "God forbid!" says I. "I'm only the doctor who was fool enough to meddle with you afterwards." She turned to the landlady. "Who took me out of the river?" she asked. The landlady told her, and mentioned your name. "Germaine?" she says to herself; "I know nobody named Germaine; I wonder whether it was the man who spoke to me on the bridge?" "Yes," says the landlady; "Mr Germaine said he met you on the bridge." Hearing that, she took a little time to think; and then she asked if she could see Mr Germaine. "Whoever he is," she says, "he has risked his life to save me, and I ought to thank him for doing that." "You can't thank him to-night," I said; "I've got him upstairs between life and death; and I've sent for his mother: wait till to-morrow." She turned on me, looking half frightened, half angry. "I can't wait," she says; "you don't know what you have done among you in bringing me back to life; I must leave this neighbourhood; I must be out of Perthshire to-morrow; when does the first coach southward pass this way?" Having nothing to do with the first coach southward, I referred her to the people of the inn. My business (now I had done with the lady) was upstairs in this room, to see how you were getting on. You were getting on as well as I could wish, and your good mother was at your bedside. I went home, to see what sick people might be waiting for me in the regular way. When I came back this morning, there was the foolish landlady with a new tale to tell. "Gone!" says she. "Who's gone?" says I. "The lady" says she, "by the first coach this morning!" '

'You don't mean to tell me that she has left the house?' I exclaimed.

'Oh, but I do!' said the doctor as positively as ever. 'Ask madam your mother here, and she'll certify it to your heart's content. I've got other sick ones to visit – and I'm away on my rounds. You'll see no more of the lady; and so much the better I'm thinking! In two hours' time I'll be back again; and, if I don't find you the worse in the interim, I'll see about having you transported from this strange place to the snug bed that knows you at home. Don't let him talk, ma'am – don't let him talk.'

With those parting words, Mr MacGlue left us to ourselves.

'Is it really true?' I said to my mother. 'Has she left the inn without waiting to see me?'

'Nobody could stop her, George,' my mother answered. 'The lady left the inn this morning by the coach to Edinburgh.'

I was bitterly disappointed. Yes! 'bitterly' is the word – though she *was* a stranger to me.

'Did you see her yourself?' I asked.

'I saw her for a few minutes, my dear, on my way up to your room.'

'What did she say?'

'She begged me to make her excuses to you. She said, "Tell Mr Germaine that my situation is dreadful: no human creature can help me. I must go away. My old life is as much at an end, as if your son had left me to drown in the river. I must find a new life for myself, in a new place. Ask Mr Germaine to forgive me for going away without thanking him. I daren't wait! I may be followed and found out. There is a person whom I am determined never to see again – never! never! never! Goodbye; and try to forgive me." She hid her face in her hands, and said no more. I tried to win her confidence – it was not to be done; I was obliged to leave her. There is some dreadful calamity, George, in that wretched woman's life. And such an interesting creature, too! It was impossible not to pity her, whether she deserves it or not. Everything about her is a mystery, my dear. She speaks English, without the slightest foreign accent – and yet she has a foreign name.'

'Did she give you her name?'

'No – and I was afraid to ask her to give it. But the landlady here is not a very scrupulous person. She told me she looked at the poor creature's linen, while it was drying by the fire. The name marked on it was: "Van Brandt."'

'Van Brandt?' I repeated. 'That sounds like a Dutch name. And yet you say she spoke like an Englishwoman. Perhaps she was born in England.'

'Or perhaps she may be married,' suggested my mother; 'and Van Brandt may be the name of her husband.'

The idea of her being a married woman had something in it repellant to me. I wished my mother had not thought of that last suggestion. I refused to receive it; I persisted in my own belief that the stranger was a single woman. In that character I could indulge myself in the luxury of thinking of her; I could consider the chances of my being able to trace this charming fugitive who had taken so strong a hold on my interest – whose desperate attempt at suicide had so nearly cost me my own life.

If she had gone as far as Edinburgh (which she would surely do, being bent on avoiding discovery) the prospect of finding her again – in that great city, and in my present weak state of health – looked doubtful indeed. Still, there was an underlying hopefulness in me which kept my spirits from being seriously depressed. I felt a purely imaginary (perhaps I ought to say, a purely superstitious) conviction, that we who had nearly died together, we who had been brought to life together, were surely destined to be involved in some future joys or sorrows common to us both. 'I fancy I shall see her again,' was my last thought before my weakness overpowered me, and I sank into a peaceful sleep.

That night I was removed from the inn to my own room at home; and that night I saw her again in a dream.

The image of her was as vividly impressed upon me as the far-different image of the child Mary, when I used to see it in the days of old. The dream-figure of the woman was robed as I had seen it robed on the bridge. She wore the same broad-brimmed garden hat of straw. She looked at me as she had looked at me when I approached her in the dim evening light. After a little her face brightened with a divinely-beautiful smile, and she whispered in my ear: 'Friend, do you know me?'

I knew her most assuredly – and yet it was with an incomprehensible after-feeling of doubt. Recognising her in my dream as the stranger who had so warmly interested me, I was nevertheless dissatisfied with myself as if it had not been the right recognition. I woke with this idea; and I slept no more that night.

In three days' time I was strong enough to go out driving with my mother, in the comfortable old-fashioned open carriage which had once belonged to Mr Germaine.

On the fourth day we arranged to make an excursion to a little waterfall in our neighbourhood. My mother had a great admiration of the place, and had often expressed a wish to possess some memorial of it. I resolved to take my sketch-book with me, on the chance that I might be able to please her by making a drawing of her favourite scene.

Searching for the sketch-book (which I had not used for years), I found it in an old desk of mine that had remained unopened since my departure for India. In the course of my investigation, I opened a drawer in the desk, and discovered a relic of the old times – my poor little Mary's first work in embroidery, the green flag!

The sight of the forgotten keepsake took my mind back to the bailiff's cottage, and reminded me of Dame Dermody, and her confident prediction about Mary and me.

I smiled as I recalled the old woman's assertion that no human power could hinder the union of the kindred spirits of the children in time to come. What had become of the prophesied dreams in which we were to communicate with each other through the term of our separation? Years had passed; and, sleeping or waking, I had seen nothing of Mary. Years had passed; and the first vision of a woman that had come to me had been my dream, a few nights since, of the stranger whom I had saved from drowning! I thought of these chances and changes in my life – but not contemptuously or bitterly. The new love that was now stealing its way into my heart had softened and humanised me. I said to myself, 'Ah, poor little Mary!' – and I kissed the green flag, in grateful memory of the days that were gone for ever.

We drove to the waterfall.

It was a beautiful day: the lonely sylvan scene was at its brightest and best. A wooden summer-house, commanding a prospect of the falling stream, had been built for the accommodation of pleasure-parties by the proprietor of the place. My mother suggested that I should try to make a sketch of the view from this point. I did my best to please her; but I was not satisfied with the result; and I abandoned my drawing before it was half finished. Leaving my sketch-book and pencil on the table of the summer-house, I proposed to my mother to cross the little wooden bridge which spanned the stream below the fall, and to see how the landscape looked from a new point of view.

The prospect of the waterfall, as seen from the opposite bank, presented even greater difficulties, to an amateur artist like me, than the prospect which we had just left. We returned to the summer-house.

I was the first to approach the open door. I stopped, checked in my advance by an unexpected discovery. The summer-house was no longer empty, as we had left it. A lady was seated at the table, with my pencil in her hand, writing in my sketch-book!

After waiting a moment I advanced a few steps nearer to the door, and stopped again, in breathless amazement. The stranger in the summer-house was now plainly revealed to me as the woman who had attempted to destroy herself from the bridge!

There was no doubt about it. There was the dress; there was the memorable face which I had seen in the evening light, which I had dreamed of only a few nights since! The woman herself – I saw her as plainly as I saw the sun shining on the waterfall – the woman herself; with my pencil in her hand; writing in my book!

My mother was close behind me: she noticed my agitation. 'George!' she exclaimed, 'what is the matter with you?'

I pointed through the open door of the summer-house.

'Well?' said my mother. 'What am I to look at?'

'Don't you see somebody, sitting at the table and writing in my sketch-book?'

My mother eyed me quickly. 'Is he going to be ill again?' I heard her say to herself.

At the same moment, the woman laid down the pencil, and rose slowly to her feet.

She looked at me with sorrowful and pleading eyes: she lifted her hand, and beckoned me to approach her. I obeyed. Moving without conscious will of my own, drawn nearer and nearer to her by an irresistible power, I ascended the short flight of stairs which led into the summer-house.

Within a few paces of her I stopped. She advanced a step towards me, and laid her hand gently on my bosom. Her touch filled me with strangely united sensations of rapture and awe. After a while she spoke, in low melodious tones, which mingled in my ear with the distant murmur of the falling water, until the two sounds became one. I heard in the murmur, I heard in the voice, these words: 'Remember me. Come to me.' Her hand dropped from my bosom; a momentary obscurity passed like a flying shadow over the bright daylight in the room. I looked for her when the light came back. She was gone.

My consciousness of passing events returned.

I saw the lengthening shadows outside, which told me that the evening was at hand. I saw the carriage approaching the summer-house to take us away. I felt my mother's hand on my arm, and heard her voice speaking to me anxiously. I was able to reply by a sign, entreating her not to be uneasy about me – but I could do no more. I was absorbed, body and soul, in the one desire to look at the sketch-book. As certainly as I had seen the woman – so certainly I had seen her with my pencil in her hand, writing in my book.

I advanced to the table on which the book was lying open. I looked at the blank space on the lower part of the page, under the foreground lines of my unfinished drawing. My mother, following me, looked at the page too.

There was the writing! The woman had disappeared – but there were her written words left behind her: visible to my mother as well as to me: readable by my mother's eyes as well as by mine!

These were the words we saw; arranged in two lines, as I copy them here:

WHEN THE FULL MOON SHINES
ON SAINT ANTHONY'S WELL.

CHAPTER V

NATURAL AND SUPERNATURAL

I pointed to the writing in the sketch-book, and looked at my mother. I was not mistaken. She *had* seen it, as I had seen it. But she refused to acknowledge that anything had happened to alarm her – plainly as I could detect it in her face.

'Somebody has been playing a trick on you, George,' she said.

I made no reply. It was needless to say anything. My poor mother was evidently as far from being satisfied with her own shallow explanation as I was. The carriage waited for us at the door. We set forth in silence on our drive home.

The sketch-book lay open on my knee. My eyes were fastened on it; my mind was absorbed in recalling the moment when the apparition beckoned me into the summer-house, and spoke. Putting the words and the writing together, the conclusion was too plain to be mistaken. The woman whom I had saved from drowning had need of me again.

And this was the same woman who, in her own proper person, had not hesitated to seize the first opportunity of leaving the house in which we had been sheltered together – without stopping to say one grateful word to the man who had preserved her from death! Four days only had elapsed, since she had left me, never (to all appearance) to see me again. And now, the ghostly apparition of her had returned, as to a tried and trusted friend; had commanded me to remember her and to go to her; and had provided against all possibility of my memory playing me false, by writing the words which invited me to meet her 'when the full moon shone on St Anthony's Well.'

What had happened in the interval? What did the supernatural manner of her communication with me mean? What ought my next course of action to be?

My mother roused me from my reflections. She stretched out her hand and suddenly closed the open book on my knee, as if the sight of the writing in it was unendurable to her.

'Why don't you speak to me, George?' she said. 'Why do you keep your thoughts to yourself?'

'My mind is lost in confusion,' I answered. 'I can suggest nothing and explain nothing. My thoughts are all bent on the one question of what I am to do next. On that point I believe I may say that my mind is made up.' I touched the sketch-book as I spoke. 'Come what may of it,' I said, 'I mean to keep the appointment.'

My mother looked at me as if she doubted the existence of her own senses.

'He talks as if it was a real thing!' she exclaimed. 'George! you don't really believe that you saw somebody in the summer-house? The place was empty. I tell you positively, when you pointed into the summer-house, the place was empty. You have been thinking and thinking of this woman till you persuade yourself that you have actually seen her.'

I opened the sketch-book again. 'I thought I saw her writing on this page,' I answered. 'Look at it – and tell me if I was wrong.'

My mother refused to look at it. Steadily as she persisted in taking the rational view, nevertheless the writing frightened her.

'It is not a week yet,' she went on, 'since I saw you lying between life and death in your bed at the inn. How can you talk of keeping the appointment, in your state of health? An appointment with a shadowy Something in your own imagination, which appears and disappears, and leaves substantial writing behind it! It's ridiculous George; I wonder you can help laughing at yourself.'

She tried to set the example of laughing at me – with the tears in her eyes, poor soul, as she made the useless effort. I began to regret having opened my mind so freely to her.

'Don't take the matter too seriously, mother,' I said. 'Perhaps I may not be able to find the place. I never heard of St Anthony's Well; I have not the least idea where it is. Suppose I make the discovery – and suppose the journey turns out to be an easy one – would you like to go with me?'

'God forbid!' cried my mother fervently. 'I will have nothing to do with it, George. You are in a state of delusion – I shall speak to the doctor.'

'By all means, my dear mother! Mr MacGlue is a sensible person. We pass his house on our way home – and we will ask him to dinner. In the meantime, let us say no more on the subject till we see the doctor.'

I spoke lightly, but I really meant what I said. My mind was sadly disturbed; my nerves were so shaken, that the slightest noises on the road startled me. The opinion of a man, like Mr MacGlue, who looked at all mortal matters from the same immovably practical point of view, might really have its use, in my case, as a species of moral remedy.

We waited until the dessert was on the table, and the servants had left the dining-room. Then, I told my story to the Scotch doctor as I have told it here; and, that done, I opened the sketch-book to let him see the writing for himself.

Had I turned to the wrong page?

I started to my feet, and held the book close to the light of the lamp that hung over the dining-table. No: I had found the right page. There was my half-finished drawing of the waterfall – but where were the two lines of writing beneath?

Gone!

I strained my eyes; I looked and looked. And the blank white paper looked back at me.

I replaced the open leaf before my mother.

'You saw it, as plainly as I did,' I said.

'Are my own eyes deceiving me? Look at the bottom of the page.'

My mother sank back in her chair with a cry of terror.

'Gone?' I asked.

'Gone!'

I turned to the doctor. He took me completely by surprise. No incredulous smile appeared on his face; no jesting words passed his lips. He was listening to us attentively. He was waiting gravely to hear more.

'I declare to you, on my word of honour,' I said to him, 'that I saw the apparition writing with my pencil at the bottom of that page. I declare that I took the book in my hand, and saw these words written in it: "When the full moon shines on Saint Anthony's Well." Not more than three hours have passed since that time – and, see for yourself, not a vestige of the writing remains.'

'Not a vestige of the writing remains,' Mr MacGlue repeated quietly.

'If you feel the slightest doubt of what I have told you,' I went on, 'ask my mother – she will bear witness that she saw the writing too.'

'I don't doubt that you both saw the writing,' answered Mr MacGlue with a composure that astonished me.

'Can you account for it?' I asked.

'Well,' said the impenetrable doctor, 'if I set my wits at work, I believe I might account for it, to the satisfaction of some people. For example, I might give you what they call, the rational explanation to begin with. I might say that you are, to my certain knowledge, in a highly-excited nervous condition; and that, when you saw the apparition (as you call it), you simply saw nothing but your own strong impression of an absent woman – who (as I greatly fear) has got on the weak or amatory side of you. I mean no offence, Mr Germaine——'

'I take no offence, doctor. But excuse me for speaking plainly – the rational explanation is thrown away on me.'

'I'll readily excuse you,' answered Mr MacGlue. 'The rather that I'm entirely of your opinion. I don't believe in the rational explanation myself.'

This was surprising, to say the least of it! 'What *do* you believe in?' I enquired. Mr MacGlue declined to let me hurry him.

'Wait a little,' he said. 'There's the *ir*-rational explanation to try next. Maybe it will fit itself to the present state of your mind better than the other. We will say, this time, that you have really seen the ghost (or double) of a living person. Very good. If you can suppose a disembodied spirit to appear in earthly clothing – of silk or merino as the case may be – it's no great stretch to suppose next that this same spirit is capable of holding a mortal pencil, and of writing mortal words in a mortal sketching-book. And, if the ghost vanishes (which your ghost did), it seems supernaturally appropriate that the writing should follow the example and vanish too. And the reason of the vanishment may be (if you want a reason), either that the ghost does not like letting a stranger like me into its secrets; or that vanishing is a settled habit of ghosts and of everything associated with them; or that this ghost has changed its mind in the course of three hours (being the ghost of a woman, I am sure that's not wonderful), and doesn't care to see you "when the full moon shines on Anthony's Well." There's the *ir*rational explanation for you. And, speaking for myself, I'm bound to add that I don't set a pin's value on *that* explanation either.'

Mr MacGlue's sublime indifference to both sides of the question began to irritate me.

'In plain words, doctor,' I said, 'you don't think the circumstances that I have mentioned to you worthy of serious investigation?'

'I don't think serious investigation capable of dealing with the circumstances,' answered the doctor. 'Put it in that way, and you put it right. Just look round you. Here we three persons are, alive and hearty at this snug table. If (which God forbid!) good Mistress Germaine, or yourself, were to fall down dead in another moment, I, doctor as I am, could no more explain what first principle of life and movement had been suddenly extinguished in you than the dog there sleeping on the hearth-rug. If I am content to sit down ignorant, in the face of such an impenetrable mystery as this – presented to me, day after day, every time I see a living creature come into the world or go out of it – why may I not sit down content in the face of your lady in the summer-house, and say, she's altogether beyond my fathoming, and there is an end of her!'

At those words, my mother joined in the conversation for the first time.

'Ah, sir,' she said, 'if you could only persuade my son to take your sensible view, how happy I should be! Would you believe it – he positively means, (if he can find the place) to go to St Anthony's Well!'

Even this revelation entirely failed to surprise Mr MacGlue.

'Aye? aye? He means to keep his appointment with the ghost – does he? Well! I can be of some service to him, if he sticks to his resolution. I can tell him of another man who kept a written appointment with a ghost, and what came of it.'

This was a startling announcement. Did he really mean what he said?

'Are you in jest or in earnest?' I asked.

'I never joke, sir!' said Mr MacGlue. 'No sick person really believes in a doctor who jokes. I defy you to show me a man at the head of our profession who has ever been discovered in high spirits (in medical hours) by his nearest and dearest friend. You may have wondered, I dare say, at seeing me take your strange narrative as coolly as I do. It comes naturally, sir. Yours is not the first story of a ghost and a pencil that I have heard.'

'Do you mean to tell me,' I said, 'that you know of another man who has seen what I have seen?'

'That's just what I mean to tell you,' rejoined the doctor. 'The man was a faraway Scots' cousin of my late wife, who bore the honourable name of Bruce, and followed a seafaring life. I'll take another glass of the sherry-wine, just to wet my whistle, as the vulgar saying is, before I begin. Well, you must know Bruce was mate of a barque, at the time I'm speaking of; and he was on a voyage from Liverpool to New Brunswick. At noon, one day, he and the captain having taken their observation of the sun, were hard at it below, working out the latitude and longitude on their slates. Bruce, in his cabin, looked across through the open door of the captain's cabin opposite. "What do you make it, sir?" says Bruce. The man in the captain's cabin looked up. And what did Bruce see? The face of the captain? Devil a bit of it – the face of a total stranger! Up jumps Bruce, with his heart going full gallop all in a moment; and searches for the captain on deck; and finds him much as usual, with his calculations done, and his latitude and longitude off his mind for the day. "There's somebody at your desk, sir," says Bruce. "He's writing on your slate, and he's a total stranger to me." "A stranger in my cabin?" says the captain. "Why, Mr Bruce, the ship has been six weeks out of port. How did he get on board?" Bruce doesn't know how, but he sticks to his story. Away goes the captain, and bursts like a whirlwind into his cabin, and finds nobody there. Bruce himself is obliged to acknowledge that the place is certainly empty. "If I didn't know you were a sober man," says the captain, "I should charge you with drinking. As it is, I'll hold you accountable for nothing worse than dreaming. Don't do it again, Mr Bruce." Bruce sticks to his story; Bruce swears he saw the man writing on the captain's slate. The captain takes up the slate, and looks at it. "Lord save us and bless us," says he, "here the writing is, sure enough!" Bruce looks at it too, and sees the writing as plain as can be, in these words: "Steer to the Nor' West." That, and no more. Ah, goodness me, narrating is dry work, Mr Germaine! With your leave, I'll take another drop of the sherry-wine.'

'Well! (It's fine old wine that; look at the oily drops running down the glass). Well, steering to the north-west, you will understand, was out of the captain's course. Nevertheless, finding no solution of the mystery on board the ship, and the weather at the time being fine, the captain determined, while the daylight lasted, to alter his course, and see what came of it. Towards three o'clock in the afternoon, an iceberg came of it; with a wrecked ship stove in, and frozen fast to the ice; and the passengers and crew nigh to death with cold and exhaustion. Wonderful enough, you will say, but more remains behind. As the mate was helping one of the rescued passengers up the side of the barque, who should he turn out to be but the very man whose ghostly appearance Bruce had seen in the captain's cabin, writing on the captain's slate! And more than that – if your capacity for being surprised·isn't clean worn out by this time – the passenger recognized the barque as the very vessel which he had seen in a dream at noon that day. He had even spoken of it to one of the officers on board the wrecked ship, when he woke. "We shall be rescued to-day," he had said – and he had exactly described the rig of the barque, hours and hours before the vessel herself hove in view. Now you know, Mr Germaine, how my wife's far-away cousin kept an appointment with a ghost, and what came of it."*

Concluding this story in these words, the doctor helped himself to another glass of 'the sherry-wine.' I was not satisfied yet – I wanted to know more.

'The writing on the slate,' I said. 'Did it remain there? or did it vanish, like the writing in my book?'

Mr MacGlue's answer disappointed me. He had never asked, and had never heard, whether the writing had remained or not. He had told me all that he knew, and he had but one thing more to say – and that was in the nature of a remark, with a moral attached to it. 'There's a marvellous resemblance, Mr Germaine, between your story and Bruce's story. The main difference, as I see it, is this. The passenger's appointment proved to be the salvation of a whole ship's company. I very much doubt whether the lady's appointment will prove to be the salvation of You.'

I silently re-considered the strange narrative which had just been related to me. Another man had seen what I had seen – had done what I proposed to do! My mother noticed with grave displeasure the strong impression which Mr MacGlue had produced on my mind.

'I wish you had kept your story to yourself, doctor,' she said sharply.

'May I ask why, madam?'

'You have confirmed my son, sir, in his resolution to go to St Anthony's Well.'

Mr MacGlue quietly consulted his pocket almanac before he replied.

'It's the full moon on the ninth of the month,' he said. 'That gives Mr Germaine some days of rest, ma'am, before he takes the journey. If he travels in his own comfortable carriage – whatever I may think, morally-speaking, of his enterprise – I can't say, medically-speaking, that I believe it will do him much harm.'

'You know where St Anthony's Well is?' I interposed.

'I must be mighty ignorant of Edinburgh not to know that,' replied the doctor.

'Is the Well in Edinburgh, then?'

'It's just outside Edinburgh – looks down on it, as you may say. You

---

* The doctor's narrative is not imaginary. It will be found related in full detail, and authenticated by names and dates, in Robert Dale Owen's very interesting work, called 'Footfalls on the Boundary of Another World.' The author gladly takes this opportunity of acknowledging his obligations to Mr Owen's remarkable book.

follow the old street called the Canongate, to the end. You turn to your right, past the famous Palace of Holyrood; you cross the Park and the Drive; and take your way upwards to the ruins of Anthony's Chapel, on the shoulder of the hill — and there you are! There's a high rock behind the Chapel; and at the foot of it, you will find the spring they call Anthony's Well. It's thought a pretty view by moonlight — and they tell me it's no longer beset at night by bad characters, as it used to be in the old time.'

My mother, in graver and graver displeasure, rose to retire to the drawing-room.

'I confess you have disappointed me,' she said to Mr MacGlue. 'I should have thought you would have been the last man to encourage my son in an act of imprudence.'

'Craving your pardon, madam, your son requires no encouragement. I can see for myself that his mind is made up. Where is the use of a person like me trying to stop him? Dear madam, if he won't profit by your advice, what hope can I have that he will take mine?'

Mr MacGlue pointed this artful compliment by a bow of the deepest respect, and threw open the door for my mother to pass out.

When we were left together over our wine, I asked the doctor how soon I might safely start on my journey to Edinburgh.

'Take three days to do the journey; and you may start, if you're bent on it, at the beginning of the week. But mind this,' added the prudent doctor, 'though I own I'm anxious to hear what comes of your expedition — understand at the same time, so far as the lady is concerned, that I wash my hands of the consequences.'

CHAPTER VI

SAINT ANTHONY'S WELL

I stood on the rocky eminence, in front of the ruins of St Anthony's Chapel, and looked on the magnificent view of Edinburgh and of the old Palace of Holyrood, bathed in the light of the full moon.

The Well, as the doctor's instructions had informed me, was behind the Chapel. I waited for some minutes in front of the ruin, partly to recover my breath, after ascending the hill; partly, I own, to master the nervous agitation which the sense of my position at that moment had aroused in me. The woman, or the apparition of the woman — it might be either — was perhaps within a few yards of the place that I occupied. Not a living creature appeared in front of the Chapel. Not a sound caught my ear, from any part of the solitary hill. I tried to fix my whole attention on the beauties of the moonlit view. It was not to be done. My mind was far away from the objects on which my eyes rested. My mind was with the woman whom I had seen in the summer-house, writing in my book.

I turned to skirt the side of the Chapel. A few steps more over the broken ground, brought me within view of the Well, and of the high boulder, or rock, from the foot of which the waters gushed bright in the light of the moon.

She was there.

I recognized her figure as she stood leaning against the rock, with her hands crossed in front of her, lost in thought. I recognized her face, as she looked up quickly, startled by the sound of my footsteps in the deep stillness of the night.

Was it the woman, or the apparition of the woman? I waited – looking at her in silence.

She spoke. The sound of her voice was not the mysterious sound that I had heard in the summer-house – it was the sound I had heard on the bridge, when we first met in the dim evening light.

'Who are you? What do you want?'

As those words passed her lips, she recognized me. '*You* here!' she went on, advancing a step in uncontrollable surprise. 'What does this mean?'

'I am here,' I answered, 'to meet you by your own appointment.'

She stepped back again, leaning against the rock. The moonlight shone full upon her face. There was terror as well as astonishment in her eyes, while they now looked at me.

'I don't understand you,' she said; 'I have not seen you since you spoke to me on the bridge.'

'Pardon me,' I replied. 'I have seen you – or the appearance of you – since that time. I heard you speak. I saw you write.'

She looked at me with the strangest expression of mingled resentment and curiosity. 'What did I say?' she asked. 'What did I write?'

'You said, "Remember me. Come to me." You wrote, 'When the full moon shines on St Anthony's Well.''

'Where?' she cried. 'Where did I do that?'

'In a summer-house which stands by a waterfall,' I answered. 'Do you know the place?'

Her head sank back against the rock. A low cry of terror burst from her. Her arm, resting on the rock, dropped at her side. I hurriedly approached her, in the fear that she might fall on the stony ground.

She rallied her failing strength. 'Don't touch me!' she exclaimed. 'Stand back, sir! You frighten me.'

I tried to soothe her. 'Why do I frighten you? You know who I am. Can you doubt my interest in you, after I have been the means of saving your life?'

Her reserve vanished in an instant. She advanced without hesitation, and took me by the hand.

'I ought to thank you,' she said; 'and I do. I am not so ungrateful as I seem. I am not a wicked woman, sir – I was mad with misery when I tried to drown myself. Don't distrust me! Don't despise me!' She stopped – I saw the tears on her cheeks. With a sudden contempt for herself, she dashed them away. Her whole tone and manner altered once more. Her reserve returned; she looked at me with a strange flash of suspicion and defiance in her eyes. 'Mind this!' she said loudly and abruptly, 'you were dreaming when you thought you saw me writing! You didn't see me; you never heard me speak. How could I say those familiar words to a stranger like you? It's all your fancy – and you try to frighten me by talking of it as if it was a real thing!' She changed again; her eyes softened to the sad and tender look which made them so irresistibly beautiful. She drew her cloak round her with a shudder as if she felt the chill of the night air. 'What is the matter with me?' I heard her say to herself. 'Why do I trust this man in my dreams? And why am I ashamed of it, when I wake?'

That strange outburst encouraged me. I risked letting her know that I had overheard her last words.

'If you trust me in your dreams, you only do me justice,' I said. 'Do me justice now; give me your confidence. You are alone – you are in trouble – you want a friend's help. I am waiting to help you.'

She hesitated. I tried to take her hand. The strange creature drew it away with a cry of alarm: her one great fear seemed to be the fear of letting me touch her.

'Give me time to think of it,' she said. 'You don't know what I have got to think of. Give me till to-morrow; and let me write. Are you staying in Edinburgh?'

I thought it wise to be satisfied – in appearance at least – with this concession. Taking out my card, I wrote on it in pencil the address of the hotel at which I was staying. She read the card by the moonlight, when I put it into her hand.

'"George!"' she repeated to herself; stealing another look at me as the name passed her lips. '"George Germaine." I never heard of "Germaine." But "George" reminds me of old times.' She smiled sadly at some passing fancy or remembrance in which I was not permitted to share. 'There is nothing very wonderful in your being called "George,"' she went on, after a while. 'The name is common enough – one meets with it everywhere as a man's name. And yet——' Her eyes finished the sentence; her eyes said to me, 'I am not so much afraid of you, now I know that you are called "George."'

So she unconsciously led me to the brink of discovery!

If I had only asked her what associations she connected with my

Christian name – if I had only persuaded her to speak in the briefest and most guarded terms of her past life – the barrier between us, which the change in our names and the lapse of ten years had raised, must have been broken down; the recognition must have followed. But I never even thought of it; and for this simple reason – I was in love with her. The purely selfish idea of winning my way to her favourable regard, by taking instant advantage of the new interest that I had awakened in her, was the one idea which occurred to my mind.

'Don't wait to write to me,' I said. 'Don't put it off till to-morrow. Who knows what may happen before to-morrow? Surely I deserve some little return for the sympathy that I feel with you? I don't ask for much. Make me happy, by making me of some service to you, before we part to-night.'

I took her hand, this time, before she was aware of me. The whole woman seemed to yield at my touch. Her hand lay unresistingly in mine; her charming figure came by soft graduations nearer and nearer to me; her head almost touched my shoulder. She murmured in faint accents, broken by sighs, 'Don't take advantage of me. I am so friendless: I am so completely in your power.' Before I could answer, before I could move, her hand closed on mine; her head sank on my shoulder: she burst into tears.

Any man, not an inbred and inborn villain, would have respected her at that moment. I put her hand on my arm, and led her away gently past the ruined chapel, and down the slope of the hill.

'This lonely place is frightening you,' I said. 'Let us walk a little, and you will soon be yourself again.'

She smiled through her tears like a child.

'Yes,' she said eagerly. 'But not that way.' I had accidentally taken the direction which led away from the city: she begged me to turn towards the houses and streets. We walked back towards Edinburgh. She eyed me, as we went on in the moonlight, with innocent wondering looks. 'What an unaccountable influence you have over me!' she exclaimed. 'Did you ever see me – did you ever hear my name – before we met that evening at the river?'

'Never!'

'And I never heard *your* name, and never saw *you* before. Strange! very strange! Ah, I remember somebody – only an old woman, sir – who might once have explained it! Where shall I find the like of her now?'

She sighed bitterly. The lost friend or relative had evidently been dear to her. 'A relation of yours?' I enquired – more to keep her talking than because I felt any interest in any member of her family but herself.

We were again on the brink of discovery. And again it was decreed that we were to advance no farther!

'Don't ask me about my relations!' she broke out. 'I daren't think of the dead and gone, in the trouble that is trying me now. If I speak of the old times at home, I shall only burst out crying again, and distress you. Talk of something else, sir, talk of something else.'

The mystery of the apparition in the summer-house was not cleared up yet. I took my opportunity of approaching the subject.

'You spoke a little while since of dreaming of me,' I began. 'Tell me your dream.'

'I hardly know whether it was a dream or whether it was something else,' she answered. 'I call it a dream for want of a better word.'

'Did it happen at night?'

'No. In the daytime – in the afternoon.'

'Late in the afternoon?'

'Yes – close on the evening.'

My memory reverted to the doctor's story of the shipwrecked passenger, whose ghostly 'double' had appeared in the vessel that was to rescue him, and who had himself seen that vessel in a dream.

'Do you remember the day of the month and the hour?' I asked.

She mentioned the day, and she mentioned the hour. It was the day when my mother and I had visited the waterfall! It was the hour when I had seen the apparition in the summer-house, writing in my book!

I stopped in irrepressible astonishment. We had walked, by this time, nearly as far on the way back to the city as the old Palace of Holyrood. My companion, after a glance at me, turned and looked at the rugged old building, mellowed into quiet beauty by the lovely moonlight.

'This is my favourite walk,' she said simply, 'since I have been in Edinburgh. I don't mind the loneliness – I like the perfect tranquillity here at night.' She glanced at me again. 'What is the matter?' she asked. 'You say nothing; you only look at me.'

'I want to hear more of your dream,' I said. 'How did you come to be sleeping in the daytime?'

'It is not easy to say what I was doing,' she replied as we walked on again. 'I was miserably anxious and ill – I felt my helpless condition keenly on that day. It was dinner-time, I remember; and I had no appetite. I went upstairs (at the inn where I was staying), and laid down, quite worn out, on my bed. I don't know whether I fainted or whether I slept. I lost all consciousness of what was going on about me; and I got some other consciousness in its place. If this was dreaming, I can only say it was the most vivid dream I ever had in my life.'

'Did it begin by your seeing me?' I enquired.

'It began by my seeing your drawing-book – lying open on a table in a summer-house.'

'Can you describe the summer-house, as you saw it?'

She described not only the summer-house, but the view of the waterfall from the door. She knew the size, she knew the binding of my sketch-book – locked up in my desk, at that moment, at home in Perthshire.

'And you wrote in the book,' I went on. 'Do you remember what you wrote?'

She looked away from me confusedly, as if she was ashamed to recall this part of her dream.

'You have mentioned it already,' she said. 'There is no need for me to go over the words again. Tell me one thing – when *you* were at the summer-house, did you wait a little on the path to the door, before you went in?'

I *had* waited – surprised by my first view of the woman writing in my book! Having answered her to this effect, I asked what she had done or dreamed of doing, at the later moment when I entered the summer-house.

'I did the strangest things,' she said in low wondering tones. 'If you had been my brother, I could hardly have treated you more familiarly! I beckoned to you to come to me – I even laid my hand on your bosom. I spoke to you – as I might have spoken to my oldest and dearest friend. I said, "Remember me. Come to me!" Oh, I was so ashamed of myself when I came to my senses again, and recollected it! Was there ever such familiarity – even in a dream – between a woman and a man whom she had only once seen, and then as a perfect stranger!'

'Did you notice how long it was,' I asked, 'from the time when you laid down on the bed, to the time when you found yourself awake again?'

'I think I can tell you,' she replied. 'It was the dinner-time of the house (as I said just now), when I went upstairs. Not long after I had come to myself, I heard a church clock strike the hour. Reckoning from one time to the other, it must have been quite three hours from the time when I first laid down, to the time when I got up again.'

Was the clue to the mysterious disappearance of the writing to be found here?

Looking back by the light of later discoveries, I am inclined to think that it was. In three hours, the lines traced by the apparition of her had vanished. In three hours, she had come to herself, and had felt ashamed of the familiar manner in which she had communicated with me in her sleeping state. While she had trusted me, in the trance – trusted me, because her spirit was then free to recognise my spirit – the writing had remained on the page. When her waking will counteracted the influence of her sleeping will, the writing disappeared. Is this the explanation? If it is not, where is the explanation to be found?

We walked on until we reached that part of the Canongate street in which she lodged. We stopped at the door.

CHAPTER VII

THE LETTER OF INTRODUCTION

I looked at the house. It was an inn – of no great size, but of respectable appearance. If I was to be of any use to her that night, the time had come to speak of other subjects than the subject of dreams.

'After all that you have told me,' I said, 'I will not ask you to admit me any farther into your confidence, until we meet again. Only let me hear how I can relieve your most pressing anxieties. What are your plans? Can I do anything to help them, before you go to rest to-night?'

She thanked me warmly, and hesitated; looking up the street and down the street, in evident embarrassment what to say next.

'Do you propose staying in Edinburgh?' I asked.

'Oh, no! I don't wish to remain in Scotland. I want to go much farther away – I think I should do better in London; at some respectable milliner's, if I could be properly recommended. I am quick at my needle, and I understand cutting out. Or I could keep accounts, if – if anybody would trust me.'

She stopped, and looked at me doubtingly – as if she felt far from sure, poor soul, of winning my confidence to begin with! I acted on that hint, with the headlong impetuosity of a man who was in love.

'I can give you exactly the recommendation you want,' I said. 'Whenever you like. Now, if you would prefer it.'

Her charming features brightened with pleasure. 'Oh, you are indeed a friend to me!' she said impulsively. Her face clouded again – she saw my proposal in a new light. 'Have I any right,' she said sadly, 'to accept what you offer me?'

'Let me give you the letter,' I answered; 'and you can decide for yourself whether you will use it or not.'

I put her arm again in mine, and entered the inn.

She shrank back, in alarm. What would the landlady think, if she saw her lodger enter the house at night, in company with a stranger, and that stranger a gentleman? The landlady appeared, as she made the objection. Reckless what I said or what I did, I introduced myself as her relative; and asked to be shown into a quiet room in which I could write a letter. After one sharp glance at me, the landlady appeared to be satisfied that she was dealing with a gentleman. She led the way into a sort of parlour behind the 'bar;' placed writing materials on the table; looked at my companion as only one woman can look at another, under certain circumstances; and left us by ourselves.

It was the first time I had ever been in a room with her, alone. The embarrassing sense of her position had heightened her colour, and brightened her eyes. She stood, leaning one hand on the table, confused and irresolute; her firm and supple figure falling into an attitude of unsought grace which it was literally a luxury to look at. I said nothing; my eyes confessed my admiration: the writing materials lay untouched before me on the table. How long the silence might have lasted I cannot say. She abruptly broke it. Her instinct warned her that silence might have its dangers, in our position. She turned to me, with an effort; she said uneasily, 'I don't think you ought to write your letter to-night, sir.'

'Why not?'

'You know nothing of me. Surely you ought not to recommend a person who is a stranger to you? And I am worse than a stranger. I am a miserable wretch who has tried to commit a great sin. I have tried to destroy myself. Perhaps the misery I was in might be some excuse for me, if you knew it. You ought to know it. But it's so late to-night; and I am so sadly tired – and there are some things, sir, which it is not easy for a woman to speak of in the presence of a man.'

Her head sank on her bosom; her delicate lips trembled a little; she said no more. The way to reassure and console her lay plainly enough before me, if I chose to take it. Without stopping to think, I took it.

Reminding her that she had herself proposed writing to me when we met that evening, I suggested that she should wait to tell the sad story of her troubles, until it was convenient to her to send me the narrative in the form of a letter. 'In the meantime,' I added, 'I have the most perfect confidence in you; and I beg as a favour that you will let me put it to the proof. I can introduce you to a dressmaker in London, who is at the head of a large establishment – and I will do it before I leave you to-night.'

I dipped my pen in the ink as I said the words. Let me confess frankly the lengths to which my infatuation led me. The dressmaker to whom I had alluded, had been my mother's maid, in former years, and had been established in business with money lent by my late stepfather, Mr Germaine. I used both their names, without scruple; and I wrote my recommendation in terms which the best of living women and the ablest of existing dressmakers could never have hoped to merit. Will anybody find excuses for me? Those rare persons who have been in love, and who have not completely forgotten it yet, may perhaps find excuses for me. It matters little; I don't deserve them.

I handed her the open letter to read.

She blushed delightfully – she cast one tenderly-grateful look at me, which I remembered but too well for many and many an after day. The next moment, to my astonishment, this changeable creature changed again. Some forgotten consideration seemed to have occurred to her. She turned pale; the soft lines of pleasure in her face hardened little by little;

she regarded me with the saddest look of confusion and distress. Putting the letter down before me on the table, she said timidly,

'Would you mind adding a postscript, sir?'

I suppressed all appearance of surprise as well as I could, and took up the pen again.

'Would you please say,' she went on, 'that I am only to be taken on trial, at first. I am not to be engaged for more——' Her voice sank lower and lower, so that I could barely hear the next words——' for more than three months, certain.'

It was not in human nature – perhaps I ought to say, it was not in the nature of a man who was in my situation – to refrain from showing some curiosity, on being asked to supplement a letter of recommendation by such a postscript as this!

'Have you some other employment in prospect?' I asked.

'None,' she answered, with her head down, and her eyes avoiding mine.

An unworthy doubt of her – the mean offspring of jealousy – found its way into my mind.

'Have you some absent friend,' I went on, 'who is likely to prove a better friend than I am, if you only give him time?'

She lifted her noble head. Her grand guileless grey eyes rested on me with a look of patient reproach.

'I have not got a friend in the world,' she said. 'For God's sake, ask me no more questions to-night.'

I rose, and gave her the letter once more – with the postscript added, in her own words.

We stood together by the table; we looked at each other, in a momentary silence.

'How can I thank you?' she murmured softly. 'Oh, sir, I will indeed be worthy of the confidence that you have shown in me!' Her eyes moistened; her variable colour came and went; her dress heaved softly over the lovely outline of her bosom. I don't believe the man lives who could have resisted her at that moment. I lost all power of restraint; I caught her in my arms; I whispered, 'I love you!' I kissed her passionately. For a moment, she lay helpless and trembling on my breast; for a moment, her fragrant lips softly returned the kiss. In an instant more it was over. She tore herself away, with a shudder that shook her from head to foot – and threw the letter that I had given her indignantly at my feet.

'How dare you take advantage of me. How dare you touch me!' she said. 'Take your letter back, sir – I refuse to receive it; I will never speak to you again. You don't know what you have done. You don't know how deeply you have wounded me. Oh!' she cried, throwing herself in despair on a sofa that stood near her – 'shall I ever recover my self-respect? shall I ever forgive myself for what I have done to-night?'

I implored her pardon; I assured her of my repentance and regret in words which did really come from my heart. The violence of her agitation more than distressed me – I was really alarmed by it.

She composed herself after a while. She rose to her feet with modest dignity, and silently held out her hand in token that my repentance was accepted.

'You will give me time for atonement?' I pleaded. 'You will not lose all confidence in me? Let me see you again, if it is only to show that I am not quite unworthy of your pardon – at your own time; in the presence of another person if you like.'

'I will write to you,' she said.

'To-morrow?'

'To-morrow.'

I took up the letter of recommendation from the floor.

'Make your goodness to me complete,' I said. 'Don't mortify me by refusing to take my letter.'

'I will take your letter,' she answered quietly. 'Thank you for writing it. Leave me now, please. Good night.'

I left her, pale and sad, with my letter in her hand. I left her, with my mind in a tumult of contending emotions, which gradually resolved themselves into two master feelings as I walked on: – Love that adored her more fervently than ever; and Hope that set the prospect before me of seeing her again on the next day.

CHAPTER VIII

THE DISASTERS OF MRS VAN BRANDT

A man who passes his evening as I had passed mine, may go to bed afterwards if he has nothing better to do. But he must not rank among the number of his reasonable anticipations the expectation of getting a night's rest. The morning was well advanced, and the hotel was astir, before I at last closed my eyes in slumber. When I awoke, my watch informed me that it was close on noon.

I rang the bell. My servant appeared with a letter in his hand. It had been left for me, three hours since, by a lady who had driven to the hotel door in a carriage, and had then driven away again. The man had found me sleeping, when he entered my bedchamber; and, having received no orders to wake me over-night, had left the letter on the sitting-room table, until he heard my bell.

Easily guessing who my correspondent was, I opened the letter. An inclosure fell out of it – to which, for the moment, I paid no attention. The letter was the one object of interest to me. I turned eagerly to the first lines. They announced that the writer had escaped me for the second time: early that morning, she had left Edinburgh! The paper enclosed proved to be my letter of introduction to the dressmaker, returned to me.

I was more than angry with her – I felt her second flight from me as a downright outrage. In five minutes I had hurried on my clothes, and was on my way to the inn in the Canongate as fast as a horse could draw me.

The servants could give me no information. Her escape had been effected without their knowledge.

The landlady, to whom I next addressed myself, deliberately declined to assist me in any way whatever. 'I have given the lady my promise,' said this obstinate person, 'to answer not one word to any question that you may ask me about her. In my belief, she is acting as becomes an honest woman in removing herself from any further communication with you. I saw you through the key-hole last night, sir. I wish you good morning.'

Returning to my hotel, I left no attempt to discover her untried. I traced the coachman who had driven her. He had set her down at a shop, and had then been dismissed. I questioned the shopkeeper. He remembered that he had sold some articles of linen to a lady with her veil down and a travelling bag in her hand, and he remembered no more. I circulated a description of her in the different coach-offices. Three 'elegant young ladies, with their veils down, and with travelling bags in their hands' answered to the description; and which of the three was the fugitive of whom I was in search, it was impossible to discover. In the days of railways and electric telegraphs, I might have succeeded in tracing her. In the days of which I am now writing, she set investigation at defiance.

I read and re-read her letter; on the chance that some slip of the pen might furnish the clue which I had failed to find in any other way. Here is the narrative that she addressed to me; copied from the original, word for word: –

'Dear Sir, – Forgive me for leaving you again, as I left you in Perthshire. After what took place last night, I have no other choice (knowing my own weakness, and the influence that you seem to have over me) than to thank you gratefully for your kindness, and to bid you farewell. My sad position must be my excuse for separating myself from you in this rude manner, and for venturing to send you back your letter of introduction. If I use the letter, I only offer you a means of communicating with me. For your sake, as well as for mine, this must not be. I must never give you a second opportunity of saying that you love me; I must go away, leaving no trace behind by which you can possibly discover me.

'But I cannot forget that I owe my poor life to your compassion and your courage. You, who saved me, have a right to know what the provocation was that drove me to drowning myself, and what my situation is, now that I am (thanks to you) still a living woman. You shall hear my sad story, sir; and I will try to tell it as briefly as possible.

'I was married, not very long since, to a Dutch gentleman whose name is Van Brandt. Please excuse my entering into family particulars. I have endeavoured to write and tell you about my dear lost father and my old home. But the tears come into my eyes when I think of my happy past life; I really cannot see the lines as I try to write them.

'Let me then only say that Mr Van Brandt was well recommended to my good father, before I married. I have only now discovered that he obtained these recommendations from his friends, under a false pretence which it is needless to trouble you by mentioning in detail. Ignorant of what he had done, I lived with him happily. I cannot truly declare that he was the object of my first love; but he was the one person in the world whom I had to look up to after my father's death. I esteemed him and admired him – and, if I may say so without vanity, I did indeed make him a good wife.

'So the time went on, sir, prosperously enough, until the evening came when you and I met on the bridge.

'I was out alone in our garden, trimming the shrubs, when the maid-servant came and told me there was a foreign lady, in a carriage at the door, who desired to say a word to Mrs Van Brandt. I sent the maid on before, to show her into the sitting-room; and I followed to receive my visitor as soon as I had made myself tidy. She was a dreadful woman, with a flushed fiery face and impudent bright eyes. "Are you Mrs Van Brandt?" she said. I answered, "Yes." "Are you really married to him?" she asked me. That question (naturally enough, I think) upset my temper. I said, "How dare you doubt it?" She laughed in my face. "Send for Van Brandt;" she said. I went out into the passage, and called him down from the room upstairs in which he was writing. "Ernest!" I said, "here is a person who has insulted me; come down directly!" He left his room the moment he heard me. The woman followed me out into the passage to meet him. She made him a low curtsey. He turned deadly pale, the moment he set eyes on her. That frightened me. I said to him, "For God's sake, what does this mean?" He took me by the arm, and he answered, "You shall know soon. Go back to your gardening, and don't return to the house till I send for you." His looks were so shocking, he was so unlike himself, that I declare he daunted me. I let him take me as far as the garden door. He squeezed my hand. "For my sake, darling," he whispered, "do what I ask of you." I went into the garden and sat me down on the nearest bench, and waited miserably for what was to come.

'How long a time passed, I don't know. My anxiety got to such a pitch at last that I could bear it no longer. I ventured back to the house.

'I listened in the passage, and heard nothing. I went close to the parlour door, and still there was silence. I took courage, and opened the door.

'The room was empty. There was a letter on the table. It was in my husband's handwriting; and it was addressed to me. I opened it and read it. The letter told me that I was deserted, disgraced, ruined. The woman with the fiery face and the impudent eyes was Van Brandt's lawful wife. She had given him his choice of going away with her at once, or of being prosecuted for bigamy. He had gone away with her – gone, and left me.

'Remember, sir, that I had lost both father and mother. I had no friends. I was alone in the world without a creature near to comfort or advise me. And please to bear in mind that I have a temper which feels even the smallest slights and injuries very keenly. Do you wonder at what I had it in my thoughts to do, that evening, on the bridge?

'Mind this! I believe I should never have attempted to destroy myself, if I could only have burst out crying. No tears came to me. A dull stunned feeling took a hold, like a vice, on my head and on my heart. I walked straight to the river. I said to myself quite calmly, as I went along: "*There* is the end of it, and the sooner the better."

'What happened after that, you know as well as I do. I may get on to the next morning – the morning when I so ungratefully left you at the inn by the river side.

'I had but one reason, sir, for going away by the first conveyance that I could find to take me – and this was the fear that Van Brandt might discover me if I remained in Perthshire. The letter that he had left on the table was full of expressions of love and remorse – to say nothing of excuses for his infamous behaviour to me. He declared that he had been entrapped into a private marriage with a profligate woman, when he was little more than a lad. They had long since separated by common consent. When he first courted me, he had every reason to believe that she was dead. How he had been deceived in this particular, and how she had discovered that he had married me, he had yet to find out. Knowing her furious temper, he had gone away with her, as the one means of preventing an application to the justices and a scandal in the neighbourhood. In a day or two, he would purchase his release from her by an addition to the allowance which she had already received from him; he would return to me, and take me abroad, out of the way of further annoyance. I was his wife in the sight of Heaven; I was the only woman he had ever loved; and so on, and so on.

'Do you now see, sir, the risk that I ran of his discovering me if I remained in your neighbourhood? The bare thought of it made my flesh creep. I was determined never again to see the man who had so cruelly deceived me. I am in the same mind still – with this difference, that I might consent to see him, if I could be positively assured first of the death of his wife. This is not likely to happen. Let me go on with my letter, and tell you that what I did on my arrival in Edinburgh.

'The coachman recommended me to the house in the Canongate where you found me lodging. I wrote the same day to relatives of my father living in Glasgow, to tell them where I was, and in what a forlorn position I found myself.

'I was answered by return of post. The head of the family and his wife requested me to refrain from visiting them in Glasgow. They had business then in hand which would take them to Edinburgh; and I might expect to see them both with the least possible delay.

'They arrived as they promised; and they expressed themselves civilly enough. Moreover, they did certainly lend me a small sum of money, when they found how poorly my purse was furnished. But I don't think either husband or wife felt much for me. They recommended me, at parting, to apply to my father's other relatives living in England. I may be doing them an injustice; but I fancy they were eager to get me (as the common phrase is) off their hands.

'The day when the departure of my relatives left me friendless, was also the day, sir, when I had that dream or vision of you which I had already related. I lingered on at the house in the Canongate; partly because the landlady was kind to me, partly because I was so depressed by my position that I really did not know what to do next.

'In this wretched condition you discovered me on that favourite walk of mine from Holyrood to St Anthony's Well. Believe me, your kind interest in my fortunes has not been thrown away on an ungrateful woman. I could ask Providence for no greater blessing than to find a brother and a friend in you. You have yourself destroyed that hope by what you said and did, when we were together in the parlour. I don't blame you; I am afraid my manner (without my knowing it) might have seemed to give you some encouragement. I am only sorry – very, very sorry, to have no honourable choice left but never to see you again.

'After much thinking, I have made up my mind to speak to those other relatives of my father to whom I have not yet applied. The chance that they may help me to earn an honest living, is the one chance that I have left. God bless you, Mr Germaine! I wish you prosperity and happiness from the bottom of my heart, and remain, your grateful servant,

'M. VAN BRANDT

'P.S. – I sign my own name (or the name which I once thought was mine) as a proof that I have honestly written the truth about myself from first to last. For the future I must for safety's sake live under some other name. I should like to go back to my name when I was a happy girl at home. But Van Brandt knows it; and besides, I have (no matter how innocently) disgraced it. Goodbye again, sir; and thank you again.'

So the letter concluded.

I read it in the temper of a thoroughly disappointed and thoroughly unreasonable man. Whatever poor Mrs Van Brandt had done, she had done wrong. It was wrong of her, in the first place, to have married at all. It was wrong of her to contemplate receiving Mr Van Brandt again, even if his lawful wife had died in the interval. It was wrong of her to return my letter of introduction, after I had given myself the trouble of altering it to suit her capricious fancy. It was wrong of her to take an absurdly prudish view of a stolen kiss and a tender declaration, and to fly from me as if I was as great a scoundrel as Mr Van Brandt himself. And last, and more than all, it was wrong of her to sign her Christian name in initial only. Here I was, passionately in love with a woman, and not knowing by what fond name to identify her in my thoughts! 'M. Van Brandt!' I might call her, Maria, Margaret, Martha, Mabel, Magdalen, Mary – no! not Mary. The old boyish love was dead and gone; but I owed some respect to the memory of it. If the 'Mary' of my early days was still living, and if I had met her, would she have treated me as *this* woman had treated me? Never! It was an injury to 'Mary,' to think even of that heartless creature by her name. Why think of her at all? Why degrade myself by trying to puzzle out a means of tracing her in her letter? It was sheer folly to attempt to trace a woman who had gone I knew not whither, and who herself informed me that she meant to pass under an assumed name. Had I lost all pride, all self-respect? In the flower of my age; with a handsome fortune; with the world before me, full of interesting female faces, and charming female figures – what course did it become me to take? To go back to my country house, and mope over the loss of a woman who had deliberately deserted me? or to send for a courier and a travelling-carriage, and forget her gaily, among foreign people and foreign scenes? In the state of my temper at that moment, the idea of a pleasure-tour in Europe fired my imagination. I first astonished the people at the hotel by ordering all further enquiries after the missing Mrs Van Brandt to be stopped – and then I opened my writing-desk and wrote to tell my mother frankly and fully of my new plans.

The answer arrived by return of post.

To my surprise and delight, my good mother was not satisfied with only formally approving of my new resolution. With an energy which I had not ventured to expect from her, she had made all her arrangements for leaving home, and had started for Edinburgh to join me as my travelling companion. 'You shall not go away alone, George' (she wrote), 'while I have strength and spirits to keep you company.'

In three days from the time when I read those words, our preparations were completed, and we were on our way to the Continent.

CHAPTER IX

NOT CURED YET

We visited France, Germany, and Italy; and we were absent from England about two years.

Had time and change justified my confidence in them? Was the image of Mrs Van Brandt an image long since dismissed from my mind?

No! Do what I might, I was still (in the prophetic language of Dame Dermody) taking the way to reunion with my kindred spirit, in the time to come. For the first two or three months of our travels, I was haunted by dreams of the woman who had so resolutely left me. Seeing her in my sleep, always graceful, always charming, always modestly tender towards me, I waited in the ardent hope of again beholding the apparition of her in my waking hours – of again being summoned to meet her at a given place and time. My anticipations were not fulfilled; no apparition showed itself. The dreams themselves grew less frequent and less vivid, and then ceased altogether. Was this a sign that the days of her adversity were at an end? Having no further need of help, had she no further remembrance of the man who had tried to help her? Were we never to meet again?

I said to myself, 'I am unworthy of the name of a man, if I don't forget her now!' She still kept her place in my memory, say what I might.

I saw all the wonders of Nature and Art which foreign countries could show me. I lived in the dazzling light of the best society that Paris, Rome, Vienna could assemble. I passed hours on hours in the company of the most accomplished and most beautiful women whom Europe could produce – and still that solitary figure at St Anthony's Well, those grand grey eyes which had rested on me so sadly at parting, held their place in my memory, stamped their image on my heart.

Whether I resisted my infatuation, or whether I submitted to it, I still longed for her. I did all I could to conceal the state of my mind from my mother. But her loving eyes discovered the secret: she saw that I suffered, and suffered with me. More than once she said, 'George, the good end is not to be gained by travelling; let us go home.' More than once I answered with the bitter and obstinate resolution of despair, 'No! let us try more new people, and more new scenes.' It was only when I found her health and strength beginning to fail under the stress of continual travelling, that I consented to abandon the hopeless search after oblivion, and to turn homeward at last.

I prevailed on my mother to wait and rest at my house in London, before she returned to her favourite abode at the country seat in Perthshire. It is needless to say that I remained in town with her. My mother now represented the one interest that held me nobly and endearingly to life. Politics, literature, agriculture – the customary pursuits of a man in my position had none of them the slightest attraction for me.

We had arrived in London, at what is called 'the height of the season.' Among the operatic attractions of that year – I am writing of the days when the ballet was still a popular form of public entertainment – there was a certain dancer whose grace and beauty were the objects of universal admiration. I was asked if I had seen her wherever I went, until my social position as the one man who was indifferent to the reigning goddess of the stage, became quite unendurable. On the next occasion when I was invited to take a seat in a friend's box, I accepted the proposal; and (far from willingly) I went the way of the world – in other words, I went to the opera.

The first part of the performance had concluded when we got to the theatre, and the ballet had not yet begun. My friends amused themselves with looking for familiar faces in the boxes and stalls. I took a chair in a corner and waited, with my mind far away from the theatre, for the dancing that was to come. The lady who sat nearest to me (like ladies in general) disliked the neighbourhood of a silent man. She determined to make me talk to her.

'Do tell me, Mr Germaine,' she said. 'Did you ever see a theatre anywhere so full as this theatre is to-night?'

She handed me her opera-glass as she spoke. I moved to the front of the box to look at the audience.

It was certainly a wonderful sight. Every available atom of space (as I gradually raised the glass from the floor to the ceiling of the building) appeared to be occupied. Looking upward and upward, my range of view gradually reached the gallery. Even at that distance, the excellent glass which had been put into my hands brought the faces of the audience close to me. I looked first at the persons who occupied the front row of seats in the gallery stalls.

Moving the opera-glass slowly along the semicircle formed by the seats, I suddenly stopped when I reached the middle.

My heart gave a great leap as if it would bound out of my body. There was no mistaking *that* face among the commonplace faces near it. I had discovered Mrs Van Brandt!

She sat in front — but not alone. There was a man in the stall immediately behind her, who bent over her and spoke to her from time to time. She listened to him, so far as I could see, with something of a sad and weary look. Who was the man? I might, or might not, find that out. Under any circumstances, I determined to speak to Mrs Van Brandt.

The curtain rose for the ballet. I made the best excuse I could to my friends, and instantly left the box.

It was useless to attempt to purchase my admission to the gallery. My money was refused. There was not even standing-room left in that part of the theatre.

But one alternative remained. I returned to the street, to wait for Mrs Van Brandt at the gallery door until the performance was over.

Who was the man in attendance on her — the man whom I had seen sitting behind her and talking familiarly over her shoulder? While I paced backwards and forwards before the door, that one question held possession of my mind, until the oppression of it grew beyond endurance. I went back to my friends in the box, simply and solely to look at the man again.

What excuses I made to account for my strange conduct I cannot now remember. Armed once more with the lady's opera-glass (I borrowed it, and kept it, without scruple), I alone, of all that vast audience, turned my back on the stage, and riveted my attention on the gallery stalls.

There he sat, in his place behind her, to all appearance spell-bound by the fascinations of the beautiful dancer. Mrs Van Brandt, on the contrary, seemed to find but little attraction in the spectacle presented by the stage. She looked at the dancing (so far as I could see) in an absent, weary manner. When the applause broke out in a perfect frenzy of cries and clapping of hands, she sat perfectly unmoved by the enthusiasm which pervaded the theatre. The man behind her (annoyed, as I supposed, by the marked indifference which she showed to the performance) tapped her impatiently on the shoulder, as if he thought that she was quite capable of falling asleep in her stall! The familiarity of the action — confirming the suspicion in my mind which had already identified him with Van Brandt — so enraged me that I said or did something which obliged one of the gentlemen in the box to interfere. 'If you can't control yourself,' he whispered, 'you had better leave us.' He spoke with the authority of an old friend. I had sense enough to take his advice, and return to my post at the gallery door.

A little before midnight the performance ended. The audience began to pour out of the theatre.

I drew back into a corner behind the door, facing the gallery stairs, and watched for her. After an interval which seemed to be endless, she and her companion appeared, slowly descending the stairs. She wore a long dark cloak: her head was protected by a quaintly-shaped hood, which looked (on *her*) the most becoming head-dress that a woman could wear. As the two passed me I heard the man speak to her in a tone of sulky annoyance.

'It's wasting money,' he said, 'to go to the expense of taking *you* to the opera.'

'I am not well,' she answered, with her head down and her eyes on the ground. 'I am out of spirits to-night.'

'Will you ride home, or walk?'

'I will walk, if you please.'

I followed them, unperceived; waiting to present myself to her until the crowd about them had dispersed. In a few minutes they turned into a quiet by-street. I quickened my pace until I was close to her side – and then I took off my hat and spoke to her.

She recognised me with a cry of astonishment. For an instant her face brightened radiantly with the loveliest expression of delight that I ever saw in any human countenance. The moment after, all was changed! The charming features saddened and hardened: she stood before me like a woman overwhelmed by shame – without uttering a word, without taking my offered hand.

Her companion broke the silence.

'Who is this gentleman?' he asked, speaking in a foreign accent, with an under-bred insolence of tone and manner.

She controlled herself the moment he addressed her. 'This is Mr Germaine,' she answered; 'a gentleman who was very kind to me in Scotland.' She raised her eyes for a moment to mine, and took refuge, poor soul, in a conventionally polite enquiry after my health. 'I hope you are quite well, Mr Germaine,' said the soft sweet voice, trembling piteously.

I made the customary reply, and explained that I had seen her at the opera. 'Are you staying in London?' I asked. 'May I have the honour of calling on you?'

Her companion answered for her before she could speak.

'My wife thanks you, sir, for the compliment you pay her. She doesn't receive visitors. We both wish you good-night.'

Saying these words he took off his hat, with a sardonic assumption of respect, and, holding her arm in his, forced her to walk on abruptly with him. Feeling certainly assured, by this time, that the man was no other than Van Brandt, I was on the point of answering him sharply, when Mrs Van Brandt checked the rash words as they rose to my lips.

'For my sake!' she whispered over her shoulder, with an imploring look that instantly silenced me. After all, she was free (if she liked) to go back to the man who had so vilely deceived and deserted her. I bowed and left them, feeling with no common bitterness the humiliation of entering into rivalry with Mr Van Brandt.

I crossed to the other side of the street. Before I had taken three steps away from her, the old infatuation fastened its hold on me again. I submitted, without a struggle against myself, to the degradation of turning spy, and followed them home. Keeping well behind, on the opposite side of the way, I tracked them to their own door, and entered in my pocket-book the name of the street and the number of the house.

The hardest critic who reads these lines cannot feel more contemptuously towards me than I felt towards myself. Could I still love a woman, after she had deliberately preferred to me a scoundrel who had married her while he was the husband of another wife? Yes! knowing what I now knew, I felt that I loved her just as dearly as ever. It was incredible; it was shocking – but it was true. For the first time in my life I tried to take refuge from my sense of my own degradation in drink. I went to my club, and joined a convivial party at a supper-table, and poured glass after glass of champagne down my throat – without feeling the slightest sense of exhilaration, without losing for an instant the consciousness of my own contemptible conduct. I went to my bed in despair; and, through the wakeful night, I weakly cursed the fatal evening at the riverside when I had met her for the first time. But revile her as I might, despise myself as I might, I loved her – I loved her still!

Among the letters laid on my table the next morning, there were two which must find their place in this narrative.

The first letter was in a handwriting which I had seen once before, at the hotel in Edinburgh. The writer was Mrs Van Brandt.

'For your own sake' (the letter ran), 'make no attempt to see me, and take no notice of an invitation which I fear you will receive with this note. I am living a degraded life – I have sunk beneath your notice. You owe it to yourself, sir, to forget the miserable woman who now writes to you for the last time, and bids you gratefully a last farewell.'

Those sad lines were signed in initials only. It is needless to say that they merely strengthened my resolution to see her at all hazards. I kissed the paper on which her hand had rested – and then I turned to the second letter. It contained the 'invitation' to which my correspondent had alluded, and it was expressed in these terms: –

'Mr Van Brandt presents his compliments to Mr Germaine, and begs to apologise for the somewhat abrupt manner in which he received Mr Germaine's polite advances. Mr Van Brandt suffers habitually from nervous irritability, and he felt particularly ill last night. He trusts Mr Germaine will receive this candid explanation in the spirit in which it is offered; and he begs to add that Mrs Van Brandt will be delighted to receive Mr Germaine, whenever he may find it convenient to favour her with a visit.'

That Mr Van Brandt had some sordid interest of his own to serve in writing this grotesquely-impudent composition, and that the unhappy woman who bore his name was heartily ashamed of the proceeding on which he had ventured, were conclusions easily drawn after reading the two letters. The suspicion of the man and of his motives which I naturally felt, produced no hesitation in my mind as to the course which I had determined to pursue. On the contrary, I rejoiced that my way to an interview with Mrs Van Brandt was smoothed, no matter with what motives, by Mr Van Brandt himself.

I waited at home until noon – and then I could wait no longer. Leaving a message of excuse for my mother (I had just sense of shame enough left to shrink from facing her), I hastened away to profit by my invitation, on the very day when I had received it!

CHAPTER X

MRS VAN BRANDT AT HOME

As I lifted my hand to ring the housebell, the door was opened from within – and no less a person than Mr Van Brandt himself stood before me! He had his hat on; we had evidently met just as he was going out.

'My dear sir, how good this is of you! You present the best of all replies to my letter, in presenting yourself. Mrs Van Brandt is at home – Mrs Van Brandt will be delighted. Pray walk in.'

He threw open the door of a room on the ground floor. His politeness was (if possible) even more offensive than his insolence. 'Be seated, Mr Germaine, I beg of you!' He turned to the open door and called up the stairs, in a loud and confident voice:

'Mary! Come down directly!'

'Mary!' I knew her Christian name at last – and knew it through Van Brandt. No words can tell how the name jarred on me, spoken by his lips! For the first time for years past, my mind went back to Mary Dermody and Greenwater Broad. The next moment, I heard the rustling of Mrs Van Brandt's dress on the stairs. As the sound caught my ear, the old times and the old faces vanished again from my thoughts as completely as if they had never existed. What had *she* in common with the frail shy little child, her namesake of other days? What similarity was perceivable in the sooty London lodging-house, to remind me of the bailiff's flower-scented cottage by the shores of the lake?

Van Brandt took off his hat, and bowed to me with sickening servility.

'I have a business appointment,' he said, 'which it is impossible to put off. Pray excuse me. Mrs Van Brandt will do the honours. Good morning.'

The house door opened and closed again. The rustling of the dress came slowly nearer and nearer. She stood before me.

'Mr Germaine!' she exclaimed, starting back as if the bare sight of me repelled her. 'Is this honourable? Is this worthy of you? You allow me to be entrapped into receiving you – and you accept as your accomplice Mr Van Brandt! Oh, sir, I have accustomed myself to look up to you as a high-minded man! How bitterly you have disappointed me!'

Her reproaches passed by me unheeded. They only heightened her colour; they only added a new rapture to the luxury of looking at her.

'If you loved me as faithfully as I love you,' I said, 'you would understand why I am here. No sacrifice is too great if it brings me into your presence again, after two years of absence.'

She suddenly approached me, and fixed her eyes in eager scrutiny on my face.

'There must be some mistake,' she said. 'You cannot possibly have received my letter? or you have not read it?'

'I have received it; and I have read it.'

'And Van Brandt's letter? You have read that, too?'

'Yes.'

She sat down by the table, and leaning her arms on it, covered her face with her hands. My answers seemed not only to have distressed her, but to have perplexed her. 'Are men all alike?' I heard her say. 'I thought I might trust in *his* sense of what was due to himself, and of what was compassionate towards me.'

I closed the door, and seated myself by her side. She removed her hands from her face when she felt me near her. She looked at me with a cold and steady surprise.

'What are you going to do?' she asked.

'I am going to try if I can recover my place in your estimation,' I said. 'I am going to ask your pity for a man whose whole heart is yours, whose whole life is bound up in you.'

She started to her feet, and looked round her incredulously, as if doubting whether she had rightly heard and rightly interpreted my last words. Before I could speak again, she suddenly faced me, and struck her open hand on the table with a passionate resolution which I now saw in her for the first time.

'Stop!' she cried. 'There must be an end to this. And an end there shall be. Do you know who that man is who has just left the house? Answer me, Mr Germaine! I am speaking in earnest.'

There was no choice but to answer her. She was indeed in earnest – vehemently in earnest.

'His letter tells me,' I said, 'that he is Mr Van Brandt.'

She sat down again, and turned her face away from me.

'Do you know how he came to write to you?' she asked. 'Do you know what made him invite you to this house?'

I thought of the suspicion that had crossed my mind when I read Van Brandt's letter – I made no reply.

'You force me to tell you the truth,' she went on. 'He asked me who you were, last night, on our way home. I knew that you were rich, and that *he* wanted money – I told him I knew nothing of your position in the world. He was too cunning to believe me; he went out to the public-house, and looked at a Directory. He came back, and said, "Mr Germaine has a house in Berkeley Square, and a country seat in the Highlands; he is not a man for a poor devil like me to offend: I mean to make a friend of him, and I expect you to make a friend of him too.' He sat down, and wrote to you. I am living under that man's protection, Mr Germaine! His wife is not dead, as you may suppose – she is living, and I know her to be living. I wrote to you that I was beneath your notice; and you have obliged me to tell you why. Am I sufficiently degraded to bring you to your senses?'

I drew closer to her. She tried to get up, and leave me. I knew my power over her, and used it (as any man in my place would have used it) without scruple. I took her hand.

'I don't believe you have voluntarily degraded yourself,' I said. 'You have been forced into your present postion – there are circumstances which excuse you, and which you are purposely keeping back from me. Nothing will convince me that you are a base woman! Should I love you as I love you, if you were really unworthy of me?'

She struggled to free her hand – I still held it. She tried to change the subject.

'There is one thing you haven't told me yet,' she said with a faint, forced smile. 'Have you seen the apparition of me again since I left you?'

'No. Have *you* ever seen *me* again, as you saw me in your dream at the inn in Edinburgh?'

'Never! Our visions of each other have left us? Can you tell why?'

If we had continued to speak on this subject, we must surely have recognized each other? But the subject dropped. Instead of answering her question, I drew her nearer to me – I returned to the forbidden subject of my love.

'Look at me,' I pleaded – 'and tell me the truth. Can you see me, can you hear me; and do you feel no answering sympathy in your own heart?

Do you really care nothing for me? Have you never once thought of me, in all the time that has passed since we last met?'

I spoke as I felt – fervently, passionately. She made a last effort to repel me; and yielded even as she made it. Her hand closed on mine; a low sigh fluttered on her lips. She answered with a sudden self-abandonment; she recklessly cast herself loose from the restraints which had held her up to this time.

'I think of you perpetually,' she said. 'I was thinking of you at the opera, last night. My heart leapt in me when I heard your voice in the street.'

'You love me!' I whispered.

'Love you?' she repeated. 'My whole heart goes out to you, in spite of myself! Degraded as I am, unworthy as I am – knowing as I do that nothing can ever come of it – I love you! I love you!'

She threw her arms round my neck, and held me to her with all her strength. The moment after, she dropped on her knees.

'Oh, don't tempt me!' she said. 'Be merciful, and leave me!'

I was beside myself; I spoke as recklessly to her as she had spoken to me.

'Prove that you love me,' I said. 'Let me rescue you from the degradation of living with that man. Leave him at once, and for ever. Leave him, and come with me to a future that is worthy of you – your future as my wife!'

'Never!' she answered, crouching low at my feet.

'Why not? What obstacle is there?'

'I can't tell you! I daren't tell you.'

'Will you write it?'

'No! I can't even write it – to *you*. Go, I implore you, before Van Brandt comes back. Go, if you love and pity me.'

She had roused my jealousy; I positively refused to leave her.

'I insist on knowing what binds you to that man,' I said. 'Let him come back! If *you* won't answer my question, I will put it to *him*.'

She looked at me wildly, with a cry of terror – she saw my resolution in my face.

'Don't frighten me,' she said. 'Let me think.'

She reflected for a moment. Her eyes brightened, as if some new way out of the difficulty had occurred to her.

'Have you a mother living?' she asked.

'Yes.'

'Do you think she would come and see me?'

'I am sure she would, if I asked her.'

She considered with herself once more. 'I will tell your mother what the obstacle is,' she said thoughtfully.

'When?'

'To-morrow – at this time.'

She raised herself on her knees; the tears suddenly filled her eyes. She drew me to her gently. 'Kiss me,' she whispered. 'You will never come here again. Kiss me for the last time.'

My lips had barely touched hers when she started to her feet, and snatched up my hat from the chair on which I had placed it.

'Take your hat,' she said. 'He has come back.'

My duller sense of hearing had discovered nothing. I rose, and took my hat to quiet her. At the same moment, the door of the room opened suddenly and softly. Mr Van Brandt came in. I saw in his face that he had some vile motive of his own for trying to take us by surprise, and that the result of the experiment had disappointed him.

'You are not going yet?' he said, speaking to me, with his eye on Mrs Van Brandt. 'I have hurried over my business, in the hope of prevailing on you to stay and take lunch with us. Put down your hat, Mr Germaine. No ceremony!'

'You are very good,' I answered. 'My time is limited to-day. I must beg you and Mrs Van Brandt to excuse me.'

I took leave of her as I spoke. She turned deadly pale when she shook hands with me at parting. Had she any open brutality to dread from Van Brandt as soon as my back was turned? The bare suspicion of it made my blood boil. But I thought of *her*. In her interests, the wise thing and the merciful thing to do, was to conciliate the fellow before I left the house.

'I am sorry not to be able to accept your invitation,' I said, as we walked together to the door. 'Perhaps, you will give me another chance?'

His eyes twinkled cunningly. 'What do you say to a quiet little dinner here?' he asked. 'A slice of mutton, you know, and a bottle of good wine. Only our three selves, and one old friend of mine, to make up four. We will have a rubber of whist in the evening. Mary and you partners – eh? When shall it be? Shall we say the day after to-morrow?'

She had followed us to the door, keeping behind Van Brandt while he was speaking to me. When he mentioned the 'old friend' and the 'rubber of whist,' her face expressed the strongest emotions of shame and disgust. The next moment (when she had heard him fix the date of the dinner for 'the day after to-morrow') her features became composed again as if a sudden sense of relief had come to her. What did the change mean? 'To-morrow' was the day she had appointed for seeing my mother. Did she really believe, when I had heard what passed at the interview, that I should never enter the house again, and never attempt to see her more? And was this the secret of her composure when she heard the date of the dinner appointed for 'the day after to-morrow?'

Asking myself these questions I accepted my invitation, and left the house with a heavy heart. That farewell kiss, that sudden composure when the day of the dinner was fixed, weighed on my spirits. I would have given twelve years of my life to have annihilated the next twelve hours.

In this frame of mind I reached home, and presented myself in my mother's sitting-room.

'You have gone out earlier than usual today,' she said. 'Did the fine weather tempt you, my dear?' She paused and looked at me more closely. 'George!' she exclaimed, 'what has happened to you? where have you been?'

I told her the truth as honestly as I have told it here.

The colour deepened in my mother's face. She looked at me, and spoke to me, with a severity which was rare indeed in my experience of her.

'Must I remind you, for the first time in your life, of what is due to your mother?' she asked. 'Is it possible that you expect me to visit a woman who, by her own confession——'

'I expect you to visit a woman who has only to say the word, and to be your daughter-in-law,' I interposed. 'Surely I am not asking what is unworthy of you, if I ask that?'

My mother looked at me in blank dismay.

'Do you mean, George, that you have offered her marriage?'

'Yes.'

'And she has said, No?'

'She has said, No – because there is some obstacle in her way. I have tried vainly to make her explain herself. She has promised to confide everything to *you*.'

The serious nature of the emergency had its effect. My mother yielded. She handed me the little ivory tablets on which she was accustomed to record her engagements. 'Write down the name and address,' she said resignedly.

'I will go with you,' I answered, 'and wait in the carriage at the door. I want to hear what has passed between you and Mrs Van Brandt the instant you have left her.'

'Is it as serious as that, George?'

'Yes, mother, it is as serious as that.'

CHAPTER XI

THE OBSTACLE BEATS ME

How long was I left alone in the carriage, at the door of Mrs Van Brandt's lodgings? Judging by my sensations, I waited half a lifetime. Judging by my watch, I waited half an hour.

When my mother returned to me, the hope which I had entertained of a happy result from her interview with Mrs Van Brandt was a hope abandoned before she had opened her lips. I saw, in her face, that an obstacle which was beyond my power of removal did indeed stand between me and the dearest wish of my life.

'Tell me the worst,' I said, as we drove away from the house; 'and tell it at once.'

'I must tell it to you, George,' my mother answered sadly, 'as she told it to me. She made no attempt to interest me in her early life as a girl. "I have innocently disgraced my father's good name," she said; "and I must beg you to excuse my saying nothing about my relatives." Beginning in those words, she passed at once to her meeting with you at Edinburgh, and to the circumstances which have led her to live as she is living now. This latter part of her narrative she especially requested me to repeat to you. Do you feel composed enough to hear it now? or would you rather wait?'

'Let me hear it now, mother – and tell it, as nearly as you can, in her own words.'

'I will repeat what she said to me, my dear, as faithfully as I can. After referring to her father's death, she told me that she had only two relatives living. "I have a married aunt in Glasgow, and a married aunt in London," she said. "When I left Edinburgh, I went to my aunt in London. She and my father had not been on good terms together; she considered that my father had neglected her. But his death had softened her towards him and towards me. She received me kindly, and she got me a situation in a shop. I kept my situation for three months; and then I was obliged to leave it."'

My mother paused. I thought directly of the strange postscript which Mrs Van Brandt had made me add to the letter that I wrote for her at the Edinburgh inn. In that case also she had only contemplated remaining in her employment for three months' time.

'Why was she obliged to leave her situation?' I asked.

'I put that question to her myself,' replied my mother. 'She made no direct reply – she changed colour and looked confused. "I will tell you afterwards, madam," she said. "Please let me go on now. My aunt was angry with me for leaving my employment – and she was more angry still when I told her the reason. She said I had failed in my duty towards her in not speaking frankly at first. We parted coolly. I had saved a little money from my wages; and I did well enough while my savings lasted. When they came to an end I tried to get employment again, and I failed. My aunt said, and said truly, that her husband's income was barely enough to support his family: she could do nothing for me, and I could do nothing for myself. I wrote to my aunt at Glasgow, and received no answer. Starvation stared me in the face, when I saw in a newspaper an advertisement addressed to me by Mr Van Brandt. He implored me to write to him; he declared that his life without me was too desolate to be endured; he solemnly promised that there should be no interruption to my tranquillity if I would return to him. If I had only had myself to think of, I would have begged my bread in the streets rather than return to him——" '

I interrupted the narrative at that point.

'What other person could she have had to think of?' I said.

'Is it possible, George,' my mother rejoined, 'that you have no suspicion of what she was alluding to when she said those words?'

The question passed by me unheeded: my thoughts were dwelling bitterly on Van Brandt and his advertisement. 'She answered the advertisement, of course?' I said.

'And she saw Mr Van Brandt,' my mother went on. 'She gave me no detailed account of the interview between them. "He reminded me," she said, "of what I knew to be true – that the woman who had entrapped him into marrying her was an incurable drunkard, and that his ever living with her again was out of the question. Still, she was alive, and she had a right to the name at least of his wife. I won't attempt to excuse my returning to him, knowing the circumstances as I did. I will only say that I could see no other choice before me, in my position at the time. It is needless to trouble you with what I have suffered since, or to speak of what I may suffer still. I am a lost woman. Be under no alarm, madam, about your son. I shall remember proudly to the end of my life that he once offered me the honour and the happiness of becoming his wife – but I know what is due to him and to you. I have seen him for the last time. The one thing that remains to be done is to satisfy him that our marriage is impossible. You are a mother; you will understand why I reveal the obstacle which stands between us – not to him, but to you." She rose saying those words, and opened the folding doors which led from the parlour into a back room. After an absence of a few minutes she returned.'

At that crowning point in the narrative my mother stopped. Was she afraid to go on? or did she think it needless to say more?

'Well?' I said.

'Must I really tell it to you in words, George? Can't you guess how it ended, even yet?'

There were two difficulties in the way of my understanding her. I had a man's bluntness of perception, and I was half maddened by suspense. Incredible as it may appear, I was too dull to guess the truth, even now.

'When she returned to me,' my mother resumed, 'she was not alone. She had with her a lovely little girl, just old enough to walk with the help of her mother's hand. She tenderly kissed the child; and then she put it on my lap. "There is my only comfort," she said simply; "and there is the obstacle to my ever becoming Mr Germaine's wife."'

Van Brandt's child! Van Brandt's child!

The postscript which she had made me add to my letter, the incomprehensible withdrawal from the employment in which she was prospering, the disheartening difficulties which had brought her to the brink of starvation, the degrading return to the man who had cruelly deceived her – all was explained, all was excused now! With an infant at the breast, how could she obtain a new employment? With famine staring her in the face, what else could the friendless woman do but return to the father of her child? What claim had I on her by comparison with *him*? What did it matter now that the poor creature secretly returned the love that I felt for her? There was the child, an obstacle between us – there was *his* hold on her, now that he had got her back! What was *my* hold worth? All social proprieties and all social laws answered the questions: – Nothing!

My head sank on my breast – I received the blow in silence.

My good mother took my hand. 'You understand it now, George?' she said, sorrowfully.

'Yes, mother, I understand it.'

'There was one thing she wished me to say to you, my dear, which I have not mentioned yet. She entreats you not to suppose that she had the faintest idea of her situation when she attempted to destroy herself. Her first suspicion that it was possible she might become a mother was conveyed to her at Edinburgh, in a conversation with her aunt. It is impossible, George, not to feel compassionately towards this poor woman. Regrettable as her position is, I cannot see that she is to blame for it. She was the innocent victim of a vile fraud when that man married her; she has suffered undeservedly since; and she has behaved nobly to you and to me. I only do her justice in saying that she is a woman in a thousand – a woman worthy, under happier circumstances, to be my daughter and your wife. I feel *for* you, and feel *with* you, my dear – I do, with all my heart.'

So this scene in my life was, to all appearance, a scene closed for ever. As it had been with my love, in the days of my boyhood, so it was again now with the love of my riper age!

Later in the day, when I had in some degree recovered my self-possession, I wrote to Mr Van Brandt – as *she* had foreseen I should write! – to apologise for breaking my engagement to dine with him.

Could I trust to a letter also, to say the farewell words for me to the woman whom I had loved and lost? No! It was better for her, and better for me, that I should not write. And yet, the idea of leaving her in silence was more than my fortitude could endure. Her last words at parting (as they were repeated to me by my mother) had expressed the hope that I should not think hardly of her, in the future. How could I assure her that I should think of her tenderly to the end of my life? My mother's delicate and true sympathy showed me the way. 'Send a little present, George,' she said, 'to the child. You bear no malice to the poor little child?' God knows I was not hard on the child! I went out myself, and bought her a toy. I brought it home, and before I sent it away, I pinned a slip of paper to it, bearing this inscription: – 'To your little daughter, from George Germaine.' There is nothing very pathetic, I suppose, in those words. And yet, I burst out crying when I had written them.

The next morning, my mother and I set forth for my country-house in Perthshire. London was now unendurable to me. Travelling abroad, I had tried already. Nothing was left but to go back to the Highlands, and to try what I could make of my life, with my mother still left to live for.

CHAPTER XII

MY MOTHER'S DIARY

There is something repellent to me, even at this distance of time, in looking back at the dreary days of seclusion which followed each other monotonously in my Highland home. The actions of my life, however trifling they may have been, I can find some interest in recalling: they associate me with my fellow-creatures; they connect me, in some degree, with the vigorous movement of the world. But I have no sympathy with the purely selfish pleasure which some men appear to derive from dwelling on the minute anatomy of their own feelings, under the pressure of adverse fortune. Let the domestic record of our stagnant life in Perthshire (so far as I am concerned in it) be presented in my mother's words, not in mine. A few lines of extract from the daily journal which it was her habit to keep will tell all that need be told, before this narrative advances to later dates and to newer scenes.

'20*th August.* – We have been two months at our home in Scotland, and I see no change in George for the better. He is as far as ever, I fear, from being reconciled to his separation from that unhappy woman. Nothing will induce him to confess it himself. He declares that his quiet life here with me is all that he desires. But I know better! I have been into his bedroom late at night. I have heard him talking of her in his sleep, and I have seen the tears on his eyelids. My poor boy! What thousands of charming women there are who would ask nothing better than to be his wife. And the one woman whom he can never marry, is the only woman whom he loves!

'25th. – A long conversation about George with Mr MacGlue. I have never liked this Scotch doctor since he encouraged my son to keep the fatal appointment at Saint Anthony's Well. But he seems to be a clever man in his profession – and I think, in his way, he means kindly towards George. His advice was given as coarsely as usual, and very positively at the same time. "Nothing will cure your son, madam, of his amatory passion for that half-drowned lady of his, but change – and another lady. Send him away by himself this time: and let him feel the want of some kind creature to look after him. And when he meets with that kind creature (they are as plenty as fish in the sea) never trouble your head about it if there's a flaw in her character. I have got a cracked tea-cup which has served me for twenty years. Marry him, ma'am, to the new one with the utmost speed and impetuosity which the law will permit." I hate Mr MacGlue's opinions – so coarse and so hard-hearted! – but I sadly fear that I must part with my son for a little while, for his own sake.

'26th. – Where is George to go? I have been thinking of it all through the night, and I cannot arrive at a conclusion. It is so difficult to reconcile myself to letting him go away alone.

'29th. – I have always believed in special Providences; and I am now confirmed in my belief. This morning has brought with it a note from our good friend and neighbour at Belhelvie. Sir James is one of the Commissioners for the Northern Lights. He is going in a government vessel to inspect the lighthouses on the north of Scotland, and on the Orkney and Shetland Islands – and, having noticed how worn and ill my poor boy looks, he most kindly invites George to be his guest on the voyage. They will not be absent for more than two months; and the sea (as Sir James reminds me) did wonders for George's health when he returned from India. I could wish for no better opportunity than this of trying what change of air and scene will do for him. However painfully I may feel the separation myself, I shall put a cheerful face on it; and I shall urge George to accept the invitation.

'30th. – I have said all I could; but he still refuses to leave me. I am a miserable selfish creature. I felt so glad when he said No.

'31st. – Another wakeful night. George must positively send his answer to Sir James to-day. I am determined to do my duty towards my son – he looks so dreadfully pale and ill this morning! Besides, if something is not done to rouse him, how do I know that he may not end in going back to Mrs Van Brandt after all? From every point of view, I feel bound to insist on his accepting Sir James's invitation. I have only to be firm, and the thing is done. He has never yet disobeyed me, poor fellow. He will not disobey me now.

'*2nd September.* – He has gone! Entirely to please me – entirely against his own wishes. Oh, how is it that such a good son cannot get a good wife! He would make any woman happy. I wonder whether I have done right in sending him away? The wind is moaning in the fir plantation at the back of the house. Is there a storm at sea? I forgot to ask Sir James how big the vessel was. The Guide to Scotland says the coast is rugged; and there is a wild sea between the north shore and the Orkney Islands. I almost regret having insisted so strongly – how foolish I am! We are all in the hands of God. May God bless and prosper my good son!

'*10th.* – Very uneasy. No letter from George. Ah, how full of trouble this life is! and how strange that we should cling to it as we do!

'*15th.* – A letter from George! They have done with the north coast; and they have crossed the wild sea to the Orkneys. Wonderful weather has favoured them so far; and George is in better health and spirits. Ah! how much happiness there is in life if we will only have the patience to wait for it.

'*2nd October.* – Another letter. They are safe in the harbour of Lerwick, the chief port in the Shetland Islands. The weather has not latterly been at all favourable. But the amendment in George's health remains. He writes most gratefully of Sir James's unremitting kindness to him. I am so happy, I declare I could kiss Sir James – though he *is* a great man, and a Commissioner for Northern Lights! In three weeks more (wind and weather permitting) they hope to get back. Never mind my lonely life here, if I can only see George happy and well again! He tells me they have passed a great deal of their time on shore; but not a word does he say about meeting any ladies. Perhaps they are scarce in those wild regions? I have heard of Shetland shawls and Shetland ponies. Are there any Shetland ladies, I wonder?'

CHAPTER XIII

SHETLAND HOSPITALITY

'Guide! Where are we?'

'I can't say for certain.'

'Have you lost your way?'

The guide looks slowly all round him, and then looks at me. That is his answer to my question. And that is enough.

The lost persons are three in number. My travelling companion, myself, and the guide. We are seated on three Shetland ponies – so small in stature, that we two strangers were at first literally ashamed to get on their backs. We are surrounded by dripping white mist, so dense that we become invisible to one another at a distance of half a dozen yards. We know that we are somewhere on the Mainland of the Shetland Isles. We see under the feet of our ponies a mixture of moorland and bog – here, the strip of firm ground that we are standing on; and there, a few feet off, the strip of watery peat-bog, which is deep enough to suffocate us if we step into it. Thus far, and no farther, our knowledge extends. The question of the moment is – What are we to do next?

The guide lights his pipe, and reminds me that he warned us against the weather before we started for our ride. My travelling companion looks at me resignedly, with an expression of mild reproach. I deserve it. My rashness is to blame for the disastrous position in which we now find ourselves.

In writing to my mother, I have been careful to report favourably of my health and spirits. But I have not confessed that I still remember the day when I parted with the one hope and renounced the one love which made life precious to me. My torpid condition of mind, at home, has simply given place to a perpetual restlessness, produced by the excitement of my new life. I must now always be doing something – no matter what, so long as it diverts me from my own thoughts. Inaction is unendurable; solitude has become horrible to me. While the other members of the party which has accompanied Sir James on his voyage of inspection among the light-houses, are content to wait in the harbour of Lerwick for a favourable change in the weather, I am obstinately bent on leaving the comfortable shelter of the vessel to explore some inland ruin of prehistoric times, of which I never heard, and for which I care nothing. The movement is all I want; the ride will fill the hateful void of time. I go, in defiance of sound advice offered to me on all sides. The youngest member of our party catches the infection of my recklessness (in virtue of his youth), and goes with me. And what has come of it? We are blinded by mist; we are lost on a moor; and the treacherous peat-bogs are round us in every direction!

What is to be done?

'Just leave it to the pownies,' the guide says.

'Do you mean leave the ponies to find the way?'

'That's it,' says the guide. 'Drop the bridle and leave it to the pownies. See for yourselves. I'm away on *my* powny.'

He drops his bridle on the pommel of his saddle, whistles to his pony, and disappears in the mist; riding with his hands in his pockets, and his pipe in his mouth, as composedly as if he was sitting by his own fireside at home.

We have no choice but to follow his example, or to be left alone on the moor. The intelligent little animals, relieved from our stupid supervision, trot off with their noses to the ground, like hounds on the scent. Where the intersecting tract of bog is wide they skirt round it; where it is narrow enough to be leaped over they cross it by a jump. Trot! trot! – away the hardy little creatures go, never stopping, never hesitating. Our 'superior intelligence,' perfectly useless in the emergency, wonders how it will end. Our guide, in front of us, answers that it will end in the ponies finding their way certainly to the nearest village or the nearest house. 'Let the bridles be,' is his one warning to us. 'Come what may of it, let the bridles be.'

It is easy for the guide to let his bridle be – he is accustomed to place himself in that helpless position under stress of circumstances, and he knows exactly what his pony can do.

To us, however, the situation is a new one, and it looks dangerous in the extreme. More than once I check myself, not without an effort, in the act of resuming the command of my pony on passing the more dangerous points in the journey. The time goes on, and no sign of an inhabited dwelling looms through the mist. I begin to get fidgety and irritable; I find myself secretly doubting the trustworthiness of the guide. While I am in this unsettled frame of mind, my pony approaches a dim black winding line, where the bog must be crossed for the hundredth time at least. The breadth of it (deceptively enlarged in appearance by the mist) looks to my eyes beyond the reach of a leap by any pony that ever was foaled. I lose my presence of mind. At the critical moment before the jump is taken, I am foolish enough to seize the bridle and suddenly check the pony. He starts, throws up his head, and falls instantly as if he had been shot. My right hand, as we drop on the ground together, gets twisted under me, and I feel that I have sprained my wrist.

If I escape with no worse injury than this I may consider myself well off. But no such good fortune is reserved for me. In his struggles to rise, before I have completely extricated myself from him, the pony kicks me, and, as my ill-luck will have it, his hoof strikes just where the poisoned spear struck me in the past days of my service in India. The old wound opens again, and there I lie bleeding on the barren Shetland moor!

This time my strength has not been exhausted in attempting to breast the current of a swift-flowing river with a drowning woman to support. I preserve my senses, and I am able to give the necessary directions for bandaging the wound with the best materials which we have at our disposal. To mount my pony again is simply out of the question. I must remain where I am, with my travelling companion to look after me, and the guide must trust his pony to discover the nearest place of shelter to which I can be removed.

Before he abandons us on the moor, the man (at my suggestion) takes our 'bearings' as correctly as he can by the help of my pocket-compass. This done, he disappears in the mist, with the bridle hanging loose and the pony's nose to the ground, as before. I am left, under my young friend's care, with a cloak to lie on and a saddle for a pillow. Our ponies composedly help themselves to such grass as they can find on the moor; keeping always near us as companionably as if they were a couple of dogs. In this position we wait events, while the dripping mist hangs thicker than ever all round us.

The slow minutes follow each other wearily in the majestic silence of the moor. We neither of us acknowledge it in words, but we both feel that hours may pass before the guide discovers us again. The penetrating damp slowly strengthens its clammy hold on me. My companion's pocket-flask of sherry has about a teaspoonful of wine left in the bottom of it. We look at one another, having nothing else to look at in the present state of the weather, and we try to make the best of it. So the slow minutes follow each other, until our watches tell us that forty minutes have elapsed since the guide and his pony vanished from our view.

My friend suggests that we may as well try what our voices can do towards proclaiming our situation to any living creature who may, by the barest possibility, be within hearing of us. I leave him to try the experiment, having no strength to spare for vocal efforts of any sort. My companion shouts at the highest pitch of his voice. Silence follows his first attempt. He tries again, and this time an answering hail reaches us faintly through the white fog. A fellow-creature of some sort, guide or stranger, is near us – help is coming at last!

An interval passes; and voices reach our ears – the voices of two men. Then, the shadowy appearance of the two becomes visible in the mist. Then, the guide advances near enough to be identified. He is followed by a sturdy fellow, in a composite dress, which presents him under the double aspect of a groom and a gardener. The guide speaks a few words of rough sympathy. The composite man stands by impenetrably silent: the sight of a disabled stranger fails entirely either to surprise or to interest the gardener-groom.

After a little private consultation, the two men decide to cross their hands, and thus make a seat for me between them. My arms rest on their shoulders; and so they carry me off. My friend trudges behind them, with the saddle and the cloak. The ponies caper and kick, in unrestrained enjoyment of their freedom; and sometimes follow, sometimes precede us, as the humour of the moment inclines them. I am, fortunately for my bearers, a light weight. After twice resting, they stop altogether, and set me down on the driest place they can find. I look eagerly through the mist, for some signs of a dwelling-house – and I see nothing but a little shelving beach, and a sheet of dark water beyond. Where are we?

The gardener-groom vanishes, and appears again on the water, looming large in a boat. I am laid down in the bottom of the boat, with my saddle-pillow; and we shove off, leaving the ponies to the desolate freedom of the moor. They will pick up plenty to eat (the guide says); and when night comes on they will find their own way to shelter in a village hard by. The last I see of the hardy little creatures they are taking a drink of water, side by side, and biting each other sportively in higher spirits than ever!

Slowly we float over the dark water – not a river, as I had at first supposed, but a lake – until we reach the shores of a little island; a flat lonely barren patch of ground. I am carried along a rough pathway made of great flat stones, until we reach the firmer earth, and discover a human dwelling-place at last. It is a long low house of one storey high; forming (as well as I can see) three sides of a square. The door stands hospitably open. The hall within is bare and cold and dreary. The men open an inner door – and we enter a long corridor, comfortably warmed by a peat fire. On one wall, I notice the closed oaken doors of rooms; on the other, rows on rows of well-filled bookshelves meet my eye. Advancing to the end of the first passage, we turn at right angles into a second. Here, a door is opened at last; I find myself in a spacious room, completely and tastefully furnished, having two beds in it, and a large fire burning in the grate. The change to this warm and cheerful place of shelter from the chilly and misty solitude of the moor is so luxuriously delightful that I am quite content, for the first few minutes, to stretch myself on a bed, in lazy enjoyment of my new position; without caring to enquire into whose house we have intruded; without even wondering at the strange absence of master, mistress, or member of the family to welcome our arrival under their roof.

After awhile, the first sense of relief passes away. My dormant curiosity revives. I begin to look about me.

The gardener-groom has disappeared. I discover my travelling companion at the farther end of the room, evidently occupied in questioning the guide. A word from me brings him to my bedside. What discoveries has he made? whose is the house in which we are sheltered? and how is it that no member of the family appears to welcome us?

My friend relates his discoveries. The guide listens as attentively to the secondhand narrative, as if it was quite new to him.

The house that shelters us belongs to a gentleman of ancient northern lineage, whose name is Dunross. He has lived in unbroken retirement on the barren island for twenty years past, with no other companion than a daughter, who is his only child. He is generally believed to be one of the most learned men living. The inhabitants of Shetland know him far and wide, under a quaintly-sounding name which means, being interpreted, 'The Master of Books.' The one occasion on which he and his daughter have been known to leave their island retreat, was at a past time when a terrible epidemic disease broke out among the villages in the neighbourhood. Father and daughter laboured day and night among their poor and afflicted neighbours, with a courage which no danger could shake, with a tender care which no fatigue could exhaust. The father had escaped infection, and the violence of the epidemic was beginning to wear itself out, when the daughter caught the disease. Her life had been preserved, but she had never completely recovered her health. She is now an incurable sufferer from some mysterious nervous disorder which nobody understands, and which has kept her a prisoner on the island, self-withdrawn from all human observation for years past. Among the poor inhabitants of the district, the father and daughter are worshipped as semi-divine beings. Their names come after the Sacred Name, in the prayers which the parents teach to the children.

Such is the household (so far as the guide's story goes) on whose privacy we have intruded ourselves! The narrative has a certain interest of its own, no doubt, but it has one defect – it fails entirely to explain the continued absence of Mr Dunross. Is it possible that he is not aware of our presence in the house? We apply to the guide, and make a few further enquiries of him.

'Are we here,' I ask, 'by permission of Mr Dunross?'

The guide stares. If I had spoken to him in Greek or Hebrew, I could hardly have puzzled him more effectually. My friend tries him with a simpler form of words.

'Did you ask leave to bring us here when you found your way to the house?'

The guide stares harder than ever, with every appearance of feeling perfectly scandalised by the question.

'Do you think,' he asks sternly, 'that I am fool enough to disturb the Master over his books, for such a little matter as bringing you and your friend into this house?'

'Do you mean that you have brought us here without first asking leave?' I exclaim in amazement.

The guide's face brightens; he has beaten the true state of the case into our stupid heads at last! 'That's just what I mean!' he says with an air of infinite relief.

The door opens before we have recovered the shock inflicted on us by this extraordinary discovery. A little lean old gentleman, shrouded in a long black dressing-gown, quietly enters the room. The guide steps forward, and respectfully closes the door for him. We are evidently in the presence of Mr Dunross!

CHAPTER XIV

THE DARKENED ROOM

The little gentleman advances to my bedside. His silky white hair flows over his shoulders; he looks at us with faded blue eyes; he bows with a sad and subdued courtesy, and says in the simplest manner, 'I bid you welcome, gentlemen, to my house.'

We are not content with merely thanking him; we naturally attempt to apologise for our intrusion. Our host defeats the attempt at the outset, by making an apology on his own behalf.

'I happened to send for my servant a minute since,' he proceeds, and I only then heard that you were here. It is the custom of the house that nobody interrupts me over my books. Be pleased, sir, to accept my excuses,' he adds, addressing himself to me, 'for not having sooner placed myself and my household at your disposal. You have met, as I am sorry to hear, with an accident. Will you permit me to send for medical help? I ask the question a little abruptly, fearing that time may be of importance, and knowing that our nearest doctor lives at some distance from this house.'

He speaks with a certain quaintly-precise choice of words – more like a man dictating a letter than holding a conversation. The subdued sadness of his manner is reflected in the subdued sadness of his face. He and sorrow have apparently been old acquaintances, and have become used to each other for years past. The shadow of some past grief rests quietly and impenetrably over the whole man; I see it in his faded blue eyes, on his broad forehead, on his delicate lips, on his pale shrivelled cheeks. My uneasy sense of committing an intrusion on him steadily increases, in spite of his courteous welcome. I explain to him that I am capable of treating my own case, having been myself in practice as a medical man; and this said, I revert to my interrupted excuses. I assure him that it is only within the last few moments that my travelling companion and I have become aware of the liberty which our guide has taken in introducing us, on his own sole responsibility, to the house. Mr Dunross looks at me, as if he, like the guide, failed entirely to understand what my scruples and excuses mean. After a while the truth dawns on him. A faint smile flickers over his face; he lays his hand in a gentle fatherly way on my shoulder.

'We are so used here to our Shetland hospitality,' he says, 'that we are slow to understand the hesitation which a stranger feels in taking advantage of it. Your guide is in no respect to blame, gentlemen. Every house in these islands which is large enough to contain a spare room, has its Guest Chamber, always kept ready for occupation. When you travel my way, you come here as a matter of course; you stay here as long as you like; and, when you go away, I only do my duty as a good Shetlander in accompanying you on the first stage of your journey to bid you God-speed. The customs of centuries past elsewhere, are modern customs here. I beg of you to give my servant all the directions which are necessary to your comfort, just as freely as you could give them in your own house.'

He turns aside to ring a handbell on the table as he speaks; and notices in the guide's face plain signs that the man has taken offence at my disparaging allusion to him.

'Strangers cannot be expected to understand our ways, Andrew,' says the Master of Books. 'But you and I understand one another – and that is enough.'

The guide's rough face reddens with pleasure. If a crowned king on a throne had spoken condescendingly to him, he could hardly have looked more proud of the honour conferred than he looks now. He makes a clumsy attempt to take the Master's hand, and kiss it. Mr Dunross gently repels the attempt, and gives him a little pat on the head. The guide looks at me and my friend, as if he had been honoured with the highest distinction that an earthly being can receive. The Master's hand had touched him kindly!

In a moment more, the gardener-groom appears at the door to answer the bell.

'You will move the medicine-chest into this room, Peter,' says Mr Dunross. 'And you will wait on this gentleman, who is confined to his bed by an accident, exactly as you would wait on me if I was ill. If we both happen to ring for you together, you will answer his bell before you answer mine. The usual changes of linen are of course ready in the wardrobe there? Very good. Go now, and tell the cook to prepare a little dinner; and get a bottle of the old Madeira out of the cellar. You will spread the table, for to-day at least, in this room. These two gentlemen will be best pleased to dine together. Return here in five minutes' time, in case you are wanted; and show my guest, Peter, that I am right in believing you to be a good nurse as well as a good servant.'

The silent and surly Peter brightens under the expression of the Master's confidence in him, as the guide brightened under the influence of the Master's caressing touch. The two men leave the room together.

We take advantage of the momentary silence that follows, to introduce ourselves by name to our host, and to inform him of the circumstances under which we happen to be visiting Shetland. He listens in his subdued courteous way; but he makes no enquiries about our relatives; he shows no interest in the arrival of the government yacht and the Commissioner for Northern Lights. All sympathy with the doings of the outer world, all curiosity about persons of social position and notoriety, is evidently at an end in Mr Dunross. For twenty years the little round of his duties and his occupations has been enough for him. Life has lost its priceless value to this man – and when Death comes to him, he will receive the king of terrors as he might receive the last of his guests.

'Is there anything else I can do,' he says, speaking more to himself than to us, 'before I go back to my books?'

Something else occurs to him, even as he puts the question. He addresses my companion, with his faint sad smile. 'This will be a dull life I am afraid, sir, for you. If you happen to be fond of angling, I can offer you some little amusement in that way. The lake is well stocked with fish; and I have a boy employed in the garden, who will be glad to attend on you in the boat.'

My friend happens to be fond of fishing, and gladly accepts the invitation. The Master says his parting words to me, before he goes back to his books.

'You may safely trust my man Peter to wait on you Mr Germaine, while you are so unfortunate as to be confined to this room. He has the advantage (in cases of illness) of being a very silent undemonstrative person. At the same time he is careful and considerate, in his own reserved way. As to what I may term, the lighter duties at your bedside – such as reading to you, writing your letters for you while your right hand is still disabled, regulating the temperature in the room, and so on – though I cannot speak positively, I think it likely that these little services may be rendered to you by another person whom I have not mentioned yet. We shall see what happens in a few hours' time. In the meanwhile, sir, I ask permission to leave you to your rest.'

With those words, he walks out of the room as quietly as he walked into it, and leaves his two guests to meditate gratefully on Shetland hospitality. We both wonder what those last mysterious words of our host mean; and we exchange more or less ingenious guesses on the subject of that nameless 'other person' who may possibly attend on me – until the arrival of dinner turns our thoughts into a new course.

The dishes are few in number, but cooked to perfection and admirably served. I am too weary to eat much: a glass of the fine old Madeira revives me. We arrange our future plans while we are engaged over the meal. Our return to the yacht in Lerwick harbour is expected on the next day at the latest. As things are, I can only leave my companion to go back to the vessel, and relieve the minds of our friends of any needless alarm about me. On the day after, I engage to send on board a written report of the state of my health, by a messenger who can bring my portmanteau back with him.

These arrangements decided on, my friend goes away (at my own request) to try his skill as an angler in the lake. Assisted by the silent Peter and the well-stocked medicine-chest, I apply the necessary dressings to my wound; wrap myself in the comfortable morning gown which is always kept ready in the Guests' Chamber; and lie down again on the bed to try the restorative virtues of sleep.

Before he leaves the room, silent Peter goes to the window, and asks in

fewest possible words if he shall draw the curtains. In fewer words still – for I
am feeling drowsy already – I answer No. I dislike shutting out the cheering
light of day. To my morbid fancy, at that moment, it looks like resigning
myself deliberately to the horrors of a long illness. The handbell is on my
bedside table; and I can always ring for Peter if the light keeps me from
sleeping. On this understanding, Peter mutely nods his head, and goes out.

For some minutes I lie in lazy contemplation of the companionable
fire. Meanwhile, the dressings on my wounds and the embrocation on my
sprained wrist steadily subdue the pains which I have felt so far. Little by
little, the bright fire seems to be fading. Little by little, sleep steals on me,
and my troubles are forgotten.

I wake, after what seems to have been a long repose – I wake, feeling
the bewilderment which we all experience on opening our eyes for the
first time in a bed and a room that are new to us. Gradually collecting my
thoughts, I find my perplexity considerably increased by a trifling but
curious circumstance. The curtains which I had forbidden Peter to touch,
are drawn – closely drawn, so as to plunge the whole room in obscurity.
And, more surprising still, a high screen with folding sides stands before
the fire, and confines the light which it might otherwise give, exclusively
to the ceiling. I am literally enveloped in shadows. Has night come?

In lazy wonder, I turn my head on the pillow, and look on the other
side of my bed.

Dark as it is, I discover instantly that I am not alone.

A shadowy figure stands by my bedside. The dim outline of the dress
tells me that it is the figure of a woman. Straining my eyes, I fancy I can
discern a wavy black object covering her head and shoulders which looks
like a large veil. Her face is turned towards me; but no distinguishing
feature in it is visible. She stands like a statue, with her hands crossed in
front of her, faintly relieved against the dark substance of her dress. This I
can see – and this is all.

There is a moment of silence. The shadowy being finds its voice, and
speaks first.

'I hope you feel better, sir, after your rest?'

The voice is low, with a certain faint sweetness of tone which falls
soothingly on my ear. The accent is unmistakably the accent of a refined
and cultivated person. After making my acknowledgments to the
unknown and half-seen lady, I venture to ask the inevitable question, 'To
whom have I the honour of speaking?'

The lady answers, 'I am Miss Dunross; and I hope, if you have no
objection to it, to help Peter in nursing you.'

This, then, is the 'other person' dimly alluded to by our host! I think
directly of the heroic conduct of Miss Dunross among her poor and
afflicted neighbours; and I do not forget the melancholy result of her

devotion to others which has left her an incurable invalid. My anxiety to see this lady more plainly increases a hundredfold. I beg her to add to my grateful sense of her kindness by telling me why the room is so dark. 'Surely,' I say, 'it cannot be night all ready?'

'You have not been asleep,' she answers, 'for more than two hours. The mist has disappeared, and the sun is shining.'

I take up the bell, standing on the table at my side.

'May I ring for Peter, Miss Dunross?'

'To open the curtains, Mr Germaine?'

'Yes – with your permission. I own I should like to see the sunlight.'

'I will send Peter to you immediately.'

The shadowy figure of my new nurse glides away. In another moment, unless I say something to stop her, the woman whom I am so eager to see will have left the room.

'Pray don't go!' I say. 'I cannot think of troubling you to take a trifling message for me. The servant will come in, if I only ring the bell.'

She pauses – more shadowy than ever – halfway between the bed and the door, and answers a little sadly.

'Peter will not let in the daylight while I am in the room. He closed the curtains, by my order.'

The reply puzzles me. Why should Peter keep the room dark, while Miss Dunross is in it? Are her eyes weak? If her eyes were weak, they would be protected by a shade. Dark as it is, her veil would surely show it, if she wore a shade? Perhaps, after all, the curtains have been drawn with a view of prolonging my slumbers? I cannot venture on asking the question – I can only make my excuses in due form.

'Invalids only think of themselves,' I say. 'I supposed that you had kindly darkened the room on my account.'

She glides back to my bedside, before she speaks again. When she does answer, it is in these startling words:

'You were mistaken, Mr Germaine. Your room has been darkened – not on your account, but on *mine*.'

CHAPTER XV

THE CATS

Miss Dunross had so completely perplexed me, that I was at a loss what to say next.

To ask her plainly why it was necessary to keep the room in darkness while she remained in it, might prove (for all I knew to the contrary) to be an act of downright rudeness. To venture on any general expression of sympathy with her, knowing absolutely nothing of the circumstances, might place us both in an embarrassing position at the outset of our acquaintance. The one thing I could do was to beg that the present arrangement of the room might not be disturbed, and to leave her to decide as to whether she should admit me to her confidence or exclude me from it, at her own sole discretion.

She perfectly understood what was going on in my mind. Taking a chair at the foot of the bed, she told me simply and unreservedly the sad secret of the darkened room.

'If you wish to see much of me, Mr Germaine,' she began, 'you must accustom yourself to the world of shadows in which it is my lot to live. Some time since, a dreadful illness raged among the people in our part of this island; and I was so unfortunate as to catch the infection. When I recovered – no! "Recovery" is not the right word to use – let me say, when I escaped death, I found myself afflicted by a nervous malady which has defied medical help from that time to this. I am suffering (as the doctors explain it to me) from a morbidly sensitive condition of the nerves near the surface to the action of light. If I were to draw the curtains, and look out at that window, I should feel the acutest pain all over my face. If I covered my face, and drew the curtains with my bare hands, I should feel the same pain in my hands. You can just see perhaps that I have a very large and very thick veil on my head. I let it fall over my face and neck and hands, when I have occasion to pass along the corridors, or to enter my father's study – and I find it protection enough. Don't be too ready to deplore my sad condition, sir! I have got so used to living in the dark that I can see quite well enough for all the purposes of *my* poor existence. I can read and write in these shadows – I can see you, and be of use to you in many little ways, if you will let me. There is really nothing to be distressed about. My life will not be a long one – I know and feel that. But I hope to be spared long enough to be my father's companion through the closing years of his life. Beyond that, I have no prospect. In the meanwhile, I have my pleasures; and I mean to add to my scanty little stock the pleasure of attending on you. You are quite an event in my life. I look forward to reading to you and writing for you, as some girls look forward to a new dress, or a first ball. Do you think it very strange of me to tell you so openly just what I have in my mind? I can't help it! I say what I think to my father, and to our poor neighbours hereabouts – and I can't alter my ways at a moment's notice. I own it when I like people; and I own it when I don't. I have been looking at you while you were asleep; and I have read your face as I might read a book. There are signs of sorrow on your forehead and your lips which it is strange to see in so young a face as yours. I am afraid I shall trouble you with many questions about yourself when we become better acquainted with each other. Let me begin with a question, in my capacity as nurse. Are your pillows comfortable? I can see they want shaking up. Shall I send for Peter to raise you? I am unhappily not strong enough to be able to help you in that way. No? You are able to raise yourself? Wait a little. There! Now lie back – and tell me if I know how to establish the right sort of sympathy between a tumbled pillow and a weary head.'

She had so indescribably touched and interested me, stranger as I was, that the sudden cessation of her faint sweet tones affected me almost with a sense of pain. In trying (clumsily enough) to help her with the pillows, I accidentally touched her hand. It felt so cold and so thin, that even the momentary contact with it startled me. I tried vainly to see her face, now that it was more within reach of my range of view. The merciless darkness kept it as complete a mystery as ever. Had my curiosity escaped her notice? Nothing escaped her notice! Her next words told me plainly that I had been discovered.

'You have been trying to see me,' she said. 'Has my hand warned you not to try again? I felt that it startled you when you touched it just now.'

Such quickness of perception as this was not to be deceived; such fearless candour demanded as a right a similar frankness on my side. I owned the truth, and left it to her indulgence to forgive me.

She returned slowly to her chair at the foot of the bed.

'If we are to be friends,' she said, 'we must begin by understanding one another. Don't associate any romantic ideas of invisible beauty with *me*, Mr Germaine. I had but one beauty to boast of before I fell ill – my complexion – and that has gone for ever. There is nothing to see in me now, but the ruin of what was once a woman.'

She stopped for a moment. I could only judge of the effort which it cost her to say those sad words, by the altered tones of her voice as she spoke. They told me plainly that she had paused, not to consider what she should say next, but to control emotions which shook her self-possession as nothing had shaken it yet.

'I don't say this to distress you,' she went on; 'I say it to reconcile you to the darkness as a perpetual obstacle, so far as your eyes are concerned, between you and me. Make the best instead of the worst of your strange position here. It offers you a new sensation to amuse you while you are ill. You have a nurse who is an impersonal creature – a shadow among shadows; a voice to speak to you, and a hand to help you, and nothing more. Enough of myself!' she exclaimed, rising and changing her tone. 'What can I do to amuse you?' She considered a little. 'I have some odd tastes,' she resumed; 'and I think I may entertain you if I make you acquainted with one of them. Are you like most other men, Mr Germaine? Do you hate cats?'

The question startled me. However, I could honestly answer that, in this respect at least, I was not like other men.

'To my thinking,' I added, 'the cat is a cruelly misunderstood creature – especially in England. Women, no doubt, generally do justice to the affectionate nature of cats. But the men treat them as if they were the natural enemies of the human race. The men drive a cat out of their presence if it ventures up stairs, and set their dogs at it if it shows itself in the street – and then they turn round and accuse the poor creature (whose genial nature must attach itself to something) of being only fond of the kitchen!'

The expression of these unpopular sentiments appeared to raise me greatly in the estimation of Miss Dunross.

'We have one sympathy in common, at any rate,' she said. 'Now I can amuse you! Prepare for a surprise.'

She drew her veil over her face as she spoke, and, partially opening the door, rang my hand-bell. Peter appeared, and received his instructions.

'Move the screen,' said Miss Dunross. Peter obeyed; the ruddy firelight streamed over the floor. Miss Dunross proceeded with her directions. 'Open the door of the cats' room, Peter; and bring me my harp. Don't suppose that you are going to listen to a great player, Mr Germaine,' she went on, when Peter had departed on his singular errand, 'or that you are likely to see the sort of harp to which you are accustomed, as a man of the modern time. I can only play some old Scotch airs; and my harp is an ancient instrument (with new strings) – an heirloom in our family, some centuries old. When you see my harp, you will think of pictures of Saint Cecilia – and you will be treating my performance kindly if you will remember, at the same time, that I am no Saint!'

She drew her chair into the firelight; and sounded a whistle which she took from the pocket of her dress. In another moment, the lithe and shadowy figures of the cats appeared noiselessly in the red light, answering their mistress's call. I could just count six of them, as the creatures seated themselves demurely in a circle round the chair. Peter followed with the harp, and closed the door after him as he went out. The streak of daylight being now excluded from the room, Miss Dunross threw back her veil, and took the harp on her knee; seating herself, I observed, with her face turned away from the fire.

'You will have light enough to see the cats by,' she said, 'without having too much light for *me*. Firelight does not give me the acute pain which I suffer when daylight falls on my face – I feel a certain inconvenience from it, and nothing more.'

She touched the strings of her instrument – the ancient harp, as she had said, of the pictured Saint Cecilia; or rather, as I thought, the ancient harp of the Welsh Bards. The sound was at first unpleasantly high in pitch, to my untutored ear. At the opening notes of the melody – a slow wailing dirge-like air – the cats began the performance by walking round their mistress. Now they followed each other singly; now, at a change in the melody, they walked two and two; and, now again, they separated into divisions of three each, and circled round the chair in opposite directions. The music quickened, and the cats quickened their pace with it. Faster and faster the notes rang out, and faster and faster in the ruddy firelight, the cats like living shadows whirled round the still black figure in the chair, with the ancient harp on its knee. Anything so weird, wild, and ghostlike I never imagined before even in a dream! The music changed, and the whirling cats began to leap. One perched itself at a bound on the pedestal of the harp. Four sprang up together, and assumed their places, two on each of her shoulders. The last and smallest of the cats took the last leap, and lighted on her head! There the six creatures kept their positions, motionless as statues! Nothing moved but the wan white hands over the harp-strings; no sound but the sound of the music stirred in the room. Once more the melody changed. In an instant, the six cats were on the floor again, seated round the chair as I had seen them on their first entrance; the harp was laid aside; and the faint sweet voice said quietly, 'I am soon tired – my cats must conclude their performances to-morrow.'

She rose, and approached the bedside.

'I leave you to see the sunset through your window,' she said. 'From the coming of the darkness to the coming of breakfast-time, you must not count on my services – I am taking my rest. I have no choice but to remain in bed (sleeping when I can) for twelve hours or more. The long repose seems to keep my life in me. Have I and my cats surprised you very much? Am I a witch; and are they my familiar spirits? Remember how few amusements I have, and you will not wonder why I devote myself to teaching these pretty creatures their tricks, and attaching them to me like dogs! They were slow at first, and they taught me excellent lessons of patience. Now, they understand what I want of them, and they learn wonderfully well. How you will amuse your friend, when he comes back from fishing, with the story of the young lady who lives in the dark, and keeps a company of performing cats! I shall expect *you* to amuse *me* to-morrow – I want you to tell me all about yourself, and how you came to visit these wild islands of ours. Perhaps, as the days go on, and we get better acquainted, you will take me a little more into your confidence, and tell me the true meaning of that story of sorrow which I read on your face while you were asleep? I have just enough of the woman left in me to be the victim of curiosity, when I meet with a person who interests me. Good-bye till to-morrow! I wish you a tranquil night, and a pleasant waking. Come, my familiar spirits – Come my cat-children! it's time we went back to our own side of the house.'

She dropped the veil over her face – and, followed by her train of cats, glided out of the room.

Immediately on her departure, Peter appeared, and drew back the curtains. The light of the setting sun streamed in at the window. At the same moment, my travelling companion returned in high spirits, eager to tell me about his fishing in the lake. The contrast between what I saw and heard now, and what I had seen and heard only a few minutes since, was so extraordinary and so startling that I almost doubted whether the veiled figure with the harp, and the dance of cats, were not the fantastic creations of a dream. I actually asked my friend whether he had found me awake or asleep when he came into the room!

Evening merged into night. Mr Dunross duly made his appearance, to receive the latest news of my health. He spoke and listened absently, as if his mind was still preoccupied by his studies – except when I referred gratefully to his daughter's kindness to me. At her name his faded blue eyes brightened; his drooping head became erect; his sad subdued voice strengthened in tone.

'Do not hesitate to let her attend on you,' he said. 'Whatever interests or amuses her, lengthens her life. In *her* life is the breath of mine. She is more than my daughter – she is the guardian-angel of the house; go where she may, she carries the air of Heaven with her. When you say your prayers, sir, pray God to leave my daughter here a little longer.'

He sighed heavily; his head dropped again on his breast – he left me.

The hour advanced; the evening meal was set by my bedside. Silent Peter, taking his leave for the night, developed into speech. 'I sleep next door,' he said. 'Ring when you want me.' My travelling-companion, taking the second bed in the room, reposed in the happy sleep of youth. In the house, there was dead silence. Out of the house, the low song of the night-wind, rising and falling over the lake and the moor, was the one sound to be heard. So the first day ended in the hospitable Shetland house.

CHAPTER XVI

THE GREEN FLAG

'I congratulate you, Mr Germaine, on your power of painting in words. Your description gives me a vivid idea of Mrs Van Brandt.'

'Does the portrait please you, Miss Dunross?'

'May I speak as plainly as usual?'

'Certainly!'

'Well, then, plainly, I don't like your Mrs Van Brandt.'

Ten days had passed; and thus far Miss Dunross had made her way into my confidence already!

By what means had she induced me to trust her with those secret and sacred sorrows of my life which I had hitherto kept for my mother's ear alone? I can easily recall the rapid and subtle manner in which her sympathies twined themselves round mine – but I fail entirely to trace the infinite gradations of approach, by which she surprised and conquered my habitual reserve. The strongest influence of all, the influence of the eye, was not hers. When the light was admitted into the room, she was shrouded in her veil. At all other times, the curtains were drawn, the screen was before the fire – I could see dimly the outline of her face, and I could see no more. The secret of her influence was perhaps partly attributable to the simple and sisterly manner in which she spoke to me, and partly to the indescribable interest which associated itself with her mere presence in the room. Her father had told me that she 'carried the air of Heaven with her.' In my experience, I can only say that she carried something with her which softly and inscrutably possessed itself of my will, and made me as unconsciously obedient to her wishes as if I had been her dog. The love-story of my boyhood, in all its particulars, down even to the gift of the green-flag; the mystic predictions of Dame Dermody; the loss of every trace of my little Mary of former days; the rescue of Mrs Van Brandt from the river; the apparition of her in the summer-house; the after-meetings with her in Edinburgh and in London; the final parting which had left its mark of sorrow on my face – all these events, all these sufferings, I confided to her as unreservedly as I have confided them to these pages. And the result, as she sat by me in the darkened room, was summed up, with a woman's headlong impetuosity of judgment, in the words I have just written – 'I don't like your Mrs Van Brandt!'

'Why not?' I asked.

She answered instantly. 'Because you ought to love nobody but Mary.'

'But Mary has been lost to me since I was a boy of thirteen.'

'Be patient – and you will find her again. Mary is patient – Mary is waiting for you. When you meet her, you will be ashamed to remember that you ever loved Mrs Van Brandt – you will look on your separation from that woman as the happiest event of your life. I may not live to hear of it – but *you* will live to own that I was right.'

Her perfectly-baseless conviction that time would yet bring about my meeting with Mary, partly irritated, partly amused me.'

'You seem to agree with Dame Dermody,' I said. 'You believe that our two destinies are one. No matter what time may elapse, or what may happen in the time, you believe my marriage with Mary is still a marriage delayed, and nothing more?'

'I firmly believe it.'

'Without knowing why – except that you dislike the idea of my marrying Mrs Van Brandt?'

She knew that this view of her motive was not far from being the right one – and womanlike, she shifted the discussion to new ground.

'Why do you call her Mrs Van Brandt?' she asked. 'Mrs Van Brandt is the namesake of your first love. If you are so fond of her, why don't you call her Mary?'

I was ashamed to give the true reason – it seemed so utterly unworthy of a man of any sense or spirit. Noticing my hesitation, she insisted on my answering her; she forced me to make my humiliating confession.

'The man who has parted us,' I said, 'called her Mary. I hate him with such a jealous hatred that he has even disgusted me with the name! It lost all its charm for me when it passed *his* lips.'

I had anticipated that she would laugh at me. No! She suddenly raised her head as if she was looking at me intently in the dark.

'How fond you must be of that woman!' she said. 'Do you dream of her now?'

'I never dream of her now.'

'Do you expect to see the apparition of her again?'

'It may be so – if a time comes when she is in sore need of help, and when she has no friend to look to but me.'

'Did you ever see the apparition of your little Mary?'

'Never!'

'But you used once to see her – as Dame Dermody predicted – in dreams?'

'Yes – when I was a lad.'

'And in the after-time, it was not Mary, but Mrs Van Brandt who came to you in dreams – who appeared to you in the spirit, when she was far away from you in the body? Poor old Dame Dermody! She little thought in her lifetime, that her prediction would be fulfilled by the wrong woman!'

To that result, her enquiries had inscrutably conducted her! If she had only pressed them a little farther – if she had not unconsciously led me astray again by the very next question that fell from her lips – she *must* have communicated to *my* mind, the idea obscurely germinating in hers – the idea of a possible identity between the Mary of my first love and Mrs Van Brandt!

'Tell me,' she went on. 'If you met with your little Mary now, what would she be like? what sort of woman would you expect to see?'

I could hardly help laughing. 'How can I tell,' I rejoined, 'at this distance of time?'

'Try!' she said.

Reasoning my way from the known personality to the unknown, I searched my memory for the image of the frail and delicate child of my remembrance; and I drew the picture of a frail and delicate woman – the most absolute contrast imaginable to Mrs Van Brandt!

The half-realised idea of identity in the mind of Miss Dunross dropped out of it instantly, expelled by the substantial conclusion which the contrast implied. Alike ignorant of the after-growth of health, strength, and beauty which time and circumstances had developed in the Mary of my youthful days, we had alike completely and unconsciously misled one another. Once more I had missed the discovery of the truth, and missed it by a hairsbreadth!

'I infinitely prefer your portrait of Mary, said Miss Dunross, 'to your portrait of Mrs Van Brandt. Mary realises my idea of what a really-attractive woman ought to be. How you can have felt any sorrow for the loss of that other person (I detest buxom women!) passes my understanding. I can't tell you how interested I am in Mary! I want to know more about her. Where is that pretty present of needlework which the poor little thing embroidered for you so industriously? Do let me see the green flag!'

She evidently supposed that I carried the green flag about me! I felt a little confused as I answered her.

'I am sorry to disappoint you. The green flag is somewhere in my house in Perthshire.'

'You have not got it with you?' she exclaimed. 'You leave her keepsake lying about anywhere? Oh, Mr Germaine, you have indeed forgotten Mary! A woman, in your place, would have parted with her life rather than part with the one memorial left of the time when she first loved!'

She spoke with such extraordinary earnestness – with such agitation, I might almost say – that she quite startled me.

'Dear Miss Dunross,' I remonstrated, 'the flag is not lost.'

'I should hope not!' she interposed quickly. 'If you lose the green flag, you lose the relic of Mary – and more than that, if *my* belief is right.'

'What do you believe?'

'You will laugh at me if I tell you. I am afraid my first reading of your face was wrong – I am afraid you are a hard man.'

'Indeed you do me an injustice. I entreat you to answer me as frankly as usual. What do I lose in losing the last relic of Mary?'

'You lose the one hope I have for you,' she answered gravely – 'the hope of your meeting and your marriage with Mary in the time to come. I was sleepless last night, and I was thinking of your pretty love story by the banks of the bright English lake. The longer I thought, the more firmly I felt the conviction that the poor child's green flag is destined to have its innocent influence in forming your future life. Your happiness is waiting for you in that artless little keepsake! I can't explain or justify this belief of mine. It is one of my eccentricities, I suppose – like training my cats to perform to the music of my harp. But, if I was your old friend, instead of being only your friend of a few days, I would leave you no peace

– I would beg and entreat and persist, as only a woman *can* persist – until I had made Mary's gift as close a companion of yours, as your mother's portrait in the locket there at your watch chain. While the flag is with you, Mary's influence is with you – Mary's love is still binding you by the dear old tie – and Mary and you, after years of separation, will meet again!'

The fancy was in itself pretty and poetical; the earnestness which had given expression to it would have had its influence over a man of a far harder nature than mine. I confess she had made me ashamed, if she had done nothing more, of my neglect of the green flag.

'I will look for it, the moment I am at home again,' I said; 'and I will take care that it is carefully preserved for the future.'

'I want more than that,' she rejoined. 'If you can't wear the flag about you, I want it always to be *with* you – to go wherever you go. When they brought your luggage here from the vessel at Lerwick, you were particularly anxious about the safety of your travelling writing-desk – the desk there on the table. Is there anything very valuable in it?'

'It contains my money, and other things that I prize far more highly – my mother's letters, and some family relics which I should be very sorry to lose. Besides, the desk itself has its own familiar interest as my constant travelling companion of many years past.'

Miss Dunross rose, and came close to the chair in which I was sitting.

'Let Mary's flag be your constant travelling companion,' she said. 'You have spoken far too gratefully of my services here as your nurse. Reward me beyond my deserts. Make allowances, Mr Germaine, for the superstitious fancies of a lonely dreamy woman. Promise me that the green flag shall take its place among the other little treasures in your desk!'

It is needless to say that I made the allowances and gave the promise – gave it, resolving seriously to abide by it. For the first time since I had known her, she put her poor wasted hand in mine, and pressed it for a moment. Acting heedlessly under my first grateful impulse, I lifted her hand to my lips, before I released it. She started – trembled – and suddenly and silently passed out of the room.

CHAPTER XVII

SHE COMES BETWEEN US

What emotion had I thoughtlessly aroused in Miss Dunross? Had I offended or distressed her? Or had I, without meaning it, forced on her inner knowledge some deeply seated feeling which she had thus far resolutely ignored?

I looked back through the days of my sojourn in the house; I
questioned my own feelings and impressions, on the chance that they
might serve me as a means of solving the mystery of her sudden flight
from the room.

What effect had she produced on me?

In plain truth, she had simply taken her place in my mind, to the
exclusion of every other person and every other subject. In ten days she
had taken a hold on my sympathies of which other women would have
failed to possess themselves in as many years. I remembered, to my
shame, that my mother had but seldom occupied my thoughts. Even the
image of Mrs Van Brandt – except when the conversation had turned on
her – had become a faint image in my mind! As to my friends at
Lerwick, from Sir James downwards, they had all kindly come to see me
– and I had secretly and ungratefully rejoiced when their departure left
the scene free for the return of my nurse. In two days more the
Government vessel was to sail on the return voyage. My wrist was still
painful when I tried to use it; but the far more serious injury presented
by the re-opened wound was no longer a subject of anxiety to myself or
to anyone about me. I was sufficiently restored to be capable of making
the journey to Lerwick – if I rested for one night at a farm half way
between the town and Mr Dunross's house. Knowing this, I had
nevertheless left the question of rejoining the vessel undecided to the
very latest moment. The motive which I pleaded to my friends was –
uncertainty as to the sufficient recovery of my strength. The motive
which I now confessed to myself was – reluctance to leave Miss Dunross.

What was the secret of her power over me? What emotion, what
passion, had she awakened in me? Was it love?

No: not love. The place which Mary had once held in my heart, the
place which Mrs Van Brandt had taken in the after-time, was not the
place occupied by Miss Dunross. How could I (in the ordinary sense of
the word) be in love with a woman whose face I had never seen? whose
beauty had faded, never to bloom again? whose wasted life hung by a
thread which the accident of a moment might snap. The senses have their
share in all love between the sexes which is worthy of the name. They
had no share in the feeling with which I regarded Miss Dunross. What
was the feeling then? I can only answer the question in one way. The
feeling lay too deep in me for my sounding.

What impression had I produced on her? What sensitive chord had I
ignorantly touched, when my lips touched her hand?

I confess I recoiled from pursuing the enquiry which I had deliberately
set myself to make. I thought of her shattered health; of her melancholy
existence in shadow and solitude; of the rich treasures of such a heart and
such a mind as hers, wasted with her wasting life – and I said to myself,

Let her secret be sacred! let me never again, by word or deed, bring the trouble which tells of it to the surface! let her heart be veiled from me in the darkness which veils her face!

In this frame of mind towards her, I waited her return.

I had no doubt of seeing her again, sooner or later, on that day. The post to the south went out on the next day; and the early hour of the morning at which the messenger called for our letters, made it a matter of ordinary convenience to write overnight. In the disabled state of my hand Miss Dunross had been accustomed to write home for me, under my dictation: she knew that I owed a letter to my mother, and that I relied as usual on her help. Her return to me, under these circumstances, was simply a question of time: any duty which she had once undertaken was an imperative duty in her estimation, no matter how trifling it might be.

The hours wore on; the day drew to its end – and still she never appeared.

I left my room to enjoy the last sunny gleam of the daylight in the garden attached to the house; first telling Peter where I might be found, if Miss Dunross wanted me. The garden was a wild place, to my southern notions; but it extended for some distance along the shore of the island; and it offered some pleasant views of the lake and the moorland country beyond. Slowly pursuing my walk, I proposed to myself to occupy my mind to some useful purpose, by arranging beforehand the composition of the letter which Miss Dunross was to write.

To my great surprise, I found it simply impossible to fix my attention on the subject. Try as I might, my thoughts persisted in wandering from the letter to my mother, and concentrated themselves instead – on Miss Dunross? No. On the question of my returning, or not returning to Perthshire by the Government vessel? No. By some capricious revulsion of feeling which it seemed impossible to account for, my whole mind (now that I was out of the atmosphere of the darkened room) was absorbed by the one subject which had been hitherto so strangely absent from it – the subject of Mrs Van Brandt!

My memory went back, in defiance of all exercise of my own will, to my last interview with her. I saw her again; I heard her again. I tasted once more the momentary rapture of our last kiss; I felt once more the pang of sorrow that wrung me when I had parted with her and found myself alone in the street. Tears – of which I was ashamed, though nobody was near to see them – filled my eyes when I thought of the months that had passed since we had last looked on one another, and of all that she might have suffered, must have suffered, in that time. Hundreds on hundreds of miles were between us – and yet she was now as near me as if she had been walking in the garden by my side!

This strange condition of my mind was matched by an equally strange condition of my body. A mysterious trembling shuddered over me faintly from head to foot. I walked without feeling the ground as I trod on it; I looked about me with no distinct consciousness of what the objects were on which my eyes rested. My hands were cold – and yet I hardly felt it. My head throbbed hotly – and yet I was not sensible of any pain. It seemed as if I was surrounded and enwrapped in some electric atmosphere which altered all the ordinary conditions of sensation. I looked up at the clear calm sky, and wondered if a thunder-storm was coming. I stopped, and buttoned my coat round me, and questioned myself if I had caught a cold, or if I was going to have a fever. The sun sank below the moorland horizon; the grey twilight trembled over the dark waters of the lake. I went back to the house; and the vivid memory of Mrs Van Brandt, still in close companionship, went back with me.

The fire in my room had burnt low in my absence. One of the closed curtains had been drawn back a few inches, so as to admit through the window a ray of the dying light. Beyond the limit where the light was bounded by the obscurity which filled the rest of the room, I saw Miss Dunross seated, with her veil drawn and her writing-case on her knee, waiting my return.

I hastened to make my excuses. I assured her that I had been careful to tell the servant where to find me. She gently checked me, before I could say more.

'It's not Peter's fault,' she said. 'I told him not to hurry your return to the house. Have you enjoyed your walk?'

She spoke very quietly. The faint sad voice was fainter and sadder than ever. She kept her head bent over her writing-case, instead of turning it towards me as usual while we were taking. I still felt the mysterious trembling which had oppressed me in the garden. Drawing a chair near the fire, I stirred the embers together, and tried to warm myself. Our positions in the room left some little distance between us. I could only see her sideways, as she sat by the window in the sheltering darkness of the curtain which still remained drawn.

'I think I have been too long in the garden,' I said. 'I feel chilled by the cold evening air.'

'Will you have some more wood put on the fire?' she asked. 'Can I get you anything?'

'No, thank you. I shall do very well here. I see you are kindly ready to write for me.'

'Yes,' she said, 'at your own convenience. When you are ready, my pen is ready.'

The unacknowledged reserve that had come between us since we had last spoken together was, I believe, as painfully felt by her as by me. We were no doubt longing to break through it on either side – if we had only known how. The writing of the letter would occupy us at any rate. I made another effort to give my mind to the subject – and once more it was an effort made in vain. Knowing what I wanted to say to my mother, my faculties seemed to be paralysed when I tried to say it. I sat cowering by the fire – and she sat waiting with her writing-case on her lap.

CHAPTER XVIII

SHE CLAIMS ME AGAIN

The moments passed; the silence between us continued. Miss Dunross made an attempt to rouse me.

'Have you decided to go back to Scotland with your friends at Lerwick?' she asked.

'It is no easy matter,' I replied, 'to decide on leaving my friends in this house.'

Her head drooped lower on her bosom; her voice sank as she answered me.

'Think of your mother,' she said. 'The first duty you owe is your duty to her. Your long absence is a heavy trial to her – your mother is suffering.'

'Suffering?' I repeated. 'Her letters say nothing——'

'You forget that you have allowed me to read her letters,' Miss Dunross interposed. 'I see the unwritten and unconscious confession of anxiety in every line that she writes to you. You know, as well as I do, that there is cause for her anxiety. Make her happy by telling her that you sail for home with your friends. Make her happier still by telling her that you grieve no more over the loss of Mrs Van Brandt. May I write it, in your name and in those words?'

I felt the strangest reluctance to permit her to write in those terms, or in any terms, of Mrs Van Brandt. The unhappy love-story of my manhood had never been a forbidden subject between us on former occasions. Why did I feel as if it had become a forbidden subject now? Why did I evade giving her a direct reply?

'We have plenty of time before us,' I said. 'I want to speak to you about yourself.'

She lifted her hand in the obscurity that surrounded her, as if to protest against the topic to which I had returned. I persisted nevertheless in returning to it.

'If I must go back,' I went on, 'I may venture to say to you at parting, what I have not said yet. I cannot, and will not, believe that you are an incurable invalid. My education, as I have told you, has been the education of a medical man. I am well acquainted with some of the greatest living physicians, in Edinburgh, as well as in London. Will you allow me to describe your malady (as I understand it) to men who are accustomed to treat cases of intricate nervous disorder? And will you let me write and tell you the result?'

I waited for her reply. Neither by word nor sign did she encourage the idea of any future communication with her. I ventured to suggest another motive which might induce her to receive a letter from me.

'In any case, I may find it necessary to write to you,' I went on. 'You firmly believe that I and my little Mary are destined to meet again. If your anticipations are realised, you will expect me to tell you of it, surely?'

Once more, I waited. She spoke – but it was not to reply: it was only to change the subject.

'The time is passing,' was all she said. 'We have not begun your letter to your mother, yet.'

It would have been cruel to contend with her any longer. Her voice warned me that she was suffering. The faint gleam of light through the parted curtains was fading fast. It was time indeed to write the letter. I could find other opportunities of speaking to her, before I left the house.

'I am ready,' I answered. 'Let us begin.'

The first sentence was easily dictated to my patient secretary. I informed my mother that my sprained wrist was nearly restored to use, and that nothing prevented my leaving Shetland, when the lighthouse commissioner was ready to return. This was all that it was necessary to say on the subject of my health; the disaster of my reopened wound having been, for obvious reasons, concealed from my mother's knowledge. Miss Dunross silently wrote the opening lines of the letter, and waited for the words that were to follow.

In my next sentence, I announced the date at which the vessel was to sail on the return voyage; and I mentioned the period at which my mother might expect to see me, weather permitting. Those words also Miss Dunross wrote – and waited again. I set myself to consider what I should say next. To my surprise and alarm, I found it impossible to fix my mind on the subject. My thoughts wandered away from my letter, in the strangest manner, to Mrs Van Brandt. I was ashamed of myself; I was angry with myself – I resolved, no matter what I said, that I would positively finish the letter. No! try as I might, the utmost effort of my will availed me nothing. Mrs Van Brandt's words at our last interview were murmuring in my ears – not a word of my own would come to me!

Miss Dunross laid down her pen, and slowly turned her head to look at me.

'Surely you have something to add to your letter?' she said.

'Certainly,' I answered. 'I don't know what is the matter with me. The effort of dictating seems to be beyond my power this evening.'

'Can I help you?' she asked.

I gladly accepted the suggestion. 'There are many things,' I said, 'which my mother would be glad to hear, if I was not too stupid to think of them. I am sure I may trust your sympathy to think of them for me.'

That rash answer offered Miss Dunross the opportunity of returning to the subject of Mrs Van Brandt. She seized the opportunity with a woman's persistent resolution when she has her end in view, and is determined to reach it at all hazards.

'You have not told your mother yet,' she said, 'that your infatuation for Mrs Van Brandt is at an end. Will you put it in your own words? Or shall I write it for you, imitating your language as well as I can?'

In the state of my mind at that moment, her perseverance conquered me. I thought to myself indolently, 'If I say No, she will only return to the subject again, and she will end (after all I owe to her kindness) in making me say Yes.' Before I could answer her, she had realised my anticipations. She returned to the subject; and she made me say Yes.

'What does your silence mean?' she said. 'Do you ask me to help you – and do you refuse to accept the first suggestion I offer?'

'Take up your pen,' I rejoined. 'It shall be as you wish.'

'Will you dictate the words?'

'I will try.'

I tried; and, this time, I succeeded. With the image of Mrs Van Brandt vividly present to my mind, I arranged the first words of the sentence which was to tell my mother that my 'infatuation' was at an end!

'You will be glad to hear,' I began, 'that time and change are doing their good work.'

Miss Dunross wrote the words, and paused in anticipation of the next sentence. The light faded and faded; the room grew darker and darker. I went on:

'I hope I shall cause you no more anxiety, my dear mother, on the subject of Mrs Van Brandt.'

In the deep silence, I could hear the pen of my secretary, travelling steadily over the paper, while it wrote those words.

'Have you written?' I asked, as the sound of the pen ceased.

'I have written,' she answered, in her customary quiet tones.

I went on again with my letter.

'The days pass now, and I seldom or never think of her; I hope I am resigned at last to the loss of Mrs Van Brandt.'

As I reached the end of the sentence, I heard a faint cry from Miss Dunross. Looking instantly towards her, I could just see, in the deepening darkness, that her head had fallen on the back of the chair. My first impulse was, of course, to rise and go to her. I had barely got to my feet, when some indescribable dread paralysed me on the instant. Supporting myself against the chimney-piece, I stood perfectly incapable of advancing a step. The effort to speak was the one effort that I could make.

'Are you ill?' I asked.

She was able to answer me; speaking in a whisper, without raising her head.

'I am frightened,' she said.

'What has frightened you?'

I heard her shudder in the darkness. Instead of answering me, she whispered to herself; 'What am I to say to him?'

'Tell me what has frightened you,' I repeated. 'You know you may trust me with the truth.'

She rallied her sinking strength. She answered in these strange words:

'Something has come between me and the letter that I am writing for you.'

'What is it?'

'I can't tell you.'

'Can you see it?'

'No.'

'Can you feel it?'

'Yes!'

'What is it like?'

'Like a breath of cold air between me and the letter.'

'Has the window come open?'

'The window is close shut.'

'And the door?'

'The door is shut also – as well as I can see. Make sure of it for yourself. Where are you? What are you doing?'

I was looking towards the window. As she spoke her last words, I was conscious of a change in that part of the room.

In the gap between the parted curtains there was a new light shining – not the dim grey twilight of Nature, but a pure and starry radiance, a pale unearthly light. While I watched it, the starry radiance quivered as if some breath of air had stirred it. When it was still again, there dawned on me through the unearthly lustre the figure of a woman. By fine and slow gradations, it became more and more distinct. I knew the noble figure; I knew the sad and tender smile. For the second time, I stood in the presence of the apparition of Mrs Van Brandt.

She was robed, not as I had last seen her, but in the dress which she had worn on the memorable evening when we met on the bridge – in the dress in which she had first appeared to me, by the waterfall in Scotland. The starry light shone round her like a halo. She looked at me with sorrowful and pleading eyes, as she had looked when I saw the apparition of her in the summer-house. She lifted her hand – not beckoning me to approach her as before, but gently signing to me to remain where I stood.

I waited – feeling awe, but no fear. My heart was all hers as I looked at her.

She moved; gliding from the window to the chair in which Miss Dunross sat; winding her way slowly round it, until she stood at the back. By the light of the pale halo that encircled the ghostly Presence, and moved with it, I could see the dark figure of the living woman, seated immovable in the chair. The writing-case was on her lap, with the letter and the pen lying on it. Her arms hung helpless at her sides; her veiled head was now bent forward. She looked as if she had been petrified in the act of trying to rise from her seat.

A moment passed – and I saw the ghostly Presence stoop over the living woman. It lifted the writing-case from her lap. It rested the writing-case on her shoulder. Its white fingers took the pen, and wrote on the unfinished letter. It put the writing-case back on the lap of the living woman. Still standing behind the chair, it turned towards me. It looked at me once more. And now it beckoned – beckoned to me to approach.

Moving without conscious will of my own, as I had moved when I first saw her in the summer-house – drawn nearer and nearer by an irresistible power – I approached, and stopped within a few paces of her. She advanced, and laid her hand on my bosom. Again I felt those strangely-mingled sensations of rapture and awe, which had once before filled me when I was conscious, spiritually, of her touch. Again she spoke, in the low melodious tones which I recalled so well. Again she said the words: 'Remember me. Come to me.' Her hand dropped from my bosom. The pale light in which she stood quivered, sank, vanished. I saw the twilight glimmering between the curtains – and I saw no more. She had spoken. She had gone.

I was near Miss Dunross – near enough, when I put out my hand, to touch her.

She started and shuddered, like a woman suddenly awakened from a dreadful dream.

'Speak to me!' she whispered. 'Let me know that it is *you* who touched me.'

I spoke a few composing words before I questioned her.

'Have you seen anything in the room?'

She answered. 'I have been filled with a deadly fear. I have seen nothing but the writing-case lifted from my lap.'

'Did you see the hand that lifted it?'

'No.'

'Did you see a starry light, and a figure standing in the light?'

'No.'

'Did you see the writing-case after it was lifted from your lap?'

'I saw it resting on my shoulder.'

'Did you see writing on the letter, which was not *your* writing?'

'I saw a darker shadow on the paper than the shadow in which I am sitting.'

'Did it move?'

'It moved across the paper.'

'In what direction did it move?'

'From right to left.'

'As a pen moves in writing?'

'Yes. As a pen moves in writing.'

'May I take the letter?'

She handed it to me.

'May I light a candle?'

She drew her veil more closely over her face, and bowed in silence.

I lit the candle on the mantel-piece behind her, and looked for the writing.

There, on the blank space in the letter – as I had seen it before on the blank space in the sketch-book – there were the written words which the ghostly Presence had left behind it; arranged once more in two lines, as I copy them here –

AT THE MONTH'S END
IN THE SHADOW OF ST PAUL'S.

CHAPTER XIX

THE KISS

She had need of me again. She had claimed me again. I felt all the old love, all the old devotion, owning her power once more. Whatever had mortified or angered me at our last interview, was forgiven and forgotten now. My whole being still thrilled with the mingled awe and rapture of beholding the Vision of her that had come to me for the second time. The minutes passed – and I stood by the fire like a man entranced; thinking only of her spoken words, 'Remember me. Come to me;' looking only at her mystic writing, 'At the month's end. In the shadow of St Paul's.'

The month's end was still far off; the apparition of her had shown itself to me, under some subtle prevision of trouble that was still in the future. Ample time was before me for the pilgrimage to which I was self-dedicated already – my pilgrimage to the shadow of St Paul's.

Other men, in my position, might have hesitated as to the right understanding of the place to which they were bidden. Other men might have wearied their memories by recalling the churches, the institutions, the streets, the towns in foreign countries, all consecrated to Christian reverence by the great Apostle's name, and might have fruitlessly asked themselves in which direction they were first to turn their steps. No such difficulty troubled me. My first conclusion was the one conclusion that was acceptable to my mind. 'St Paul's' meant the famous Cathedral of London. Where the shadow of the great church fell, there, at the month's end, I should find her, or the trace of her. In London once more, and nowhere else, I was destined to see the woman I loved, in the living body, as certainly as I had just seen her in the ghostly presence.

Who could interpret the mysterious sympathies that still united us, in defiance of distance, in defiance of time? Who could predict to what end our lives were tending in the years that were to come?

Those questions were still present to my thoughts; my eyes were still fixed on the mysterious writing – when I became instinctively aware of the strange silence in the room. Instantly, the lost remembrance of Miss Dunross came back to me. Stung by my own sense of self-reproach, I turned with a start, and looked towards her chair by the window.

The chair was empty. I was alone in the room.

Why had she left me secretly, without a word of farewell? Because she was suffering, in mind or body? Or because she resented, naturally resented, my neglect of her?

The bare suspicion that I had given her pain was intolerable to me. I rang the bell, to make enquiries.

The bell was answered, not as usual by the silent servant Peter, but by a woman of middle age, very quietly and neatly dressed, whom I had once or twice met on the way to and from my room, and of whose exact position in the house I was still ignorant.

'Do you wish to see Peter?' she asked.

'No. I wish to know where Miss Dunross is.'

'Miss Dunross is in her room. She has sent me to you with this letter.'

I took the letter, feeling some surprise and uneasiness. It was the first time Miss Dunross had communicated with me in that formal way. I tried to gain further information by questioning her messenger.

'Are you Miss Dunross's maid?' I asked.

'I have served Miss Dunross for many years,' was the answer, spoken very ungraciously.

'Do you think she would receive me, if I sent you with a message to her?'

'I can't say, sir. The letter may tell you. You will do well to read the letter.'

We looked at each other. The woman's pre-conceived impression of me was evidently an unfavourable one. Had I indeed pained or offended Miss Dunross? And had the servant – perhaps the faithful servant who loved her – discovered and resented it? The woman frowned as she looked at me. It would be a mere waste of words to persist in questioning her. I let her go.

Left by myself again, I read the letter. It began, without any form of address, in these lines:

'I write, instead of speaking to you, because my self-control has already been severely tried, and I am not strong enough to bear more. For my father's sake – not for my own – I must take all the care I can of the little health that I have left.

'Putting together what you have told me of the visionary creature whom you saw in the summer-house in Scotland, and what you said when you questioned me in your room a little while since, I cannot fail to infer that the same Vision has shown itself to you, for the second time. The fear that I felt, the strange things that I saw (or thought I saw), may have been imperfect reflections in my mind of what was passing in yours. I do not stop to enquire whether we are both the victims of a delusion, or whether we are the chosen recipients of a supernatural communication. The result, in either case, is enough for me. You are once more under the influence of Mrs Van Brandt. I will not trust myself to tell you of the anxieties and forebodings by which I am oppressed: I will only acknowledge that my one hope for you is in your speedy re-union with the worthier object of your constancy and devotion. I still believe, and am consoled in believing, that you and your first love will meet again.

'Having written so far, I leave the subject – not to return to it, except in my own thoughts.

'The necessary preparations for your departure to-morrow are all made. Nothing remains but to wish you a safe and pleasant journey home. Do not, I entreat you, think me insensible of what I owe to you, if I say my farewell words here.

'The little services which you have allowed me to render you have brightened the closing days of my life. You have left me a treasury of happy memories which I shall hoard, when you are gone, with miserly care. Are you willing to add new claims to my grateful remembrance? I ask it of you, as a last favour – do not attempt to see me again! Do not expect me to take a personal leave of you! The saddest of all words is "Goodbye:" I have fortitude enough to write it, and no more. God preserve and prosper you – farewell!'

'One more request. I beg that you will not forget what you promised me, when I told you my foolish fancy about the green flag. Wherever you go, let Mary's keepsake go with you. No written answer is necessary. – I would rather not receive it. Look up, when you leave the house to-morrow, at the centre window over the doorway – that will be answer enough.'

To say that these melancholy lines brought the tears into my eyes, is only to acknowledge that I had sympathies which could be touched. When I had in some degree recovered my composure, the impulse which urged me to write to Miss Dunross was too strong to be resisted. I did not trouble her with a long letter – I only entreated her to reconsider her decision, with all the art of persuasion which I could summon to help me. The answer was brought back by the servant who waited on Miss Dunross, in three resolute words: – 'It cannot be.' This time the woman spoke out before she left me. 'If you have any regard for my mistress,' she said sternly, 'don't make her write to you again.' She looked at me with a last lowering frown, and left the room.

It is needless to say that the faithful servant's words only increased my anxiety to see Miss Dunross once more before we parted – perhaps for ever. My one last hope of success in attaining this object lay in approaching her directly through the intercession of her father.

I sent Peter to enquire if I might be permitted to pay my respects to his master that evening. My messenger returned with an answer which was a new disappointment to me. Mr Dunross begged that I would excuse him if he deferred the proposed interview until the next morning. The next morning was the morning of my departure. Did the message mean that he had no wish to see me again until the time had come to take leave of him? I enquired of Peter whether his master was particularly occupied that evening. He was unable to tell me. 'The Master of Books' was not in his study as usual. When he sent his message to me, he was sitting by the sofa in his daughter's room.

Having answered in those terms, the man left me by myself until the next morning. I do not wish my bitterest enemy a sadder time in his life than the time I passed, on the last night of my residence under Mr Dunross's roof.

After walking to and fro in the room until I was weary, I thought of trying to divert my mind from the sad thoughts that oppressed it, by reading. The one candle which I had lit failed to sufficiently illuminate the room. Advancing to the mantelpiece to light the second candle which stood there, I noticed the unfinished letter to my mother lying where I had placed it, when Miss Dunross's servant first presented herself before me. Having lit the second candle, I took up the letter to put it away among my other papers. Doing this (while my thoughts were still dwelling on Miss Dunross), I mechanically looked at the letter again – and instantly discovered a change in it.

The written characters traced by the hand of the apparition had vanished! Below the last lines written by Miss Dunross, nothing met my eye now but the blank white paper!

My first impulse was to look at my watch.

When the ghostly Presence had written in my sketch-book, the characters had disappeared after an interval of three hours. On this occasion, as nearly as I could calculate, the writing had vanished in one hour only.

Reverting to the conversation which I had held with Mrs Van Brandt when we met at Saint Anthony's Well, and to the discoveries which followed at a later period of my life, I can only repeat that she had again been the subject of a trance or dream, when the apparition of her showed itself to me for the second time. As before, she had freely trusted me and freely appealed to me to help her, in the dreaming state, when her spirit was free to recognise my spirit. When she had come to herself, after an interval of an hour, she had again felt ashamed of the familiar manner in which she had communicated with me in the trance; had again unconsciously counteracted by her waking-will the influence of her sleeping-will; and had thus caused the writing once more to disappear, in an hour from the moment when the pen had traced (or seemed to trace) it.

This is still the one explanation that I can offer. At the time when the incident happened, I was far from being fully admitted to the confidence of Mrs Van Brandt; and I was necessarily incapable of arriving at any solution of the mystery right or wrong. I could only put away the letter, doubting vaguely whether my own senses had not deceived me. After the distressing thoughts which Miss Dunross's letter had roused in my mind, I was in no humour to employ my ingenuity in finding a clue to the mystery of the vanished writing. My nerves were irritated; I felt a sense of angry discontent with myself and with others. 'Go where I may' (I thought impatiently), 'the disturbing influence of women seems to be the only influence that I am fated to feel.' As I still paced backwards and forwards in my room, – it was useless to think now of fixing my attention on a book – I fancied I understood the motives which made men as young as I was retire to end their lives in a monastery. I drew aside the window curtains, and looked out. The only prospect that met my view was the black gulf of darkness in which the lake lay hidden. I could see nothing; I could do nothing; I could think of nothing. The one alternative before me was the alternative of trying to sleep. My medical knowledge told me plainly that natural sleep was, in my nervous condition, one of the unattainable luxuries of life, for that night. The medicine-chest which Mr Dunross had placed at my disposal remained in the room. I mixed for myself a strong sleeping draught, and sullenly took refuge from my troubles in bed.

It is a peculiarity of most of the soporific drugs that they not only act in a totally different manner on different constitutions, but that they are not even to be depended on to act always in the same manner on the same person. I had taken care to extinguish the candles before I got into my bed. Under ordinary circumstances, after I had laid quietly in the darkness for half-an-hour, the draught that I had taken would have sent me to sleep. In the present state of my nerves the draught stupefied me, and did no more.

Hour after hour, I lay perfectly still, with my eyes closed, in the semi-sleeping, semi-wakeful state which is so curiously characteristic of the ordinary repose of a dog. As the night wore on, such a sense of heaviness oppressed my eyelids that it was literally impossible for me to open them – such a masterful languor possessed all my muscles that I could no more move on my pillow than if I had been a corpse. And yet, in this somnolent condition, my mind was able to pursue lazy trains of pleasant thought. My sense of hearing was so acute that it caught the faintest sounds made by the passage of the night breeze through the rushes of the lake. Inside my bedchamber, I was even more keenly sensible of those weird night-noises in the heavy furniture of a room, of those sudden settlements of extinct coals in the grate, so familiar to bad sleepers, so startling to overwrought nerves! It is not a scientifically correct statement, but it exactly describes my condition, that night, to say that one-half of me was asleep and the other half awake.

How many hours of the night had passed, when my irritable sense of hearing became aware of a new sound in the room, I cannot tell. I can only relate that I found myself of a sudden listening intently, with fast-closed eyes. The sound that disturbed me was the faintest sound imaginable, as of something soft and light travelling slowly over the surface of the carpet, and brushing it just loud enough to be heard.

Little by little, the sound came nearer and nearer to my bed – and then suddenly stopped just as I fancied it was close by me.

I still lay immovable, with closed eyes; drowsily waiting for the next sound that might reach my ears; drowsily content with the silence, if the silence continued. My thoughts (if thoughts they could be called) were drifting back again into their former course, when I became suddenly conscious of soft breathing just above me. The next moment, I felt a touch on my forehead – light, soft, tremulous, like the touch of lips that had kissed me. There was a momentary pause. Then, a low sigh trembled through the silence. Then, I heard again the still small sound of something brushing its way over the carpet; travelling this time *from* my bed, and moving so rapidly that in a moment more it was lost in the silence of the night.

Still stupefied by the drug that I had taken, I could lazily wonder what had happened, and I could do no more. Had living lips really touched me? Was the sound that I had heard really the sound of a sigh? Or was it all delusion, beginning and ending in a dream? The time passed without my deciding, or caring to decide, those questions. Minute by minute, the composing influence of the draught began at last to strengthen its hold on my brain. A cloud seemed to pass softly over my last waking impressions. One after another, the ties broke gently that held me to conscious life. I drifted peacefully into perfect sleep.

Shortly after sunrise I awoke. When I regained the use of my memory, my first clear recollection was the recollection of the soft breathing which I had felt above me – then of the touch on my forehead, and of the sigh which I had heard after it. Was it possible that someone had entered my room in the night? It was quite possible. I had not locked the door – I had never been in the habit of locking the door during my residence under Mr Dunross's roof.

After thinking it over a little, I rose to examine my room.

Nothing in the shape of a discovery rewarded me, until I reached the door. Though I had not locked it overnight, I had certainly satisfied myself that it was closed before I went to bed. It was now ajar. Had it opened again, through being imperfectly shut? or had a person, after entering and leaving my room, forgotten to close it?

Accidentally looking downwards while I was weighing these probabilities, I noticed a small black object on the carpet, lying just under the key, on the inner side of the door. I picked the thing up, and found that it was a torn morsel of black lace.

The instant I saw the fragment, I was reminded of the long black veil, hanging below her waist, which it was the habit of Miss Dunross to wear. Was it *her* dress then that I had heard softly travelling over the carpet; *her* kiss that had touched my forehead; *her* sigh that had trembled through the silence? Had the ill-fated and noble creature taken her last leave of me in the dead of night; trusting the preservation of her secret to the deceitful appearances which persuaded her that I was asleep? I looked again at the fragment of black lace. Her long veil might easily have been caught, and torn, by the projecting key, as she passed rapidly through the door on her way out of my room. Sadly and reverently I laid the morsel of lace among the treasured memorials which I had brought with me from home. To the end of her life, I vowed it, she should be left undisturbed in the belief that her secret was safe in her own breast! Ardently as I still longed to take her hand at parting, I now resolved to make no further effort to see her. I might not be master of my own emotions; something in my face or in my manner might betray me to her quick and delicate perception. Knowing what I now knew, the last sacrifice I could make to her, would be to obey her wishes. I made the sacrifice.

In an hour more Peter informed me that the ponies were at the door, and that the Master was waiting for me in the outer hall.

I noticed that Mr Dunross gave me his hand, without looking at me. His faded blue eyes, during the few minutes while we were together, were not once raised from the ground.

'God speed you on your journey, sir, and guide you safely home,' he said. 'I beg you to forgive me if I fail to accompany you on the first few miles of your journey. There are reasons which oblige me to remain with my daughter in the house.'

He was scrupulously, almost painfully, courteous – but there was something in his manner which, for the first time in my experience which, for the first time in my experience, seemed designedly to keep me at a distance from him. Knowing the intimate sympathy, the perfect confidence, which existed between the father and daughter, a doubt crossed my mind, whether the secret of the past night was entirely a secret to Mr Dunross. His next words set that doubt at rest, and showed me the truth.

In thanking him for his good wishes, I attempted also to express to him (and through him to Miss Dunross) my sincere sense of gratitude for the kindness which I had received under his roof. He stopped me, politely and resolutely; speaking with that quaintly precise choice of language which I had remarked as characteristic of him at our first interview.

'It is in your power, sir,' he said, 'to return any obligation which you may think you have incurred on leaving my house. If you will be pleased to consider your residence here as an unimportant episode in your life, which ends – *absolutely* ends – with your departure, you will more than repay any kindness that you may have received as my guest. In saying this, I speak under a sense of duty which does entire justice to *you*, as a gentleman and a man of honour. I am sure I may trust to your discretion, not to misjudge my motives, if I abstain from explaining myself any farther.'

A faint colour flushed his pale cheeks. He waited, with a certain proud resignation, for my reply. I respected her secret, respected it more resolutely than ever, before her father.

'After all that I owe to you, sir,' I answered, 'your wishes are my commands.' Saying that, and saying no more, I bowed to him with marked respect, and left the house.

Mounting my pony at the door, I looked up at the centre window, as she had bidden me. It was open; but dark curtains, jealously closed, kept out the light from the room within. At the sound of the pony's hoofs on the rough island road, as the animal moved, the curtains were parted for a few inches only. Through the gap in the dark draperies, a wan white hand appeared; waved tremulously a last farewell; and vanished from my view. The curtains closed again on her dark and solitary life. The dreary wind sounded its long low dirge over the rippling waters of the lake. The ponies took their places in the ferry-boat which was kept for the passage of animals to and from the island. With slow regular strokes the men rowed us to the mainland, and took their leave. I looked back at the distant house. I thought of her in the dark room, waiting patiently for death. Burning tears blinded me. The guide took my bridle in his hand.

'You're not well, sir,' he said; 'I will lead the pony.'

When I looked again at the landscape round me, we had descended in the interval from the higher ground to the lower. The house and the lake had disappeared, to be seen no more.

CHAPTER XX

IN THE SHADOW OF SAINT PAUL'S

In ten days I was at home again – and my mother's arms were round me.

I had left her for my sea voyage very unwillingly – seeing that she was in delicate health. On my return, I was grieved to observe a change for the worse, for which her letters had not prepared me. Consulting our medical friend Mr MacGlue, I found that he too had noticed my mother's failing health, but that he attributed it to an easily removable cause – to the climate of Scotland. My mother's childhood and early life had been passed on the southern shores of England. The change to the raw keen air of the north had been a trying change to a person at her age. In Mr MacGlue's opinion, the wise course to take would be to return to the south before the autumn was farther advanced, and to make our arrangements for passing the coming winter at Penzance or Torquay.

Resolved as I was to keep the mysterious appointment which summoned me to London at the month's end, Mr MacGlue's suggestion met with no opposition on my part. It had, to my mind, the great merit of obviating the necessity of a second separation from my mother – assuming that she approved of the doctor's advice. I put the question to her the same day. To my infinite relief she was not only ready, but eager, to take the journey to the south. The season had been unusually wet, even for Scotland; and my mother reluctantly confessed that she 'did feel a certain longing' for the mild air and genial sunshine of the Devonshire coast.

We arranged to travel in our own comfortable carriage by post – resting of course at inns on the road at night. In the days before railways it was no easy matter for an invalid to travel from Perthshire to London – even with a light carriage and four horses. Calculating our rate of progress from the date of our departure, I found that we had just time, and no more, to reach London on the last day of the month.

I shall say nothing of the secret anxieties which weighed on my mind, under these circumstances. Happily for me, on every account, my mother's strength held out. The easy, and (as we then thought) the rapid rate of travelling, had its invigorating effect on her nerves. She slept better when we rested for the night than she had slept at home. After twice being delayed on the road, we arrived in London at three o'clock on the afternoon of the last day of the month. Had I reached my destination in time?

As I interpreted the writing of the apparition, I had still some hours at my disposal. The phrase, 'at the month's end,' meant, as I understood it, at the last hour of the last day in the month. If I took up my position 'under the shadow of St Paul's (say), at ten that night, I should arrive at the place of meeting with two hours to spare, before the last stroke of the clock marked the beginning of the new month.

At half-past nine, I left my mother to rest after her long journey, and privately quitted the house. Before ten, I was at my post. The night was fine and clear; and the huge shadow of the cathedral marked distinctly the limits within which I had been bidden to wait, on the watch for events.

The great clock of St Paul's struck ten – and nothing happened.

The next hour passed very slowly. I walked up and down; at one time absorbed in my own thoughts; at another, engaged in watching the gradual diminution in the number of foot passengers who passed me as the night advanced. The City (as it is called) is the most populous part of London in the daytime. But, at night, when it ceases to be the centre of commerce, its busy population melts away, and the empty streets assume the appearance of a remote and deserted quarter of the metropolis. As the half-hour after ten struck – then the quarter to eleven – then the hour – the pavement steadily became more and more deserted. I could count the foot passengers now by twos and threes; and I could see the places of public refreshment within my view beginning already to close for the night.

I looked at the clock: it pointed to ten minutes past eleven. At that hour, could I hope to meet Mrs Van Brandt alone, in the public street?

The more I thought of it, the less likely such an event seemed to be. The more reasonable probability was that I might meet her once more, accompanied by some friend – perhaps under the escort of Van Brandt himself. I wondered whether I should preserve my self-control, in the presence of that man, for the second time.

While my thoughts were still pursuing this direction, my attention was recalled to passing events by a sad little voice, putting a strange little question close at my side.

'If you please, sir, do you know where I can find a chemist's shop open at this time of night?'

I looked round, and discovered a poorly clad little boy, with a basket over his arm, and a morsel of paper in his hand.

'The chemists' shops are all shut,' I said. 'If you want any medicine, you must ring the night-bell.'

'I dursn't do it, sir,' replied the small stranger. 'I am such a little boy, I'm afraid of their beating me if I ring them up out of their beds, without somebody to speak for me.'

The little creature looked at me under the street lamp with such a forlorn experience of being beaten for trifling offences in his face, that it was impossible to resist the impulse to help him.

'Is it a serious case of illness?' I said.

'I don't know, sir.'

'Have you got a doctor's prescription?'

He held out his morsel of paper.

'I have got this,' he said.

I took the paper from him, and looked at it.

It was an ordinary prescription for a tonic mixture. I looked first at the doctor's signature: it was the name of a perfectly obscure person in the profession. Below it was written the name of the patient for whom the medicine had been prescribed. I started as I read it. The name was 'Mrs Brand.'

The idea instantly struck me that this (so far as sound went, at any rate) was the English equivalent of Brandt.

'Do you know the lady who sent you for the medicine?' I asked.

'Oh, yes, sir! She lodges with mother – and she owes for rent. I have done everything she told me except getting the physic. I've pawned her ring, and I've bought the bread and butter and eggs, and I've taken care of the change. Mother looks to the change for her rent. It isn't my fault, sir, that I've lost myself. I am but ten years old – and all the chemists' shops are shut up!'

Here my little friend's sense of his unmerited misfortunes overpowered him, and he began to cry.

'Don't cry, my man!' I said: 'I'll help you. Tell me something more about the lady first. Is she alone?'

'She's got her little girl with her, sir.'

My heart quickened its beat. The boy's answer reminded me of that other little girl whom my mother had once seen.

'Is the lady's husband with her?' I asked next.

'No, sir – not now. He was with her; but he went away – and he hasn't come back yet.'

I put a last conclusive question.

'Is her husband an Englishman?' I enquired.

'Mother says he is a foreigner,' the boy answered.

I turned away to hide my agitation. Even the child might have noticed it.

Passing under the name of 'Mrs Brand' – poor, so poor that she was obliged to pawn her ring – left by a man who was a foreigner, alone with her little girl – was I on the trace of her at that moment? Was this lost child destined to be the innocent means of leading me back to the woman I loved, in her direst need of sympathy and help? The more I thought of it, the more strongly the idea of returning with the boy to the house in which his mother's lodger lived, fastened itself on my mind. The clock struck the quarter past eleven. If my anticipations ended in misleading me I had still three-quarters of an hour to spare, before the month reached its end.

'Where do you live?' I asked.

The boy mentioned a street, the name of which I then heard for the first time. All he could say, when I asked for further particulars, was that he lived close by the river – in which direction he was too confused and too frightened to be able to tell me.

While we were still trying to understand each other, a cab passed slowly at some little distance. I hailed the man, and mentioned the name of the street to him. He knew it perfectly well. The street was rather more than a mile away from us, in an easterly direction. He undertook to drive me there, and to bring me back to St Paul's (if necessary) in less than twenty minutes. I opened the door of the cab, and told my little friend to get in. The boy hesitated.

'Are we going to the chemist's, if you please, sir?' he asked.

'No. You are going home first, with me.'

The boy began to cry again.

'Mother will beat me, sir, if I go back without the medicine.'

'I will take care that your mother doesn't beat you. I am a doctor myself; and I want to see the lady before we get the medicine for her.'

The announcement of my profession appeared to inspire the boy with a certain confidence. But he still showed no disposition to accompany me to his mother's house.

'Do you mean to charge the lady anything?' he asked. 'The money I've got on the ring isn't much. Mother won't like having it taken out of her rent.'

'I won't charge the lady a farthing,' I answered.

The boy instantly got into the cab. 'All right,' he said, 'as long as mother gets her money.'

Alas for the poor! The child's education in the sordid anxieties of life was completed already at ten years old!

We drove away.

CHAPTER XXI

I KEEP MY APPOINTMENT

The poverty-stricken aspect of the street, when we entered it; the dirty and dilapidated condition of the house, when we drew up at the door, would have warned most men, in my position, to prepare themselves for a distressing discovery when they were admitted to the interior of the dwelling. The first impression which the place produced on *my* mind suggested on the contrary that the boy's answers to my questions had led me astray. It was simply impossible to associate Mrs Van Brandt (as I remembered her) with the spectacle of such squalid poverty as I now beheld. I rang the door-bell, feeling persuaded beforehand that my enquiries would lead to no useful result.

As I lifted my hand to the bell, my little companion's dread of a beating revived in full force. He hid himself behind me; and when I asked what he was about, he answered confidentially, 'Please stand between us, sir, when mother opens the door!'

A tall and truculent woman answered the bell. No introduction was necessary. Holding a cane in her hand, she stood self-proclaimed as my small friend's mother.

'I thought it was that vagabond of a boy of mine,' she explained, as an apology for the exhibition of the cane. 'He has been gone on an errand more than two hours. What did you please to want, sir?'

I interceded for the unfortunate boy, before I entered on my own business.

'I must beg you to forgive your son, this time,' I said. 'I found him lost in the streets; and I have brought him home.'

The woman's astonishment when she heard what I had done, and discovered her son behind me, literally struck her dumb. The language of the eye, superseding on this occasion the language of the tongue, plainly revealed the impression that I had produced on her: – 'You bring my lost brat home in a cab? Mr Stranger, you are mad.'

'I hear that you have a lady named Brand lodging in the house,' I went on. 'I dare say I am mistaken in supposing her to be a lady of the same name whom I know. But I should like to make sure whether I am right or wrong. Is it too late to disturb your lodger to-night?'

The woman recovered the use of her tongue.

'My lodger is up and waiting for that little fool, who doesn't know his way about London yet!' She emphasised those words by shaking her brawny fist at her son – who instantly returned to his place of refuge behind the tail of my coat. 'Have you got the money?' enquired this terrible person, shouting at her hidden offspring over my shoulder. 'Or have you lost *that* as well as your own stupid little self?'

The boy showed himself again, and put the money into his mother's knotty hand. She counted it, with eyes which satisfied themselves fiercely that each coin was of genuine silver – and then became partially pacified.

'Go along upstairs,' she growled, addressing her son; 'and don't keep the lady waiting any longer. They're half-starved, she and her child,' the woman proceeded, turning to me. 'The food my boy has got for them in his basket will be the first food the mother has tasted to-day. She's pawned everything by this time; and what she's to do unless you help her is more than I can say. The doctor does what he can – but he told me today, if she wasn't better nourished it was no use sending for *him*. Follow the boy; and see for yourself if it's the lady you know.'

I listened to the woman, still feeling persuaded that I had acted under a delusion in going to her house. How was it possible to associate the charming object of my heart's worship with the miserable story of destitution which I had just heard? I stopped the boy on the first landing, and told him to announce me simply as a doctor, who had been informed of Mrs Brand's illness and who had called to see her.

We ascended a second flight of stairs, and a third. Arrived now at the top of the house, the boy knocked at the door that was nearest to us on the landing. No audible voice replied. He opened the door without ceremony, and went in. I waited outside to hear what was said. The door was left ajar. If the voice of 'Mrs Brand' was (as I believed it would prove it to be) the voice of a stranger, I resolved to offer her delicately such help as lay within my power, and to return forthwith to my post under 'the shadow of St Paul's.'

The first voice that spoke to the boy was the voice of a child.

'I'm so hungry, Jemmy – I'm so hungry!'

'All right, missy – I've got you something to eat.'

'Be quick, Jemmy! Be quick!'

There was a momentary pause – and then I heard the boy's voice once more.

'There's a slice of bread-and-butter, Missy. You must wait for your egg till I can boil it. Don't you eat too fast, or you'll choke yourself. What's the matter with your mamma? Are you asleep, ma'am?'

I could barely hear the answering voice – it was so faint; and it uttered but one word: 'No!'

The boy spoke again.

'Cheer up, Missus. There's a doctor waiting outside to see you.'

This time there was no audible reply. The boy showed himself to me at the door. 'Please to come in, sir. I can't make anything of her.'

It would have been misplaced delicacy to have hesitated any longer to enter the room. I went in.

There, at the opposite end of a miserably furnished bedchamber, lying back feebly in a tattered old arm-chair, was one more among the thousands of forlorn creatures, starving that night in the great city. A white handkerchief was laid over her face as if to screen it from the flame of the fire hard by. She lifted the handkerchief, startled by the sound of my footsteps as I entered the room. I looked at her, and saw in the white, wan, deathlike face – the face of the woman I loved!

For a moment, the horror of the discovery turned me faint and giddy. In another instant I was kneeling by her chair. My arm was round her – her head lay on my shoulder. She was past speaking, past crying out: she trembled silently, and that was all. I said nothing. No words passed my lips, no tears came to my relief. I held her to me; and she let me hold her. The child devouring its bread and butter at a little round table, stared at us. The boy, on his knees before the grate, stared at us. And the slow minutes lagged on – and the buzzing of a fly in a corner was the only sound in the room.

The instincts of the profession to which I had been trained, rather than any active sense of the horror of the situation in which I was placed, roused me at last. She was starving! I saw it in the deadly colour of her skin; I felt it in the faint quick flutter of her pulse. I called the boy to me; and sent him to the nearest public-house for wine and biscuits. 'Be quick about it,' I said, 'and you shall have more money for yourself than ever you had in your life!' The boy looked at me – spat on the coins in his hand – said, 'That's for luck!' – and ran out of the room as never boy ran yet.

I turned to speak my first words of comfort to the mother. The cry of the child stopped me.

'I'm so hungry! I'm so hungry!'

I set more food before the famished child, and kissed her. She looked up at me with wondering eyes.

'Are you a new papa?' the little creature asked. 'My other papa never kisses me.'

I looked at the mother. Her eyes were closed; the tears flowed slowly

over her worn white cheeks. I took her frail hand in mine. 'Happier days
are coming,' I said; 'you are *my* care now.' There was no answer. She still
trembled silently – and that was all.

In less than five minutes the boy returned, and earned his promised
reward. He sat on the floor by the fire counting his treasure, the one
happy creature in the room. I soaked some crumbled morsels of biscuit in
the wine – and, little by little, I revived her failing strength by
nourishment administered at intervals in that cautious form. After awhile
she raised her head, and looked at me, with wondering eyes that were
pitiably like the eyes of her child. A faint delicate flush began to show
itself in her face. She spoke to me, for the first time, in whispering tones
that I could just hear as I sat close at her side.

'How did you find me? Who showed you the way to this place?'

She paused; painfully recalling the memory of something that was slow
to come back. Her colour deepened; she found the lost remembrance,
and looked at me with a timid curiosity. 'What brought you here?' she
asked. 'Was it my dream?'

'Wait, dearest, till you are stronger; and I will tell you all.'

I lifted her gently, and laid her on the wretched bed. The child
followed us, and, climbing to the bedstead with my help, nestled at her
mother's side. I sent the boy away to tell the mistress of the house that I
should remain with my patient, watching her progress towards recovery,
through the night. He went out, jingling his money joyfully in his
pocket. We three were left together.

As the long hours followed each other, she fell at intervals into a
broken sleep; waking with a start, and looking at me wildly as if I had
been a stranger at her bedside. Towards morning, the nourishment which
I still carefully administered wrought its healthful change in her pulse,
and composed her to quieter slumbers. When the sun rose she was
sleeping as peacefully as the child at her side. I was able to leave her, until
my return later in the day, under the care of the woman of the house.
The magic of money transformed this termagant and terrible person into
a docile and attentive nurse – so eager to follow my instructions exactly
that she begged me to commit them to writing before I went away. For a
moment, I still lingered alone at the bedside of the sleeping woman; and
satisfied myself for the hundredth time that her life was safe, before I left
her. It was the sweetest of all rewards to feel sure of this – to touch her
cool forehead lightly with my lips – to look, and look again, at the poor
worn face, always dear, always beautiful, to *my* eyes, change as it might. I
closed the door softly, and went out in the bright morning, a happy man
again. So close together rise the springs of joy and sorrow in human life!
So near in our heart, as in our heaven, is the brightest sunshine to the
blackest cloud!

CHAPTER XXII

CONVERSATION WITH MY MOTHER

I reached my own house in time to snatch two or three hours of repose, before I paid my customary morning visit to my mother in her own room. I observed in her reception of me, on this occasion, certain peculiarities of look and manner which were far from being familiar in my experience of her.

When our eyes first met, she regarded me with a wistful questioning look, as if she was troubled by some doubt which she shrank from expressing in words. And, when I enquired after her health as usual, she surprised me by answering as impatiently as if she resented my having mentioned the subject. For a moment, I was inclined to think these changes signified that she had discovered my absence from home during the night, and that she had some suspicion of the true cause of it. But she never alluded, even in the most distant manner, to Mrs Van Brandt; and not a word dropped from her lips which implied, directly or indirectly, that I had pained or disappointed her. I could only conclude that she had something important to say, in relation to herself or to me – and that for reasons of her own she abstained from giving expression to it for the present.

Reverting to our ordinary topics of conversation, we touched on the subject (always interesting to my mother) of my visit to Shetland. Speaking of this, we naturally spoke also of Miss Dunross. Here again, when I least expected it, there was another surprise in store for me.

'You were talking, the other day,' said my mother, 'of the green flag which poor Dermody's daughter worked for you, when you were both children. Have you really kept it all this time?'

'Yes.'

'Where have you left it? In Scotland?'

'I have brought it with me to London.'

'Why?'

I mentioned the promise which I had given to Miss Dunross.

My mother smiled.

'Is it possible, George, that you think about this as the young lady in Shetland thinks? After all the years that have passed, do you believe in the green flag being the means of bringing Mary Dermody and yourself together again?'

'Certainly not! I am only humouring one of the fancies of poor Miss Dunross. Could I refuse to grant her trifling request, after all I owed to her kindness?'

The smile left my mother's face. She looked at me attentively.

'Miss Dunross seems to have produced a very favourable impression on you,' she said.

'I own it. I feel deeply interested in her.'

'If she had not been an incurable invalid, George, I too might have become interested in Miss Dunross – perhaps in the character of my daughter-in-law?'

'It is useless, mother, to speculate on what *might* have happened. The sad reality is enough.'

My mother paused a little, before she put her next question to me.

'Did Miss Dunross always keep her veil drawn, in your presence, when there happened to be a light in the room?'

'Always.'

'She never even let you catch a momentary glance at her face?'

'Never.'

'And the only reason she gave you was that the light caused her a painful sensation if it fell on her uncovered skin?'

'You say that, mother, as if you doubt whether Miss Dunross told me the truth.'

'No, George. I only doubt whether she told you *all* the truth.'

'What do you mean?'

'Don't be offended, my dear. I believe Miss Dunross has some more serious reason for keeping her face hidden than the reason that she gave *you*.'

I was silent. The suspicion which those words implied had never occurred to my mind. I had read in medical books of cases of morbid nervous sensitiveness exactly similar to the case of Miss Dunross, as described by herself – and that had been enough for me. Now that my mother's idea had found its way from her mind to mine, the impression produced on me was painful in the last degree. Horrible imaginings of deformity possessed my brain, and profaned all that was purest and dearest in my recollections of Miss Dunross. It was useless to change the subject – the evil influence that was on me was too potent to be charmed away by talk. Making the best excuse that I could think of for leaving my mother's room, I hurried away to seek a refuge from myself, where alone I could hope to find it, in the presence of Mrs Van Brandt.

CHAPTER XXIII

CONVERSATION WITH MRS VAN BRANDT

The landlady was taking the air at her own door, when I reached the house. Her reply to my enquiries justified my most hopeful anticipations. The poor lodger looked already 'like another woman;' and the child was at that moment posted on the stairs, watching for the return of her 'new papa.'

'There's one thing I should wish to say to you, sir, before you go up stairs,' the woman went on. 'Don't trust the lady with more money, at a time, than the money that is wanted for the day's housekeeping. If she has any to spare, it's as likely as not to be wasted on her good-for-nothing husband.'

Absorbed in the higher and dearer interests that filled my mind, I had thus far forgotten the very existence of Mr Van Brandt.

'Where is he?' I asked.

'Where he ought to be,' was the answer. 'In prison for debt.'

In those days, a man imprisoned for debt was not infrequently a man imprisoned for life. There was little fear of my visit being shortened by the appearance on the scene of Mr Van Brandt.

Ascending the stairs, I found the child waiting for me on the upper landing, with a ragged doll in her arms. I had bought a cake for her on my way to the house. She forthwith turned over the doll to my care, and, trotting before me into the room with her cake in her arms, announced my arrival in these words:

'Mamma, I like this papa better than the other. You like him better too.'

The mother's wasted face reddened for a moment, then turned pale again, as she held out her hand to me. I looked at her anxiously, and discerned the welcome signs of recovery, clearly revealed. Her grand grey eyes rested on me again with a glimmer of their old light. The hand that had lain so cold in mine on the past night had life and warmth in it now.

'Should I have died before the morning, if you had not come here?' she asked softly. 'Have you saved my life for the second time? I can well believe it!'

Before I was aware of her, she bent her head over my hand, and touched it tenderly with her lips. 'I am not an ungrateful woman,' she murmured – 'and yet, I don't know how to thank you.'

The child looked up quickly from her cake. 'Why don't you kiss him?' the quaint little creature asked, with a broad stare of astonishment.

Her head sank on her breast. She sighed bitterly.

'No more of Me!' she said, suddenly recovering her composure, and suddenly forcing herself to look at me again. 'Tell me what happy chance brought you here last night?'

'The same chance,' I answered, 'which took me to Saint Anthony's Well.'

She raised herself eagerly in the chair.

'You have seen me again – as you saw me in the summer-house by the waterfall!' she exclaimed. 'Was it in Scotland once more?'

'No. Farther away than Scotland – as far away as Shetland.'

'Tell me about it! Pray, pray tell me about it!'

I related what had happened as exactly as I could – consistently with maintaining the strictest reserve on one point. Discreetly concealing the existence of Miss Dunross, I left her to suppose that the master of the house was the one person whom I had found to receive me, during my sojourn under Mr Dunross's roof.

'That is strange!' she exclaimed, after she had heard me attentively to the end.

'What is strange?' I asked.

She hesitated, searching my face earnestly with her large grave eyes.

'I hardly like speaking of it,' she said. 'And yet I ought to have no concealments, in such a matter, from you. I understand everything that you have told me – with one exception. It seems strange to me that you should only have had one old man for your companion while you were at the house in Shetland.'

'What other companion did you expect to hear of?' I enquired.

'I expected,' she answered, 'to hear of a lady in the house.'

I cannot positively say that the reply took me by surprise: it forced me to reflect before I spoke again. I knew, by my past experience, that she must have seen me, in my absence from her, while I was spiritually present to her mind in a trance or dream. Had she also seen the daily companion of my life in Shetland – Miss Dunross?

I put the question in a form which left me free to decide whether I should take her unreservedly into my confidence or not.

'Am I right,' I began, 'in supposing that you dreamed of me in Shetland, as you once before dreamed of me when I happened to be in Scotland?'

'Yes,' she answered. 'It was at the close of evening, this time. I fell asleep, or became insensible – I cannot say which. And I saw you again, in a vision or a dream.'

'Where did you see me?'

'I first saw you on the bridge over the Scotch river – just as we both met on the evening when you saved my life. After awhile, the stream and the landscape about it, faded, and you faded with them, into darkness. I waited a little – and the darkness melted away slowly. I stood, as it seemed to me, in a circle of starry light; fronting a window, with a lake behind me, and before me a darkened room. And I looked into the room, and the starry light showed you to me again.'

'When did this happen? Do you remember the date?'

'I remember that it was at the beginning of the month. The misfortunes which have since brought me so low, had not then fallen on me – and yet, as I stood looking at you, I had the strangest prevision of calamity that was to come. I felt the same absolute reliance on your power to help me that I felt when I first dreamed of you in Scotland.

And I did the same familiar things. I laid my hand on your bosom. I said to you, "Remember me. Come to me." I even wrote——'

She stopped, shuddering, as if a sudden fear had laid its hold on her. Seeing this, and dreading the effect of any violent agitation, I hastened to suggest that we should say no more, for that day, on the subject of her dream.

'No,' she answered firmly. 'There is nothing to be gained by giving me time. My dream has left one horrible remembrance on my mind. As long as I live, I believe I shall tremble when I think of what I saw near you, in that darkened room.'

She stopped again. Was she approaching the subject of the shrouded figure, with the black veil over its head? Was she about to describe her first discovery, in the dream, of Miss Dunross?

'Tell me one thing first,' she resumed. 'Have I been right in what I have said to you, so far? Is it true that you were in a darkened room, when you saw me?'

'Quite true.'

'Was the date the beginning of the month? and was the hour the close of evening?'

'Yes.'

'Were you alone in the room? Answer me truly!'

'I was not alone.'

'Was the master of the house with you? or had you some other companion?'

It would have been worse than useless (after what I had now heard) to attempt to deceive her.

'I had another companion,' I answered. 'The person in the room with me was a woman.'

Her face showed, as I spoke, that she was again shaken by the terrifying recollection to which she had just alluded. I had, by this time, some difficulty myself in preserving my composure. Still, I was determined not to let a word escape me which could operate as a suggestion on the mind of my companion.

'Have you any other question to ask me?' was all I said.

'One more,' she answered. 'Was there anything unusual in the dress of your companion?'

'Yes. She wore a long black veil, which hung over her head and face, and dropped to below her waist.'

Mrs Van Brandt leaned back in her chair, composing herself before she spoke again.

'I understand your motive for concealing from me the presence of that miserable woman in the house,' she said. 'It is good and kind like all your motives; but it is useless. While I lay in the trance I saw everything exactly as it was in the reality; and I, too, saw that frightful face!'

Those words literally electrified me.

My conversation of that morning with my mother instantly recurred to my memory. I started to my feet.

'Good God!' I exclaimed, 'what do you mean?'

'Don't you understand yet?' she asked, in amazement on her side. 'Must I speak more plainly still? When you saw the apparition of me, did you see me write?'

'Yes. On a letter that the lady was writing for me. I saw the words afterwards; the words that brought me to you last night: – At the month's end. In the shadow of Saint Paul's.'

'How did I appear to write on the unfinished letter?'

'You lifted the writing-case, on which the letter and the pen lay, off the lady's lap; and, while you wrote, you rested the case on her shoulder.'

'Did you notice if the lifting of the case produced any effect on her?'

'I saw no effect produced. She remained immovable in her chair.'

'I saw it differently in my dream. She raised her hand – not the hand that was nearest to you, but nearest to me. As *I* lifted the writing-case, *she* lifted her hand, and parted the folds of the veil from off her face – I suppose to see more clearly. It was only for a moment; and, in that moment, I saw what the veil hid. Don't let us speak of it! You must have shuddered at that frightful sight in the reality, as I shuddered at it in the dream. You must have asked yourself, as I did: Is there nobody to poison the terrible creature, and hide her mercifully in the grave?'

At those words, she abruptly checked herself. I could say nothing – my face spoke for me. She saw it, and guessed the truth.

'Good heavens!' she cried. 'You have *not* seen her! She must have kept her face hidden from you behind the veil! Oh, why, why did you cheat me into talking of it? I will never speak of it again. See, we are frightening the child! Come here, darling; there is nothing to be afraid of. Come, and bring your cake with you. You shall be a great lady, giving a grand dinner; and we will be two friends whom you have invited to dine with you; and the doll shall be the little girl who comes in after dinner, and has fruit at dessert!' So she ran on, trying vainly to forget the shock that she had inflicted on me, in talking nursery nonsense to the child.

Recovering my composure in some degree, I did my best to second the effort that she had made. My quieter thoughts suggested that she might well be self-deceived in believing the horrible spectacle presented to her in the vision to be actual reflection of the truth. In common justice towards Miss Dunross, I ought surely not to accept the conviction of her deformity on no better evidence than the evidence of a dream? Reasonable as it undoubtedly was, this view left certain doubts still lingering in my mind. The child's instinct soon discovered that her mother and I were playfellows who felt no genuine enjoyment of the game. She dismissed her make-believe guests without ceremony, and went back with her doll to the favourite play-ground on which I had met her – the landing outside the door. No persuasion on her mother's part or on mine, succeeded in luring her back to us. We were left together, to face each other as best we might – with the forbidden subject of Miss Dunross between us.

CHAPTER XXIV

LOVE AND MONEY

Feeling the embarrassment of the moment most painfully on her side, Mrs Van Brandt spoke first.

'You have said nothing to me about yourself,' she began. 'Is your life a happier one than it was when we last met?'

'I cannot honestly say that it is,' I answered.

'Is there any prospect of your being married?'

'My prospect of being married still rests with you.'

'Don't say that!' she exclaimed, with an entreating look at me. 'Don't spoil my pleasure in seeing you again, by speaking of what can never be! Have you still to be told how it is that you find me here alone with my child?'

I forced myself to mention Van Brandt's name, rather than hear it pass *her* lips.

'I have been told that Mr Van Brandt is in prison for debt,' I said. 'And I saw for myself last night that he had left you helpless.'

'He left me the little money he had with him when he was arrested,' she rejoined sadly. 'His cruel creditors are more to blame than he is for the poverty that has fallen on us.'

Even this negative defence of Van Brandt stung me to the quick.

'I ought to have spoken more guardedly of him,' I said bitterly. 'I ought to have remembered that a woman can forgive almost any wrong that a man can inflict on her – when he is the man whom she loves.'

She put her hand on my mouth, and stopped me before I could say any more.

'How can you speak so cruelly to me?' she asked. 'You know – to my shame I confessed it to you the last time we met – you know that my heart, in secret, is all yours. What "wrong" are you talking of? Is it the wrong I suffered when Van Brandt married me, with a wife living at the time (and living still)? Do you think I can ever forget the great misfortune of my life – the misfortune that has made me unworthy of you? It is no fault of mine – God knows – but it is not the less true that I am not married, and that the little darling who is playing out there with her doll is my child. And you talk of my being your wife – knowing that!'

'The child accepts me as her second father,' I said. 'It would be better and happier for us both, if you had as little pride as the child.'

'Pride?' she repeated. 'In such a position as mine? A helpless woman, with a mock-husband in prison for debt! Say that I have not fallen quite so low yet as to forget what is due to you – and you will pay me a compliment that will be nearer to the truth. Am I to marry you for my food and shelter? Am I to marry you, because there is no lawful tie that binds me to the father of my child? Cruelly as he has behaved, he has still *that* claim upon me. Bad as he is, he has not forsaken me; he has been forced away. My only friend! is it possible that you think me ungrateful enough to consent to be your wife? The woman (in my situation) must be heartless indeed who could destroy your place in the estimation of the world, and the regard of your friends! The wretchedest creature that walks the streets would shrink from treating you in that way. Oh! what are men made of? How *can* you – how *can* you speak of it!'

I yielded – and spoke of it no more. Every word she uttered only increased my admiration of the noble creature whom I had loved, and lost. What refuge was now left to me? But one refuge; I could still offer to her the sacrifice of myself. Bitterly as I hated the man who had parted us, I loved her dearly enough to be even capable of helping him, for her sake. Hopeless infatuation! I don't deny it; I don't excuse it – hopeless infatuation!

'Forgive me,' I said sadly; 'and let me deserve to be forgiven. It is something to be your only friend. You must have plans for the future – tell me unreservedly how I can help you.'

'Complete the good work that you have begun,' she answered gratefully. 'Help me back to health. Make me strong enough to submit to a doctor's estimate of my chances of living for some years yet.'

'A doctor's estimate of your chances of living?' I repeated. 'What do you mean?'

'I hardly know how to tell you,' she said, 'without speaking again of Mr Van Brandt.'

'Does speaking of him again mean speaking of his debts?' I asked. 'Why need you hesitate? You know that there is nothing I will not do to relieve *your* anxieties.'

She looked at me for a moment, in silent distress.

'Oh! do you think I would let you give your money to Van Brandt?' she asked as soon as she could speak. 'I, who owe everything to your devotion to me? Never! Let me tell you the plain truth. There is a serious necessity for his getting out of prison. He must pay his creditors; and he has found out a way of doing it – with my help.'

'Your help!' I exclaimed.

'Yes! This is his position, in two words. A little while since, he obtained an excellent offer of employment abroad, from a rich relative of his; and he had made all his arrangements to accept it. Unhappily, he returned to tell me of his good fortune; and the same day he was arrested for debt. His relative has offered to keep the situation open for a certain time – and the time has not yet expired. If he can pay a dividend to his creditors they will give him his freedom; and he believes he can raise the money if I consent to insure my life.'

To insure her life! The snare that had been set for her was plainly revealed in those four words.

In the eye of the law, she was of course a single woman: she was of age, she was to all intents and purposes her own mistress. What was there to prevent her from insuring her life, if she pleased, and from so disposing of the insurance as to give Van Brandt a direct interest in her death? Knowing what I knew of him, believing him as I did to be capable of any atrocity, I trembled at the bare idea of what might have happened, if I had failed to find my way back to her until a later date. Thanks to the happy accident of my position, the one certain way of protecting her lay easily within my reach. I could offer to lend the scoundrel the money that he wanted, at an hour's notice – and he was the man to accept my proposal quite as easily as I could make it.

'You don't seem to approve of our idea,' she said, noticing in evident perplexity the effect which she had produced on me. 'I am very unfortunate – I seem to have innocently disturbed and annoyed you for the second time.'

'You are quite mistaken,' I replied. 'I am only doubting whether your plan for relieving Mr Van Brandt of his embarrassments is quite so simple as you suppose. Are you aware of the delays that are likely to take place, before it will be possible to borrow money on your policy of insurance?'

'I know nothing about it,' she said sadly.

'Will you let me ask the advice of my lawyers? They are trustworthy and experienced men – and I am sure they can be of use to you.'

Cautiously as I had expressed myself, her delicacy took the alarm.

'Promise that you won't ask me to borrow money of you for Mr Van Brandt,' she rejoined; 'and I will accept your help gratefully.'

I could honestly promise that. My one chance of saving her lay in keeping from her knowledge the course that I had now determined to pursue. I rose to go, while my resolution still sustained me. The sooner I made my enquiries (I reminded her), the more speedily our present doubts and difficulties would be resolved.

She rose, as I rose – with the tears in her eyes and the blush on her cheeks.

'Kiss me,' she whispered, 'before you go! And don't mind my crying. I am quite happy now. It is only your goodness that overpowers me.'

I pressed her to my heart, with the unacknowledged tenderness of a parting embrace. It was impossible to disguise the position in which I had now placed myself – I had, so to speak, pronounced my own sentence of banishment. When my interference had restored my unworthy rival to his freedom, could I submit to the degrading necessity of seeing her in his presence, of speaking to her under his eyes? *That* sacrifice of myself was beyond me – and I knew it. 'For the last time!' I thought, as I held her to me for a moment longer – 'for the last time!'

The child ran to meet me with open arms, when I stepped out on the landing. My manhood had sustained me through the parting with the mother. It was only when the child's round innocent little face laid itself lovingly against mine that my fortitude gave way. I was past speaking – I put her down gently in silence, and waited on the lower flight of stairs until I was fit to face the world outside.

CHAPTER XXV

OUR DESTINIES PART US

Descending to the ground floor of the house, I sent to request a moment's interview with the landlady. I had yet to learn in which of the London prisons Van Brandt was confined; and she was the only person to whom I could venture to address the question.

Having answered my enquiries, the woman put her own sordid construction on my motive for visiting the prisoner.

'Has the money you left upstairs gone into his greedy pockets already?' she asked. 'If I was as rich as you are, I should let it go. In your place, I wouldn't touch him with a pair of tongs!'

The woman's coarse warning actually proved useful to me – it started a new idea in my mind! Before she spoke, I had been too dull or too pre-occupied to see that it was quite needless to degrade myself by personally communicating with Van Brandt in his prison. It only now occurred to me that my legal advisers were, as a matter of course, the proper persons to represent me in the matter – with this additional advantage, that they could keep my share in the transaction a secret even from Van Brandt himself.

I drove at once to the office of my lawyers. The senior partner – the tried friend and adviser of our family – received me.

My instructions naturally enough astonished him. He was immediately to satisfy the prisoner's creditors, on my behalf, without mentioning my name to anyone. And he was gravely to accept as security for repayment – Mr Van Brandt's note of hand.

'I thought I was well acquainted with the various methods by which a gentleman can throw away his money,' the senior partner remarked. 'I congratulate you, Mr Germaine, on having discovered an entirely new way of effectually emptying your purse. Founding a newspaper, taking a theatre, keeping race-horses, gambling at Monaco – are highly efficient as modes of losing money. But they all yield, sir, to the paying the debts of Mr Van Brandt!'

I left him, and went home.

The servant who opened the door had a message for me from my mother. She wished to see me as soon as I was at leisure to speak to her.

I presented myself at once in my mother's sitting-room.

'Well, George?' she said, without a word to prepare me for what was coming. 'How have you left Mrs Van Brandt?'

I was completely thrown off my guard.

'Who has told you that I have seen Mrs Van Brandt?' I asked.

'My dear! your face has told me. Don't I know by this time, how you look and how you speak when Mrs Van Brandt is in your mind? Sit down by me. I have something to say to you, which I wanted to say this morning – but, I hardly know why, my heart failed me. I am bolder now; and I can say it. My son! you still love Mrs Van Brandt. You have my permission to marry her.'

Those were the words! Hardly an hour had elapsed since Mrs Van Brandt's own lips had told me that our union was impossible. Not even half an hour had passed, since I had given the directions which would restore to liberty the man who was the one obstacle to my marriage. And this was the time that my mother had innocently chosen for consenting to receive as her daughter-in-law, Mrs Van Brandt!

'I see that I surprise you,' she resumed. 'Let me explain my motives as plainly as I can. I should not be speaking the truth, George, if I told you that I had ceased to feel the serious objections that there are to your marrying this lady. The only difference in my way of thinking is, that I am now willing to set my objections aside, out of regard for your happiness. I am an old woman, my dear. In the course of Nature I cannot hope to be with you much longer. When I am gone, who will be left to care for you and love you, in the place of your mother? No one will be left – unless you marry Mrs Van Brandt. Your happiness is my first consideration; and the woman you love (sadly as she has been led astray) is a woman worthy of a better fate. Marry her.'

I could not trust myself to speak. I could only kneel at my mother's feet, and hide my face on her knees, as if I had been a boy again.

'Think of it, George,' she said. 'And come back to me when you are composed enough to speak as quietly of the future as I do.'

She lifted my head, and kissed me. As I rose to leave her, I saw something in the dear old eyes that met mine so tenderly, which struck a sudden fear through me – keen and cutting like a stroke from a knife.

The moment I had closed the door, I went downstairs to the porter in the hall.

'Has my mother left the house,' I asked, 'while I have been away?'

'No, sir.'

'Have any visitors called?'

'One visitor has called, sir.'

'Do you know who it was?'

The porter mentioned the name of a celebrated physician – a man at the head of his profession, in those days. I instantly took my hat, and went to his house.

He had just returned from his round of visits. My card was taken to him, and was followed at once by my admission to his consulting-room.

'You have seen my mother,' I said. 'Is she seriously ill – and have you not concealed it from her? For God's sake tell me the truth; I can bear it.'

The great man took me kindly by the hand.

'Your mother stands in no need of any warning; she is herself aware of the critical state of her health,' he said. 'She sent for me to confirm her own conviction. I could not conceal from her – I must not conceal from you – that the vital energies are sinking. She may live for some months longer in a milder air than the air of London. That is all I can say. At her age, her days are numbered.'

He gave me time to steady myself under the blow; and then he placed his vast experience, his matured and consummate knowledge, at my disposal. From his dictation, I committed to writing the necessary instructions for watching over the frail tenure of my mother's life.

'Let me give you one word of warning,' he said, as we parted. 'Your mother is especially desirous that you should know nothing of the precarious condition of her health. Her one anxiety is to see you happy. If she discovers your visit to me, I will not answer for the consequences. Make the best excuse you can think of for at once taking her away from London – and, whatever you may feel in secret, keep up an appearance of good spirits in her presence.'

That evening I made my excuse. It was easily found. I had only to tell my poor mother of Mrs Van Brandt's refusal to marry me; and there was an intelligible motive assigned for my proposing to leave London. The same night I wrote to inform Mrs Van Brandt of the sad event which was the cause of my sudden departure, and to warn her that there no longer existed the slightest necessity for insuring her life. 'My lawyers' (I wrote) 'have undertaken to arrange Mr Van Brandt's affairs immediately. In a few hours he will be at liberty to accept the situation that has been offered to him.' The last lines of the letter assured her of my unalterable love, and entreated her to write to me before she left England.

This done, all was done. I was conscious, strange to say, of no acutely painful suffering at this saddest time of my life. There is a limit, morally as well as physically, to our capacity for endurance. I can only describe my sensations under the calamities that had now fallen on me, in one way – I felt like a man whose mind had been stunned.

The next day, my mother and I set forth on the first stage of our journey to the south coast of Devonshire.

CHAPTER XXVI

A GLANCE BACKWARDS

Three days after we had comfortably established ourselves at Torquay, I received Mrs Van Brandt's answer to my letter. After the opening sentences (informing me that Van Brandt had been set at liberty, under circumstances painfully suggestive to the writer of some unacknowledged sacrifice on my part), the letter proceeded in these terms:–

'The new employment which Mr Van Brandt is to undertake secures to us the comforts, if not the luxuries, of life. For the first time since my troubles began, I have the prospect before me of a peaceful existence, among a foreign people from whom all that is false in my position may be concealed – not for my sake, but for the sake of my child. To more than this, to the happiness which some women enjoy, I must not, I dare not, aspire.

'We leave for the Continent early to-morrow morning. Shall I tell you in what part of Europe my new residence is to be?

'No! You might write to me again; and I might write back. The one return I can make to the good angel of my life, is to help him to forget me. What right have I to cling to my usurped place in your regard? The time will come when you will give your heart to a woman who is worthier of it than I am. Let me drop out of your life – except as an occasional remembrance, when you sometimes think of the days that have gone for ever.

'I shall not be without some consolation on my side, when I too look back at the past. I have been a better woman since I met with you. Live as long as I may, I shall always remember that.

'Yes! the influence that you have had over me has been from first to last an influence for good. Allowing that I have done wrong (in my position) to love you — and worse even than that, to own it — still the love has been innocent, and the effort to control it has been an honest effort at least. But, apart from this, my heart tells me that I am the better for the sympathy which has united us. I may confess to you what I have never yet acknowledged — now that we are so widely parted, and so little likely ever to meet again. Whenever I have given myself up unrestrainedly to my own better impulses, they have always seemed to lead me to You. Whenever my mind has been most truly at peace, and I have been able to pray with a pure and penitent heart, I have felt as if there was some unseen tie that was drawing us nearer and nearer together. And, strange to say, this has always happened to me (just as my dreams of you have always come to me) when I have been separated from Van Brandt. At such times, thinking or dreaming, it has always appeared to me that I knew you far more familiarly than I know you when we meet face to face. Is there really such a thing I wonder, as a former state of existence? And were we once constant companions in some other sphere, thousands of years since? These are idle guesses! Let it be enough for me to remember that I have been the better for knowing you — without enquiring how or why.

'Farewell, my beloved benefactor, my only friend! The child sends you a kiss; and the mother signs herself your grateful and affectionate,

'M. VAN BRANDT'

When I first read those lines, they once more recalled to my memory — very strangely as I then thought — the predictions of Dame Dermody in the days of my boyhood. Here were the foretold sympathies which were spiritually to unite me to Mary, realised by a stranger whom I had met by chance in the later years of my life!

Thinking in this direction, did I advance no farther? Not a step farther? Not a suspicion of the truth presented itself to my mind, even yet.

Was my own dullness of apprehension to blame for this? Would another man, in my position, have discovered what I failed to see?

I look back along the chain of events which runs through my narrative; and I ask myself, Where are the possibilities to be found — in my case, or in the case of any other man — of identifying the child who was Mary Dermody with the woman who was Mrs Van Brandt? Was there anything left in our faces, when we met again by the Scotch river, to remind us of our younger selves? We had developed, in the interval, from boy and girl, to man and woman: no outward traces were discernible in us of the George and Mary of other days. Disguised from each other by our faces, we were also disguised by our names. Her mock-marriage had changed her surname. My stepfather's Will had changed mine. Her Christian name was the commonest of all names of women; and mine was almost as far from being remarkable among the names of men. Turning next to the various occasions on which we had met, had we seen enough of each other to drift into recognition on either side, in the ordinary course of talk? We had met but four times in all: once on the bridge, once again in Edinburgh, twice more in London. On each of these occasions the absorbing anxieties and interests of the passing moment had filled her mind and mine, had inspired her words and mine. When had the events which brought us together, left us with leisure enough and tranquillity enough to look back idly through our lives, and calmly to compare the recollections of our youth? Never! From first to last, the course of events had borne us farther and farther away from any result that could have led even to a suspicion of the truth. She could only believe when she wrote to me on leaving England, and I could only believe when I read her letter, that we had first met at the river, and that our divergent destinies had ended in parting us for ever.

Reading her farewell letter in later days, by the light of my matured experience, I note how remarkably Dame Dermody's faith in the purity of the tie that united us, as kindred spirits, was justified by the result.

It was only when my unknown Mary was parted from Van Brandt – in other words, it was only when she was a pure spirit – that she felt my influence over her as a refining influence on her life, and that the apparition of her communicated with me in the visible and perfect likeness of herself. On my side, when was it that I dreamed of her (as in Scotland), or felt the mysterious warning of her presence in my waking moments (as in Shetland)? Always at the time when my heart opened most tenderly towards her and towards others – when my mind was most free from the bitter doubts, the self-seeking aspirations, which degrade the divinity within us. Then, and then only, my sympathy with her was the perfect sympathy which holds its fidelity unassailable by the chances and changes, the delusions and temptations of mortal life.

CHAPTER XXVII

MISS DUNROSS

Absorbed in watching over the closing days of my mother's life, I found in devoting myself to this sacred duty my only consolation under the overthrow of my last hope of marriage with Mrs Van Brandt.

By degrees, my mother felt the reviving influences of a quiet life and a soft air. The improvement in her health could, as I but too well knew, be only an improvement for a time. Still, it was a relief to see her free from pain, and innocently happy in the presence of her son. Excepting those hours of the day and night which were dedicated to repose, I was never away from her. To this day, I remember with a tenderness which attaches to no other memories of mine, the books that I read to her, the sunny corner on the seashore where I sat with her, the games of cards that we played together, the little trivial gossip that amused her when she was strong enough for nothing else. These are my imperishable relics; these are the deeds of my life that I shall love best to look back on, when the all-enfolding shadows of death are closing round me.

In the hours when I was alone, my thoughts – occupying themselves mostly among the persons and events of the past – wandered back many and many a time to Shetland and Miss Dunross.

My haunting doubt as to what the black veil had really hidden from me, was no longer accompanied by a feeling of horror when it now recurred to my mind. The more vividly my later remembrances of Miss Dunross were associated with the idea of an unutterable bodily affliction, the higher the noble nature of the woman seemed to rise in my esteem.

For the first time since I had left Shetland, the temptation now came to me to disregard the injunction which her father had laid on me at parting. When I thought again of the stolen kiss, in the dead of night; when I recalled the appearance of the frail white hand, waving to me through the dark curtains its last farewell – and when there mingled with these memories the later remembrance of what my mother had suspected, and of what Mrs Van Brandt had seen in her dream – the longing in me to find a means of assuring Miss Dunross that she still had her place apart in my memory and my heart, was more than mortal fortitude could resist. I was pledged in honour not to return to Shetland, and not to write. How to communicate with her secretly, in some other way, was the constant question in my mind, as the days went on. A hint to enlighten me was all that I wanted – and, as the irony of circumstances ordered it, my mother was the person who gave me the hint.

We still spoke at intervals of Mrs Van Brandt. Watching me on those occasions when we were in the company of acquaintances at Torquay, my mother plainly discerned that no other woman, whatever her attractions might be, could take the place in my heart of the woman whom I had lost. Seeing but one prospect of happiness for me, she refused to abandon the idea of my marrying Mrs Van Brandt. When a woman has owned that she loves a man (so my mother used to express her opinion) it is that man's fault, no matter what the obstacles may be, if he fails to make her his wife. Reverting to this view in various ways, she pressed it on my consideration one day, in these words:

'There is one drawback, George, to my happiness in being here with you. I am an obstacle in the way of your communicating with Mrs Van Brandt.'

'You forget,' I said, 'that she has left England, without telling me where to find her.'

'If you were free from the incumbrance of your mother, my dear, you could easily find her. Even as things are, you might surely write to her? Don't mistake my motives, George! If I had any hope of your forgetting her – if I saw you only moderately attracted by one or other of the charming women whom we know here – I should say let us never speak again, or think again, of Mrs Van Brandt. But, my dear, your heart is closed to every woman but one. Be happy in your own way, and let me see it before I die. The wretch to whom that poor creature is sacrificing her life, will sooner or later ill-treat her, or desert her – and then she must turn to you. Don't let her think you are resigned to the loss of her. The more resolutely you set her scruples at defiance, the more she will love and admire you in secret. Women are like that. Send her a letter – and follow it with a little present. You talked of taking me to the studio of the young artist here, who left his card the other day. I am told that he paints admirable portraits in miniature. Why not send your portrait to Mrs Van Brandt?'

Here was the idea of which I had been vainly in search! Quite superfluous as a method of pleading my cause with Mrs Van Brandt, the portrait offered the best of all means of communicating with Miss Dunross – without absolutely violating the engagement to which her father had pledged me. In this way, without writing a word, without even sending a message, I might tell her how gratefully she was remembered; I might remind her of me tenderly in the bitterest moments of her sad and solitary life.

The same day, I went to the artist privately. The sittings were afterwards continued during the hours while my mother was resting in her room, until the portrait was completed. I caused it to be enclosed in a plain gold locket, with a chain attached; and I forwarded my gift, in the first instance, to the one person whom I could trust to assist me in arranging for the conveyance of it to its destination. This was the old friend (alluded to in these pages as 'Sir James') who had taken me with him to Shetland in the Government yacht.

I had no reason, in writing the necessary explanations, to express myself to Sir James with any reserve. On the voyage back, we had more than once spoken together confidentially of Miss Dunross. Sir James had heard her sad story from the resident medical man at Lerwick, who had been an old companion of his in their college days. Requesting him to confide my gift to this gentleman, I did not hesitate to acknowledge the doubt that oppressed me, in relation to the mystery of the black veil. It was of course impossible to decide whether the doctor would be able to relieve that doubt. I could only venture to suggest that the question might be guardedly put, in making the customary enquiries after the health of Miss Dunross.

In those days of slow communication, I had to wait, not for days but for weeks, before I could expect to receive Sir James's answer. His letter only reached me after an unusually long delay. For this, or for some other reason which I cannot divine, I felt so strongly the foreboding of bad news that I abstained from breaking the seal in my mother's presence. I waited until I could retire to my own room – and then I opened the letter.

My presentiment had not deceived me. Sir James's reply contained these words only: 'The lines that I enclose tell their own sad story, without help from me. I cannot grieve for *her*. I feel heartily sorry for *you*.'

The letter thus described was addressed to Sir James by the doctor at Lerwick. I copy it without comment, in these words:–

'The late stormy weather has delayed the vessel, by means of which we communicate with the mainland. I have only received your letter to-day. With it, there has arrived a little box, containing a gold locket and chain; being the present which you ask me to convey privately to Miss Dunross, from a friend of yours whose name you are not at liberty to mention.

'In transmitting these instructions, you have innocently placed me in a position of extreme difficulty.

'The poor lady for whom the gift is intended, is near the end of her life – a life of such complicated and terrible suffering that death comes, in her case, literally as a mercy and a deliverance. Under these melancholy circumstances, I am, I think, not to blame, if I hesitate to give her the locket in secret; not knowing with what associations this keepsake is connected, or of what serious agitation it may not possibly be the cause.

'In this state of doubt, I have ventured on opening the locket – and my hesitation is naturally increased. I am quite ignorant of the remembrances which my unhappy patient may connect with the portrait. I don't know whether it will give her pleasure or pain to receive it, in her last moments on earth. I can only resolve to take it with me, when I see her to-morrow, and to let circumstances decide whether I shall risk giving it to her or not. Our post to the south, only leaves this place in three days' time. So I can keep my letter open, and let you know the result.

'I have seen her; and I have just returned to my own house. My distress of mind is great. But I will do my best to write intelligibly and fully of what has happened.

'Her sinking energies, when I first saw her this morning, had rallied for the moment. The nurse informed me that she slept during the early hours of the new day. Previously to this there were symptoms of fever; accompanied by some slight delirium. The words that escaped her in this condition, appear to have related mainly to an absent person whom she spoke of by the name of "George." Her one anxiety, I am told, was to see "George" again before she died.

'Hearing this, it struck me as barely possible, that the portrait in the locket might be the portrait of the absent person. I sent her nurse out of the room; and took her hand in mine. Trusting partly to her own admirable courage and strength of mind, and partly to the confidence which I knew she placed in me as an old friend and adviser, I adverted to the words which had fallen from her in the feverish state. And then I said, "You know that any secret of yours is safe in my keeping. Tell me, do you expect to receive any little keepsake or memorial from George?"

'It was a risk to run. The black veil which she always wears was over her face. I had nothing to tell me of the effect which I was producing on her, except the changing temperature or the partial movement of her hand, as it lay in mine, just under the silk coverlet of the bed.

'She said nothing at first. Her hand turned suddenly from cold to hot, and closed with a quick pressure on mine. Her breathing became oppressed. When she spoke, it was with difficulty. She told me nothing; she only put a question.

'"Is he here?" she asked.

'I said, "Nobody is here but myself."

'"Is there a letter?"

'I said, "No."

'She was silent for awhile. Her hand turned cold; the grasp of her fingers loosened. She spoke again: "Be quick, doctor! Whatever it is, give it to me before I die."

'I risked the experiment; I opened the locket, and put it into her hand.

'So far as I could discover, she refrained from looking at it, at first. She said, "Turn me in the bed, with my face to the wall." I obeyed her. With her back turned towards me, she lifted up her veil; and then (as I suppose) she looked at the portrait. A long low cry − not of sorrow or pain; a cry of rapture and delight − burst from her. I heard her kiss the portrait. Accustomed as I am in my profession to piteous sights and sounds, I never remember so completely losing my self-control as I lost it at that moment. I was obliged to turn away to the window.

'Hardly a minute could have passed before I was back again at the bedside. The veil was drawn once more over her face. Her voice had sunk again; I could only hear what she said, by leaning over her, and placing my ear close to her lips.

"'Put it round my neck," she whispered.

'I clasped the chain of the locket round her neck. She tried to lift her hand to it — but her strength failed her.

"'Help me to hide it," she said.

'I guided her hand. She hid the locket in her bosom, under the white dressing-gown which she wore that day. The oppression in her breathing increased. I raised her on the pillow. The pillow was not high enough. I rested her head on my shoulder; and partially opened her veil. She spoke again; feeling a momentary relief.

"'Promise," she said, "that no stranger's hand shall touch me. Promise to bury me, as I am now."

'I gave her my promise.

'Her failing breath quickened. She was just able to articulate the next words:

"'Cover my face again."

'I drew the veil over her face. She rested awhile in silence. Suddenly, the sound of her labouring respiration ceased. She started and raised her head from my shoulder.

"'Are you in pain?" I asked.

"'I am in Heaven!" she answered.

'Her head dropped back on my breast as she spoke. In that last outburst of joy, her last breath had passed. The moment of her supreme happiness, and the moment of her death were one. The mercy of God had found her at last.'

'I return to my letter before the post goes out.

'I have taken the necessary measures for the performance of my promise. She will be buried, with the locket hidden in her bosom, and with the black veil over her face. No nobler creature ever breathed the breath of life. Tell the stranger who sent her his portrait that her last moments were joyful moments — through his remembrance of her, as expressed by his gift.

'I observe a passage in your letter to which I have not yet replied. You ask me if there was any more serious reason for the persistent hiding of her face under the veil, than the reason she was accustomed to give to the persons about her. It is true that she suffered under a morbid sensitiveness to the action of light. It is also true that this was not the only result, or the worst result of the malady that afflicted her. She *had* another reason for keeping her face hidden — a reason known to two persons only: to the doctor who lives in the village near her father's house, and to myself. We are both pledged never to divulge to any living creature what our eyes alone have seen. We have kept our terrible secret, even from her father, and we shall carry it with us to our graves. I have no more to say on this melancholy subject to the person in whose interests you write. When he thinks of her now, let him think of the beauty which no bodily affliction can profane – the beauty of the freed Spirit, eternally happy in its union with the angels of God.

'I may add, before I close my letter, that the poor old father will not be left in cheerless solitude at the lake-house. He will pass the remainder of his days under my roof; with my good wife to take care of him, and my children to remind him of the brighter side of life.'

So the letter ended. I put it away, and went out. The solitude of my room forewarned me unendurably of the coming solitude in my own life. My interests in this busy world were now narrowed to one object – to the care of my mother's failing health. Of the two women whose hearts had once beaten in loving sympathy with mine, one lay in her grave, and the other was lost to me in a foreign land. On the drive by the sea I met my mother, in her little pony-chaise, moving slowly under the mild wintry sunshine. I dismissed the man who was in attendance on her, and walked by the side of the chaise with the reins in my hand. We chatted quietly on trivial subjects. I closed my eyes to the dreary future that was before me; and tried, in the intervals of the heart-ache, to live resignedly in the passing hour.

CHAPTER XXVIII

THE PHYSICIAN'S OPINION

Six months have elapsed. Summer-time has come again.

The last parting is over. Prolonged by my care, the days of my mother's life have come to their end. She has died in my arms; her last words have been spoken to me, her last look on earth has been mine. I am now, in the saddest and plainest meaning of the words, alone in the world.

The affliction which has befallen me has left certain duties to be performed that require my presence in London. My house is let; I am staying at an hotel. My friend, Sir James (also in London on business), has rooms near mine. We breakfast and dine together, in my sitting-room. For the moment, solitude is dreadful to me – and yet, I cannot go into society; I shrink from persons who are mere acquaintances. At Sir James's suggestion, however, one visitor to our hotel has been asked to dine with us, who claims distinction as no ordinary guest. The physician who first warned me of the critical state of my mother's health, is anxious to hear what I can tell him of her last moments. His time is too precious to be wasted in the earlier hours of the day; and he joins us at the dinner-table when his patients leave him free to visit his friends.

The dinner is nearly at an end. I have made the effort to preserve my self-control; and, in few words, I have told the simple story of my mother's last peaceful days on earth. The conversation turns next on topics of little interest to me: my mind rests after the effort that it has made; my observation is left free to exert itself as usual.

Little by little, while the talk goes on, I observe something in the conduct of the celebrated physician which first puzzles me, and then arouses my suspicion of some motive for his presence, which has not been acknowledged, and in which I am concerned.

Over and over again, I discover that his eyes are resting on me with a furtive interest and attention which he seems anxious to conceal. Over and over again, I notice that he contrives to divert the conversation from general topics, and to lure me into talking of myself; and, stranger still (unless I am quite mistaken), Sir James understands and encourages him. Under various pretences, I am questioned about what I have suffered in the past, and what plans of life I have formed for the future. Among other subjects of personal interest to me, the subject of supernatural appearances is introduced. I am asked if I believe in occult spiritual sympathies, and in ghostly apparitions of dead or distant persons. I am dexterously led into hinting that my views on this difficult and debateable question are in some degree influenced by experiences of my own. Hints, however, are not enough to satisfy the doctor's innocent curiosity: he tries to induce me to relate in detail what I have myself seen and felt. But, by this time, I am on my guard; I make excuses; I steadily abstain from taking my friend into my confidence. It is more and more plain to me that I am being made the subject of an experiment in which Sir James and the physician are equally interested. Outwardly assuming to be guiltless of any suspicion of what is going on, I inwardly determine to discover the true motive for the doctor's presence that evening, and for the part that Sir James has taken in inviting him to be my guest.

Events favour my purpose, soon after the dessert has been placed on the table.

The waiter enters the room, with a letter for me, and announces that the bearer waits to know if there is any answer. I open the envelope, and find inside a few lines from my lawyers, announcing the completion of some formal matter of business. I at once seize the opportunity that is offered to me. Instead of sending a verbal message downstairs, I make my apologies, and use the letter as a pretext for leaving the room.

Dismissing the messenger who waits below, I return to the corridor in which my rooms are situated, and softly open the door of my bedchamber. A second door communicates with the sitting-room, and has a ventilator in the upper part of it. I have only to stand under the ventilator, and every word of the conversation between Sir James and the physician reaches my ears.

'Then you think I am right?' are the first words I hear, in Sir James's voice.

'Quite right,' the doctor answers.

'I have done my best to make him change his dull way of life,' Sir James proceeds. 'I have asked him to pay a visit to my house in Scotland; I have proposed travelling with him on the Continent; I have offered to take him with me, on my next voyage in the yacht. He has but one answer – he simply says No to everything that I can suggest. You have heard from his own lips that he has no definite plans for the future. What is to become of him? what had we better do?'

'It is not easy to say,' I hear the physician reply. 'To speak plainly, the man's nervous system is seriously deranged. I noticed something strange in him when he first came to consult me about his mother's health. The mischief has not been caused entirely by the affliction of her death. In my belief, his mind has been – what shall I say? – unhinged, for some time past. He is a very reserved person. I suspect he has been oppressed by anxieties which he has kept secret from everyone. At his age, the unacknowledged troubles of life are generally troubles caused by women. It is in his temperament to take the romantic view of love; and some matter-of-fact woman of the present day may have bitterly disappointed him. Whatever may be the cause, the effect is plain – his nerves have broken down; and his brain is necessarily affected by whatever affects his nerves. I have known men in his condition who have ended badly. He may drift into insane delusions, if his present course of life is not altered. Did you hear what he said when we talked about ghosts?'

'Sheer nonsense!' Sir James remarks.

'Sheer delusion would be the more correct form of expression,' the doctor rejoins. 'And other delusions may flow out of it, at any moment.'

'What is to be done?' persists Sir James; 'I may really say for myself, doctor, that I feel a fatherly interest in the poor fellow. His mother was one of my oldest and dearest friends – and he has inherited many of her engaging and endearing qualities. I hope you don't think the case is bad enough to be a case for restraint?'

'Certainly not, as yet,' answers the doctor. 'So far there is no positive brain disease; and there is accordingly no sort of reason for placing him under restraint. It is essentially a doubtful and a difficult case. Have him privately looked after by a competent person, and thwart him in nothing, if you can possibly help it. The merest trifle may excite his suspicions – and, if that happens, we lose all control over him.'

'You don't think he suspects us already – do you, doctor?'

'I hope not. I saw him once or twice look at me rather strangely — and he has certainly been a long time out of the room.'

Hearing this, I wait to hear no more. I return to the sitting-room (by way of the corridor) and resume my place at the table.

The indignation that I feel — naturally enough, I think, under the circumstances — makes a good actor of me, for once in my life. I invent the necessary excuse for my long absence, and take my part in the conversation; keeping the strictest guard on every word that escapes me, without betraying any appearance of restraint in my manner. Early in the evening, the Doctor leaves us, to go to a scientific meeting. For half an hour more Sir James remains with me. By way as I suppose, of further testing the state of my mind, he renews the invitation to his house in Scotland. I pretend to feel flattered by his anxiety to secure me as his guest. I undertake to reconsider my first refusal, and to give him a definite answer when we meet the next morning at breakfast. Sir James is delighted; we shake hands cordially, and wish each other good night. At last I am left alone.

My resolution as to my next course of proceeding is formed without a moment's hesitation. I determine to leave the hotel privately the next morning, before Sir James is out of his bedroom.

To what destination I am to betake myself is naturally the next question that arises — and this also I easily decide. During the last days of my mother's life, we spoke together frequently of the happy past days when we were living on the banks of the Greenwater lake. The longing thus inspired to look once more at the old scenes, to live for awhile again among the old associations, has grown on me since my mother's death. I have, happily for myself, not spoken of this feeling to Sir James, or to any other person. When I am missed at the hotel, there will be no suspicion of the direction in which I have turned my steps. To the old home in Suffolk I resolve to go the next morning. Wandering among the scenes of my boyhood, I can consider with myself how I may best bear the burden of the life that lies before me.

After what I have heard this evening, I confide in nobody. For all I know to the contrary, my own servant may be employed to-morrow as the spy who watches my actions. When the man makes his appearance to take his orders for the night, I tell him to wake me at six o'clock the next morning, and release him from further attendance.

I next employ myself in writing two letters. They will be left on the table, to speak for themselves after my departure.

In the first letter, I briefly inform Sir James that I have discovered his true reason for inviting the doctor to dinner. While I thank him for the interest he takes in my welfare, I decline to be made the subject of any further medical enquiries as to the state of my mind. In due course of time, when my plans are settled, he will hear from me again. Meanwhile, he need feel no anxiety about my safety. It is one among my other delusions to believe that I am still perfectly capable of taking care of myself. My second letter is addressed to the landlord of the hotel, and simply provides for the disposal of my luggage, and the payment of my bill.

I enter my bedroom next, and pack a travelling-bag with the few things that I can carry with me. My money is in my dressing-case. Opening it, I discover my pretty keepsake – the green flag. Can I return to Greenwater Broad, can I look again at the bailiff's cottage, without the one memorial of little Mary that I possess? Besides, have I not promised Miss Dunross that Mary's gift shall always go with me, wherever I go; and is the promise not doubly sacred, now that she is dead? For awhile, I sit idly looking at the device on the flag – the white dove, embroidered on the green ground, with the golden olive-branch in its beak. The innocent love-story of my early life returns to my memory – and shows me in horrible contrast the life that I am leading now. I fold up the flag, and place it carefully in my travelling-bag. This done, all is done. I may rest till the morning comes.

No! I lie down in bed – and I discover that there is no rest for me, that night.

Now that I have no occupation to keep my energies employed – now that my first sense of triumph in the discomfiture of the friends who have plotted against me has had time to subside – my mind reverts to the conversation that I have overheard, and considers it from a new point of view. For the first time the terrible question confronts me: – The doctor's opinion on my case has been given very positively: how do I know that the doctor is not right?

This famous physician has risen to the head of his profession, entirely by his own abilities. He is not one of the medical men who succeed by means of an ingratiating manner and the dexterous handling of good opportunities. Even his enemies admit that he stands unrivalled in the art of separating the true conditions from the false in the discovery of disease, and in tracing effects accurately to their distant and hidden cause. Is such a man as this likely to be mistaken about me? Is it not far more probable that I am mistaken in my judgment of myself?

When I look back over past years, am I quite sure that the strangest events which I recall may not, in certain cases, be the visionary product of my own disordered brain – realities to me, and to no one else? What are the dreams of Mrs Van Brandt, what are the ghostly apparitions of her which I believe myself to have seen? Delusions which have been the stealthy growth of years? Delusions which are leading me by slow degrees nearer and nearer to madness in the end? Is it insane suspicion which has made me so angry with the good friends who have been trying to save my reason? Is it insane terror which sets me on escaping from the hotel like a criminal escaping from prison?

These are the questions that torment me, while I am alone in the dead of night. My bed becomes a place of unendurable torture. I rise and dress myself; and wait for the daylight, looking through my open window into the street.

The summer night is short. The grey light of dawn comes to me like a deliverance; the glow of the glorious sunrise cheers my soul once more. Why should I wait in the room that is still haunted by my horrible doubts of the night? I take up my travelling-bag; I leave my letters on the sitting-room table; and I descend the stairs to the house-door. The night-porter at the hotel is slumbering in his chair. He wakes as I pass him; and (God help me!) he too looks as if he thought I was mad.

'Going to leave us already, sir?' he says, looking at the bag in my hand.

Mad or sane, I am ready with my reply. I tell him I am going out for a day in the country – and to make it a long day I must start early.

The man still stares at me. He asks if he shall find somebody to carry my bag. I decline to let anybody be disturbed. He enquires if I have any message to leave for my friend. I inform him that I have left written messages upstairs for Sir James and the landlord. Upon this, he draws the bolts and opens the door. To the last he looks at me as if he thought I was mad.

Is he right or wrong? Who can answer for himself? How can I tell?

CHAPTER XXIX

A LAST LOOK AT GREENWATER BROAD

My spirits rose as I walked through the bright empty streets, and breathed the fresh morning air.

Making my way eastward through the great city, I stopped at the first office that I passed, and secured my place by the early coach to Ipswich. Thence, I travelled with post horses to the market-town which was nearest to Greenwater Broad. A walk of a few miles in the cool evening brought me, through well-remembered bye-roads to our old house. By the last rays of the setting sun, I looked at the familiar row of windows in front, and saw that the shutters were all closed. Not a living creature was visible anywhere. Not even a dog barked, as I rang the great bell at the door. The place was deserted; the house was shut up.

After a long delay, I heard heavy footsteps in the hall. An old man opened the door.

Changed as he was, I remembered him as one of our tenants in the bygone time. To his astonishment, I greeted him by his name. On his side, he tried hard to recognise me, and evidently tried in vain. No doubt I was the most sadly changed of the two – I was obliged to introduce myself. The poor fellow's withered face brightened slowly and timidly, as if he was half incapable, half afraid, of indulging in the unaccustomed luxury of a smile. In his confusion, he bade me welcome home again, as if the house had been mine!

Taking me into the little back room which he inhabited, the old man gave me all he had to offer – a supper of bacon and eggs, and a glass of home-brewed beer. He was evidently puzzled to understand me, when I informed him that the only object of my visit was to look once more at the familiar scenes round my old home. But he willingly placed his services at my disposal; and he engaged to do his best, if I wished it, to make me up a bed for the night.

The house had been closed, and the establishment of servants had been dismissed, for more than a year past. A passion for horse-racing, developed late in life, had ruined the rich retired tradesman who had become our tenant at the time of our family troubles. He had gone abroad with his wife, to live on the little income that had been saved from the wreck of his fortune; and he had left the house and lands in such a state of neglect that no new tenant had thus far been found to take them. My old friend, now 'past his work,' had been put in charge of the place. As for Dermody's cottage, it was empty like the house. I was at perfect liberty to look over it if I liked. There was the key of the door, on the bunch with the others; and here was the old man, with his old hat on his head, ready to accompany me wherever I pleased to go. I declined to trouble him to accompany me, or to make me up a bed in the lonely house. The night was fine, the moon was rising. I had supped; I had rested. When I had seen what I wanted to see, I could easily walk back to the market-town, and sleep at the inn.

Taking the key in my hand, I set forth alone on the way through the grounds which led to Dermody's cottage.

Again I followed the woodland paths, along which I had once idled so happily with my little Mary. At every step, I saw something that reminded me of her. Here was the rustic bench, on which we had sat together under the shade of the old cedar tree, and vowed to be constant to each other to the end of our lives. There was the bright little water-spring, from which we drank when we were weary and thirsty in sultry summer-days, still bubbling its way downward to the lake as cheerily as ever. As I listened to the companionable murmur of the stream, I almost expected to see her again, in her simple white frock and straw hat, singing to the music of the rivulet, and freshening her nosegay of wild flowers by dipping it in the cold water. A few steps farther on, and I reached a clearing in the wood, and stood on a little promontory of rising ground, which commanded the prettiest view of the Greenwater lake. A platform of wood was built out from the bank, to be used for bathing by good swimmers, who were not afraid of a plunge into deep water. I stood on the platform, and looked round me. The trees that fringed the shore on either side murmured their sweet sylvan music in the night air; the moonlight trembled softly on the rippling water. Away on my right hand, I could just see the old wooden shed that once sheltered my boat, in the days when Mary went sailing with me, and worked the green flag. On my left, was the wooden paling that followed the curves of the winding creek; and beyond it rose the brown arches of the Decoy for wild fowl, now falling to ruin for want of use. Guided by the radiant moonlight, I could see the very spot on which Mary and I had stood to watch the snaring of the ducks. Through the hole in the paling, before which the decoy-dog had shown himself at Dermody's signal, a water-rat now passed, like a little black shadow on the bright ground, and was lost in the waters of the lake. Look where I might, the happy by-gone time looked back in mockery; and the voices of the past came to me with their burden of reproach: See what your life was once! Is your life worth living, now?

I picked up a stone, and threw it into the lake. I watched the circling ripples round the place at which it had sunk. I wondered whether a practised swimmer like myself had ever tried to commit suicide by drowning, and had been so resolute to die that he had resisted the temptation to let his own skill keep him from sinking. Something in the lake itself, or something in connection with the thought that it had put into my mind, revolted me. I turned my back suddenly on the lovely view, and took the path through the wood which led to the bailiff's cottage.

Opening the door with my key, I groped my way into the well-remembered parlour; and, unbarring the window-shutters, I let in the light of the moon.

With a heavy heart, I looked round me. The old furniture, renewed perhaps in one or two places, asserted its mute claim to my recognition in every part of the room. The tender moonlight streamed into the corner in which little Mary and I used to nestle together, while Dame Dermody was at the window reading her mystic books. Over-shadowed by the obscurity in the opposite corner, I discovered the high-backed armchair of carved oak in which the Sibyl of the cottage sat, on the memorable day when she warned us of our coming separation, and gave us her blessing for the last time. Looking next round the walls of the room, I recognised old friends wherever my eyes happened to rest – the gaudily-coloured prints; the framed pictures in fine needlework which we thought wonderful efforts of art; the old circular mirror to which I used to lift Mary when she wanted to 'see her face in the glass.' Wherever the moonlight penetrated, there it showed me some familiar object that recalled my happiest days. Again, the by-gone time looked back in mockery. Again, the voices of the past came to me with their burden of reproach: See what your life was once! Is your life worth living now?

I sat down at the window, where I could just discover, here and there between the trees, the glimmer of the waters of the lake. I thought to myself: – 'Thus far, my mortal journey has brought me. Why not end it here?'

Who would grieve for me, if my suicide was reported to-morrow? Of all living men, I had perhaps the smallest number of friends; the fewest duties to perform towards others; the least reason to hesitate at leaving a world which had no place in it for my ambition, no creature in it for my love.

Besides, what necessity was there for letting it be known that my death was a death of my own seeking? It could easily be left to represent itself as a death by accident.

On that fine summer night, and after a long day of travelling, might I not naturally take a bath in the cool water before I went to bed? And practised as I was in the exercise of swimming, might it not nevertheless be my misfortune to be attacked by cramp? On the lonely shores of Greenwater Broad, the cry of a drowning man would bring no help at night: 'the fatal' accident would explain itself. There was literally but one difficulty in my way – the difficulty which had already occurred to my mind. Could I sufficiently master the animal instinct of self preservation, to deliberately let myself sink at the first plunge?

The atmosphere in the room felt close and heavy. I went out, and walked to and fro – now in the shadow, and now in the moonlight – under the trees before the cottage door.

Of the normal objections to suicide, not one had any influence over me now. I, who had once found it impossible to excuse, impossible even to understand, the despair which had driven Mrs Van Brandt to attempt self-destruction – I now contemplated with composure the very act which had horrified me when I saw it committed by another person! Well may we hesitate to condemn the frailties of our fellow-creatures – for the one unanswerable reason that we can never feel sure how soon similar temptations may not lead us to be guilty of the same frailties ourselves. Looking back at the events of that night, I can recall but one consideration that stayed my feet on the fatal path which led back to the lake. I still doubted whether it would be possible for such a swimmer as I was to drown himself. This was all that troubled my mind. For the rest, my Will was made; and I had few others affairs which remained unsettled. No lingering hope was left in me of a re-union in the future with Mrs Van Brandt. She had never written to me again: I had never, since our last parting, seen her again in my dreams. She was doubtless reconciled to her life abroad. I forgave her for having forgotten me. My thoughts of her, and of others, were the forbearing thoughts of a man whose mind was withdrawn already from the world, whose views were narrowing fast to the one idea of his own death.

I grew weary of walking up and down. The loneliness of the place began to oppress me. The sense of my own indecision irritated my nerves. After a long look at the lake, through the trees, I came to a positive conclusion at last. I determined to try if a good swimmer could drown himself.

CHAPTER XXX

A VISION OF THE NIGHT

Returning to the cottage parlour, I took a chair by the window, and opened my pocket-book at a blank page. I had certain directions to give to my representatives, which might spare them some trouble and uncertainty in the event of my death. Disguising my last instructions, under the commonplace heading of 'Memoranda on my return to London,' I began to write.

I had filled one page of the pocket-book, and had just turned to the next – when I became conscious of a difficulty in fixing my attention on the subject that was before it. I was at once reminded of the similar difficulty which I felt, in Shetland, when I had tried vainly to arrange the composition of the letter to my mother which Miss Dunross was to write. By way of completing the parallel my thoughts wandered now, as they had wandered then, to my latest remembrances of Mrs Van Brandt. In a minute or two I began to feel once more the strange physical sensations which I had first experienced in the garden at Mr Dunross's house. The same mysterious trembling shuddered through me from head to foot. I looked about me again, with no distinct consciousness of what the objects were on which my eyes rested. My nerves trembled, on that lovely summer night, as if there had been an electric disturbance in the atmosphere, and a storm coming. I laid my pocket-book and pencil on the table, and rose to go out again under the trees. Even the trifling effort to cross the room proved to be an effort that was beyond my power. I stood rooted to the spot, with my face turned towards the moonight streaming in at the open door.

An interval passed; and, as I still looked out through the door, I became aware of something moving, far down among the trees that fringed the shore of the lake. The first impression produced on me was of two grey shadows winding their way slowly towards me between the trunks of the trees. By fine degrees, the shadows assumed a more and more marked outline, until they presented themselves in the likeness of two robed figures, one taller than the other. While they glided nearer and nearer, their grey obscurity of hue melted away. They brightened softly with an inner light of their own, as they approached the open space before the door. For the third time, I stood in the ghostly Presence of Mrs Van Brandt – and with her, holding her hand, I beheld a second apparition never before revealed to me, the apparition of her child.

Hand in hand, shining in their unearthly brightness through the bright moonlight itself, the two stood before me. The mother's face looked at me once more with the sorrowful and pleading eyes which I remembered so well. But the face of the child was innocently radiant with an angelic smile. I waited, in unutterable expectation, for the word that was to be spoken, for the movement that was to come. The movement came first. The child released its hold on the mother's hand; and, floating slowly upward, remained poised in mid air – a softly-glowing Presence, shining out of the dark background of the trees. The mother glided into the room, and stopped at the table on which I had laid my pocket-book and pencil, when I could no longer write. As before, she took the pencil, and wrote on the blank page. As before, she beckoned to me to step nearer to her. I approached her outstretched hand; and felt once more the mysterious rapture of her touch on my bosom; and heard once more her low melodious tones, repeating the words: 'Remember me. Come to me.' Her hand dropped from my bosom. The pale light which revealed her to me quivered, sank, vanished. She had spoken. She had gone.

I drew to me the open pocket-book. And, this time, I saw in the writing of the ghostly hand these words only:

'FOLLOW THE CHILD.'

I looked out again at the lonely night landscape.

There, in mid air, shining softly out of the dark background of the trees, still hovered the starry apparition of the child.

Advancing, without conscious will of my own, I crossed the threshold of the door. The softly-glowing Vision of the child moved away before me among the trees. I followed, like a man spell-bound. The apparition, floating slowly onward, led me out of the wood and past my old home, back to the lonely bye-roads along which I had walked from the market-town to the house. From time to time, as we two went on our way, the bright figure of the child paused, hovering low in the cloudless sky. Its radiant face looked down smiling on me: it beckoned with its little hand – and floated on again, leading me as the Star led the Eastern Sages in the olden times.

I reached the town. The airy figure of the child paused, hovering over the house at which I had left my travelling-carriage in the evening. I ordered the horses to be harnessed again for another journey. The postillion waited for his further directions. I looked up. The child's hand was pointing southward along the road that led to London. I gave the man instructions to return to the place at which I had hired the carriage. At intervals, as we proceeded, I looked out through the window. The bright figure of the child still floated on before me, gliding low in the cloudless sky. Changing the horses stage by stage, I went on till the night ended – went on till the sun rose in the eastern heaven. And still, whether it was night or whether it was day, the figure of the child floated on before me in its changeless and mystic light. Mile after mile, it still led the way southward till we left the country behind us, and, passing through the din and turmoil of the great city, stopped under the shadow of the ancient Tower, within view of the river that runs by it.

The postillion came to the carriage door, to ask if I had further need of his services. I had called to him to stop, when I saw the figure of the child pause on its airy course. I looked upward again. The child's hand pointed towards the river. I paid the postillion, and left the carriage. Floating on before me, the child led the way to a wharf, crowded with travellers and their luggage. A vessel lay alongside the wharf, ready to sail. The child led me on board the vessel, and paused again, hovering over me in the smoky air.

I looked up. The child looked back at me with its radiant smile; and pointed eastward down the river towards the distant sea. While my eyes were still fixed on the softly-glowing figure, I saw it fade away, upward and upward into the higher light, as the lark vanishes upward and upward in the morning sky. I was alone again with my earthly fellow-beings – left, with no clue to guide me but the remembrance of the child's hand, pointing eastward to the distant sea.

A sailor was near me, coiling a loosened mooring-rope on the deck. I asked him to what port the vessel was bound. The man looked at me in surly amazement, and answered:

'To Rotterdam.'

CHAPTER XXXI

BY LAND AND SEA

It mattered little to me to what port the vessel was bound. Go where I might, I knew that I was on my way to Mrs Van Brandt. She had need of me again; she had claimed me again. Where the visionary hand of the child had pointed – abroad or at home, it mattered nothing – thither I was destined to go. When I next set my foot on the land, I should be further directed on the journey which lay before me. I believed this as firmly as I believed that I had been guided thus far by the vision of the child.

For two nights I had not slept – my weariness overpowered me. I descended to the cabin, and found an unoccupied corner in which I could lie down to rest. When I awoke, it was night already: the vessel was at sea.

I went on deck to breathe the fresh air. Before long the sensation of drowsiness returned; I slept again, for hours together. My friend the physician would no doubt have attributed this prolonged need of repose to the exhausted condition of my brain, excited by delusions which had lasted uninterruptedly for many hours together. Let the cause be what it might, during the greater part of the voyage I was awake at intervals only. The rest of the time I lay like a weary animal, lost in sleep.

When I stepped on shore at Rotterdam, my first proceeding was to ask my way to the English consulate. I had but a small sum of money left; and, for all I knew to the contrary, it might be well, before I did anything else, to take the necessary measures for replenishing my purse.

I had my travelling-bag with me. On the journey to Greenwater Broad, I had left it at the inn in the market-town; and the waiter had placed it in the carriage, when I started on my return to London. The bag contained my cheque-book, and certain letters which assisted me in proving my identity to the consul. He kindly gave me the necessary introduction to the correspondents at Rotterdam of my bankers in London.

Having obtained my money, and having purchased certain necessaries of which I stood in need, I walked slowly along the street; knowing nothing of what my next proceeding was to be, and waiting confidently for the event which was to guide me. I had not walked a hundred yards before I noticed the name of 'Van Brandt,' inscribed on the window-blinds of a house which appeared to be devoted to mercantile purposes.

The street door stood open. A second door, on one side of the passage, led into the office. I entered the room, and enquired for Mr Van Brandt. A clerk who spoke English was sent for to communicate with me. He told me there were three partners of that name in the business, and enquired which of them I wished to see. I remembered Van Brandt's Christian name and mentioned it. No such person as 'Mr Ernest Van Brandt' was known at the office.

'We are only the branch-house of the firm of Van Brandt here,' the clerk explained. The head-office is at Amsterdam. They may know where Mr Ernest Van Brandt is to be found, if you enquire there.'

It mattered nothing to me where I went, so long as I was on my way to Mrs Van Brandt. It was too late to travel that day; I slept at an hotel. The night passed quietly and uneventfully. The next morning I set forth by the public conveyance for Amsterdam.

Repeating my enquiries at the head-office, on my arrival, I was referred to one of the partners in the firm. He spoke English perfectly; and he received me with an appearance of interest which I was at a loss to account for at first.

'Mr Ernest Van Brandt is well known to me,' he said. 'May I ask if you are a relative or friend of the English lady who has been introduced here as his wife?'

I answered in the affirmative; adding, 'I am here to give any assistance to the lady of which she may stand in need.'

The merchant's next words explained the appearance of interest with which he had received me.

'You are most welcome,' he said. 'You relieve my partners and myself of a great anxiety. I can only explain what I mean by referring for a moment to the business affairs of my firm. We have a fishing establishment at the ancient city of Enkhuizen, on the shores of the Zuyder-Zee. Mr Ernest Van Brandt had a share in it, at one time, which he afterwards sold. Of late years our profits from this source have been diminishing; and we think of giving up the fishery, unless our prospects in that quarter improve after a further trial. In the meantime, having a vacant situation in the counting house at Enkhuizen, we thought of Mr Ernest Van Brandt, and offered him the opportunity of renewing his connection with us in the capacity of a clerk. He is related to one of my partners; but I am bound in truth to tell you that he is a very bad man. He has rewarded us for our kindness to him by embezzling our money; and he has taken to flight – in what direction we have not yet discovered. The English lady and her child are left deserted at Enkhuizen – and until you came here to-day, we were quite at a loss to know what to do with them. I don't know whether you are already aware of it, sir – but the lady's position is made doubly distressing by doubts which we entertain of her being really Mr Ernest Van Brandt's wife. To our certain knowledge, he was privately married to another woman, some years since – and we have no evidence whatever that the first wife is dead. If we can help you, in any way, to assist your unfortunate countrywoman, pray believe that our services are at your disposal.'

With what breathless interest I listened to these words, it is needless to say. Van Brandt had deserted her! Surely (as my poor mother had said) 'she must turn to me now'? The hopes that had abandoned me filled my heart once more; the future which I had so long feared to contemplate, showed itself again, bright with the promise of coming happiness, to my view. I thanked the good merchant with a fervour that surprised him. 'Only help me to find my way to Enkhuizen,' I said; 'and I will answer for the rest.'

'The journey will put you to some expense,' the merchant replied. 'Pardon me if I ask the question bluntly. Have you money?'

'Plenty of money!'

'Very good! The rest will be easy enough. I will place you under the care of a countryman of yours, who has been employed in our office for many years. The easiest way for you, as a stranger, will be to go by sea; and the Englishman will show you where to hire a boat.'

In a few minutes more the clerk and I were on our way to the harbour.

Difficulties which I had not anticipated occurred in finding the boat and in engaging a crew. This done, it was next necessary to purchase provisions for the voyage. Thanks to the experience of my companion, and to the hearty goodwill with which he exerted it, my preparations were completed before nightfall. I was able to set sail for my destination on the next day.

The boat had the double advantage in navigating the Zuyder-Zee, of being large, and of drawing very little water. The captain's cabin was at the stern; and the two or three men who formed his crew were berthed forward, in the bows. The whole middle of the boat, partitioned off on the one side and on the other from the captain and the crew, was assigned to me for my cabin. Under these circumstances, I had no reason to complain of want of space; the vessel measuring between fifty and sixty tons. I had a comfortable bed, a table, and chairs. The kitchen was well away from me, in the forward part of the boat. At my own request, I set forth on the voyage without servant or interpreter. I preferred being alone. The Dutch captain had been employed, at a former period of his life, in the mercantile navy of France; and we could communicate, whenever it was necessary or desirable, in the French language.

We left the spires of Amsterdam behind us, and sailed over the smooth waters of the river Y on our way to the Zuyder-Zee.

The history of this remarkable Sea is a romance in itself. In the days when Rome was mistress of the world it had no existence. Where the waves now roll, vast tracts of forest surrounded a great inland lake, with but one river to serve it as an outlet to the sea. Swelled by a succession of tempests the lake overflowed its boundaries; its furious waters, destroying every obstacle in their course, rested only when they reached the farthest limits of the land. The great Northern Ocean burst its way in, through the gaps of ruin; and, from that time, the Zuyder-Zee existed as we know it now. The years advanced; the generations of man succeeded each other; and on the shores of the new ocean there rose great and populous cities, rich in commerce, renowned in history. For centuries their prosperity lasted, before the next in this mighty series of changes ripened and revealed itself. Isolated from the rest of the world; vain of themselves and their good fortune; careless of the march of progress in the nations round them, the inhabitants of the Zuyder-Zee cities sank into the fatal torpor of a secluded people. The few members of the population who still preserved the relics of their old energy emigrated; while the mass left behind witnessed resignedly the diminution of their commerce and the decay of their institutions. As the years advanced to the nineteenth century, the population was reckoned by hundreds, where it had once been numbered by thousands. Trade disappeared; whole streets were left desolate. Harbours once filled with shipping were destroyed by the unresisted accumulation of sand. In our times, the decay of these once flourishing cities is so completely beyond remedy, that the next great change in contemplation is the draining of the now dangerous and useless tract of water, and the profitable cultivation of the reclaimed land by generations that are still to come. Such, briefly told, is the strange story of the Zuyder-Zee.

As we advanced on our voyage, and left the river, I noticed the tawny hue of the sea, caused by sandbanks which colour the shallow water, and which make the navigation dangerous to inexperienced seamen. We found our moorings for the night at the fishing-island of Marken — a low, lost, desolate-looking place, as I saw it under the last gleams of the twilight. Here and there, the gabled cottages, perched on hillocks, rose black against the dim grey sky. Here and there, a human figure appeared at the waterside, standing fixed in contemplation of the strange boat. And that was all I saw of the island of Marken.

Lying awake in the still night, alone on a strange sea, there were moments when I found myself beginning to doubt the reality of my own position.

Was it all a dream? My thoughts of suicide; my vision of the mother and daughter; my journey back to the metropolis, led by the apparition of the child; my voyage to Holland; my night-anchorage in the unknown sea — were these, so to speak, all pieces of the same morbid mental puzzle, all delusions from which I might wake at any moment, and find myself restored to my senses again in the hotel at London? Bewildered by doubts which led me farther and farther from any definite conclusion, I left my bed, and went on deck to change the scene. It was a still and cloudy night. In the black void round me, the island was a blacker shadow yet, and nothing more. The one sound that reached my ears was the heavy breathing of the captain and his crew, sleeping on either side of me. I waited, looking round and round the circle of darkness in which I stood. No new vision showed itself. When I returned again to the cabin, and slumbered at last, no dreams came to me. All that was mysterious, all that was marvellous, in the later events of my life, seemed to have been left behind me in England. Once in Holland, my course had been influenced by circumstances which were perfectly natural, by commonplace discoveries which might have revealed themselves to any man in my position. What did this mean? Had my gifts as a seer of visions departed from me in the new land and among the strange people? Or had my Destiny led me to the place at which the troubles of my mortal pilgrimage were to find their end? Who could say?

Early the next morning, we set sail once more.

Our course was nearly northward. On one side of me was the tawny sea, changing under certain conditions of the weather to a dull pearl-grey. On the other side, was the flat winding coast, composed alternately of yellow sand and bright green meadowlands: diversified at intervals by towns and villages, whose red-tiled roofs and quaint church steeples rose gaily against the clear blue sky. The captain suggested to me to visit the famous towns of Edam and Hoorn, but I declined to go on shore. My one desire was to reach the ancient city in which Mrs Van Brandt had been left deserted. As we altered our course to make for the promontory on which Enkhuizen is situated, the wind fell – then shifted to another quarter, and blew with a force which greatly increased the difficulties of navigation. I still insisted, as long as it was possible to do so, on holding on our course. After sunset, the strength of the wind abated. The night came without a cloud; and the starry firmament gave us its pale and melancholy light. In an hour more the capricious wind shifted back again in our favour. Towards ten o'clock we sailed into the desolate harbour of Enkhuizen.

The captain and crew, fatigued by their exertions, ate their frugal suppers, and went to rest. In a few minutes, I was the only person left awake in the boat.

I ascended to the deck, and looked about me.

Our boat was moored to a deserted quay. Excepting a few small vessels visible near us, the harbour of this once prosperous place was a vast solitude of water, varied here and there by dreary banks of sand. Looking inland, I saw the lonely buildings of the Dead City – black, grim and dreadful, under the mysterious starlight. Not a human creature, not even a stray animal, was to be seen anywhere. The place might have been desolated by a pestilence, so empty and so lifeless did it now appear. Little more than a hundred years ago, the record of its population reached sixty thousand. The inhabitants had dwindled to a tenth of that number when I looked at Enkhuizen now!

I considered with myself what my next course of proceeding was to be.

The chances were certainly against my discovering Mrs Van Brandt if I ventured alone and unguided into the city at night. On the other hand, now that I had reached the place in which she and her child were living, friendless and deserted, could I patiently wait through the weary interval that must elapse before the morning came and the town was astir? I knew my own self-tormenting disposition too well to accept this latter alternative. Whatever came of it, I determined to walk through Enkhuizen, on the bare chance of passing the office of the fishery, and of so discovering Mrs Van Brandt's address.

First taking the precaution of locking my cabin door, I stepped from the bulwark of the vessel to the lonely quay, and set forth upon my night wanderings through the Dead City.

CHAPTER XXXII

UNDER THE WINDOW

I set the position of the harbour by my pocket-compass, and followed the course of the first street that lay before me.

On either side, as I advanced, the desolate old houses frowned on me. There were no lights in the windows, no lamps in the street. For a quarter of an hour at least I penetrated deeper and deeper on my way into the city, without encountering a living creature – with only the starlight to guide me. Turning by chance into a street broader than the rest, I at last saw a moving figure, just visible ahead, under the shadows of the houses. I quietened my pace, and found myself following a man in the dress of peasant. Hearing my footsteps behind him, he turned and looked at me. Discovering that I was a stranger, he lifted a thick cudgel that he carried with him, shook it threateningly, and called to me in his own language (as I gathered by his actions) to stand back. A stranger in Enkhuizen at that time of night was evidently reckoned as a robber in the estimation of this citizen! I had learnt on the voyage, from the captain of the boat, how to ask my way in Dutch, if I happened to be by myself in a strange town; and I now repeated my lesson, asking my way to the fishing office of Van Brandt. Either my foreign accent made me unintelligible, or the man's suspicions disinclined him to trust me. Again he shook his cudgel; and again he signed to me to stand back. It was useless to persist. I crossed to the opposite side of the way, and soon afterwards lost sight of him under the portico of a house.

Still following the windings of the deserted streets, I reached what I at first supposed to be the end of the town.

Before me, for half a mile or more as well as I could guess, rose a tract of meadowland, with sheep dotted over it at intervals, reposing for the night. I advanced over the grass, and observed here and there where the ground rose a little, some mouldering fragments of brickwork. Looking onward, as I reached the middle of the meadow, I perceived on its farther side, towering gaunt and black in the night, a lofty arch or gateway, without walls at its sides, without a neighbouring building of any sort visible, far or near. This (as I afterwards learnt) was one of the ancient gates of the city. The walls, crumbling to ruin, had been destroyed as useless obstacles that cumbered the ground. On the waste meadowland round me had once stood the shops of the richest merchants, the palaces of the proudest nobles, of North Holland. I was actually standing on what had formerly been the wealthiest quarter of Enkhuizen. And what was left of it now? A few mounds of broken bricks, a pasture-land of sweet-smelling grass, and a little flock of sheep sleeping.

The mere desolation of the view (apart altogether from its history) struck me with a feeling of horror. My mind seemed to lose its balance, in the dreadful stillness that was round me. I felt unutterable forebodings of calamity to come. For the first time, I repented having left England. My thoughts turned regretfully to the woody shores of Greenwater Broad. If I had only held to my resolution, I might have been at rest now in the deep waters of the lake. For what had I lived, and planned, and travelled, since I left Dermody's cottage? Perhaps, only to find that I had lost the woman whom I loved – now that I was in the same town with her!

Regaining the outer rows of houses still left standing, I looked about me, intending to return by the street along which I had advanced. Just as I thought I had discovered it, I noticed another living creature in the solitary city. A man was standing at the door of one of the outermost houses, on my right hand, looking at me.

At the risk of meeting with another rough reception, I determined to make a last effort to discover Mrs Van Brandt, before I returned to the boat.

Seeing that I was approaching him, the stranger met me midway. His dress and manner showed plainly that I had not encountered, this time, a person in the lower ranks of life. He answered my question civilly in his own language. Seeing that I was at a loss to understand what he said, he invited me by signs to follow him.

After walking for a few minutes in a direction which was quite new to me, we stopped in a gloomy little square, with a plot of neglected garden ground in the middle of it. Pointing to a lower window in one of the houses, in which a light dimly appeared, my guide said in Dutch, 'Office of Van Brandt, sir' – bowed – and left me.

I advanced to the window. It was open; and it was just high enough to be above my head. The light in the room found its way outward through the interstices of closed wooden shutters. Still haunted by misgivings of trouble to come, I hesitated to announce my arrival precipitately by ringing the house bell. How did I know what new calamity might not confront me when the door was opened? I waited under the window – and listend.

Hardly a minute had passed before I heard a woman's voice in the room. There was no mistaking the charm of those tones. It was the voice of Mrs Van Brandt.

'Come, darling!' she said. 'It is very late – you ought to have been in your bed two hours ago.'

The child's voice answered, 'I am not sleepy, mamma.'

'But, my dear, remember you have been ill. You may be ill again, if you keep out of bed so late as this. Only lie down, and you will soon fall asleep when I put the candle out.'

'You must *not* put the candle out,' the child returned with strong emphasis. 'My new papa is coming. How is he to find his way to us, if you put out the light?'

The mother replied sharply, as if the child's strange words had irritated her.

'You are talking nonsense,' she said; 'and you must go to bed. Mr Germaine knows nothing about us. Mr Germaine is in England.'

I could restrain myself no longer. I called out under the window,

'Mr Germaine is here!'

CHAPTER XXXIII

LOVE AND PRIDE

A cry of terror from the room told me that I had been heard. For a moment more, nothing happened. Then the child's voice reached me, wild and shrill: 'Open the shutters, mamma! I said he was coming; I want to see him!'

There was still an interval of hesitation before the mother opened the shutters. She did it at last. I saw her darkly at the window, with the light behind her, and the child's head just visible above the lower part of the window-frame. The quaint little face moved rapidly up and down, as if my self-appointed daughter was dancing for joy!

'Can I trust my own senses?' said Mrs Van Brandt. 'Is it really Mr Germaine?'

'How do you do, new papa?' cried the child. 'Push open the big door – and come in. I want to kiss you.'

There was a world of difference between the coldly-doubtful tone of the mother and the joyous greeting of the child. Had I forced myself too suddenly on Mrs Van Brandt? Like all sensitively-organised persons, she possessed the inbred sense of self-respect which is pride under another name. Was her pride wounded by the bare idea of my seeing her, deserted as well as deceived – abandoned contemptuously, a helpless burden on strangers, by the man for whom she had sacrificed and suffered so much? And that man a thief, flying from the employers whom he had cheated! I pushed open the heavy oaken door, fearing that this might be the true explanation of the change which I had already remarked in her. My apprehensions were confirmed, when she unlocked the inner-door leading from the court-yard to the sitting-room, and let me in.

As I took her by both hands and kissed her, she quickly turned her head, so that my lips touched her cheek only. She flushed deeply; her eyes were on the ground, as she expressed in a few formal words her surprise at seeing me. When the child flew to my arms, she cried out irritably, 'Don't trouble Mr Germaine!' I took a chair with the little one on my knee. Mrs Van Brandt seated herself at a distance from me. 'It is needless, I suppose, to ask if you know what has happened?' she said; turning pale again as suddenly as she had turned red, and keeping her eyes fixed obstinately on the floor.

Before I could answer, the child burst out gaily with the news of her father's disappearance: 'My other papa has run away! My other papa has stolen money! It's time I had a new one – isn't it?' She put her arms round my neck. 'And now I've got him!' she cried, at the shrillest pitch of her voice.

The mother looked at us. For a while, the proud sensitive woman struggled successfully with herself. But the pang that wrung her was not to be endured in silence. With a low cry of pain, she hid her face in her hands. Overwhelmed by the sense of her own degradation, she was even ashamed to let the man who loved her see that she was in tears.

I took the child off my knee. There was a second door in the sitting-room, which happened to be left open. It showed me a bedchamber within, and a candle burning on the toilette-table.

'Go in there, and play,' I said. 'I want to talk to your mamma.'

The child pouted: my proposal did not appear to tempt her. 'Give me something to play with,' she said. 'I'm tired of my toys. Let me see what you have got in your pockets.'

Her busy little hands began to search in my coat-pockets. I let her take what she pleased, and so bribed her to run away into the inner room. As soon as she was out of sight, I approached the poor mother and seated myself by her side.

'Think of it as I do,' I said. 'Now that he has forsaken you, he has left you free to be mine.'

She lifted her head instantly.

'Now that he has forsaken me,' she answered, 'I am more unworthy of you than ever!'

'Why?' I asked.

'Why!' she repeated passionately. 'Has a woman not reached the lowest depths of degradation, when she had lived to be deserted by a thief?'

It was hopeless to attempt to reason with her, in her present frame of mind. I tried to attract her attention to a less painful subject, by referring to the strange succession of events which had brought me to her for the third time. She stopped me wearily at the outset.

'It seems useless to say once more, what we have said on other occasions,' she answered. 'I understand what has brought you here. I have appeared to you again in a dream or a vision, just as I appeared to you twice before.'

'No,' I said. 'Not as you appeared to me twice before. This time, I saw you with the child by your side.'

That reply roused her. She started, and looked nervously towards the bedchamber door.

'Don't speak loud!' she said. 'Don't let the child hear us! My dream of you this time has left a painful impression on my mind. The child is mixed up in it – and I don't like that. Then, the place in which I dreamt that I saw you, is associated——' She paused, leaving the sentence unfinished. 'I am nervous and wretched to-night,' she resumed; 'and I don't want to speak of it. And yet, I should like to know whether you really were in *that* cottage, of all the places in the world?'

I was at a loss to understand the embarrassment which she appeared to feel in putting her question. There was nothing very wonderful, to my mind, in the discovery that she had been in Suffolk, and that she was acquainted with Greenwater Broad. The lake was known all over the county, as a favourite resort of pic-nic parties; and Dermody's pretty cottage used to be one of the popular attractions of the scene. What really surprised me was to see, as I now plainly saw, that she had some painful associations with my old home. I decided on answering her question in such terms as might encourage her to take me into her confidence. In a moment more, I should have told her that my boyhood had been passed at Greenwater Broad – in a moment more we should have recognised each other – when a trivial interruption suspended the words on my lips. The child ran out of the bedchamber with a quaintly-shaped key in her hand.

'What is this?' she asked, as she approached me.

'My key,' I answered, recognising one of the things which she had taken out of my pockets.

'What does it open?'

'The cabin door, on board my boat.'

'Take me to your boat.'

Her mother interposed. A new discussion followed, on the question of going, or not going, to bed. By the time the little creature had left us again, with permission to play for a few minutes longer, the conversation between Mrs Van Brandt and myself had taken a new direction. Speaking now of the child's health, we were led naturally to the subject of the child's connection with her mother's dream.

'She had been ill with fever,' Mrs Van Brandt began; 'and she was just getting better again on the day when I was left deserted in this miserable place. Towards evening, she had another attack that frightened me dreadfully. She became perfectly insensible – her little limbs were stiff and cold. There is one doctor here who has not yet abandoned the town. Of course, I sent for him. He thought her insensibility was caused by a sort of cataleptic seizure. At the same time, he comforted me by saying that she was in no immediate danger of death; and he left me certain remedies to be given, if certain symptoms appeared. I took her to bed; and held her to me, with the idea of keeping her warm. Without believing in mesmerism, do you think it likely that we might have had some influence over each other which may explain what followed?'

'Quite likely. At the same time, the mesmeric theory (if you could believe in it) would carry the explanation farther still. Mesmerism would assert, not only that you and the child influenced each other, but that – in spite of the distance – you both influenced *me*. And, in that way, mesmerism would account for my vision as the necessary result of a highly-developed sympathy between us. Tell me, did you fall asleep with the child in your arms?'

'Yes. I was completely worn out; and I fell asleep in spite of my resolution to watch through the night. In my forlorn situation, forsaken in a strange place, with a sick child, I dreamed of you again, and I appealed to you again as my one protector and friend. The only new thing in the dream was that I thought I had the child with me when I approached you, and that she put the words into my mind, when I wrote in your book. You saw the words, I suppose? and they vanished, no doubt, as before? When I woke, I found my little darling still lying like a dead creature in my arms. All through the night, there was no change in her. She only recovered her senses at noon the next day. Why do you start? What have I said that surprises you?'

There was good reason for my feeling startled, and showing it. On the day and at the hour when the child had come to herself, I had stood on the deck of the vessel, and had seen the apparition of her disappear from my view!

'Did she say anything,' I asked, 'when she recovered her senses?'

'Yes. She, too, had been dreaming – dreaming that she was in company with You. She said, "He is coming to see us, mamma; and I have been showing him the way." I asked her where she had seen you. She spoke confusedly of more places than one. She talked of trees, and a cottage, and a lake. Then of fields and hedges and lonely lanes. Then of a carriage and horses, and a long white road. Then of crowded streets and houses, and a river, and a ship. As to these last objects, there is nothing very wonderful in what she said. The houses, the river, and the ship which she saw in her dream, she saw in the reality when we took her from London to Rotterdam, on our way here. But as to the other places, especially the cottage and the lake (as she described them), I can only suppose that her dream was the reflection of mine. *I* had been dreaming of the cottage and the lake, as I once knew them in years long gone by; and – Heaven only knows why – I had associated You with the scene. Never mind going into that now! I don't know what infatuation it is that makes me trifle in this way with old recollections which affect me painfully in my present position. We were talking of the child's health – let us go back to that.'

It was not easy to return to the topic of her child's health. She had revived my curiosity on the subject of her associations with Greenwater Broad. The little one was still quietly at play in the bedchamber. My second opportunity was before me. I took it.

'I won't distress you,' I said. 'I will only ask leave, before we change the subject, to put one question to you about the cottage and the lake.'

As the fatality that pursued us willed it, it was *her* turn now to be innocently an obstacle in the way of our discovering each other.

'I can tell you nothing more to-night,' she interposed, rising impatiently. 'It is time I put the child to bed – and, besides, I can't talk of things that distress me. You must wait for the time – if it ever comes! – when I am calmer and happier than I am now.'

She turned to enter the bedchamber. Acting headlong on the impulse of the moment, I took her by the hand, and stopped her.

'You have only to choose,' I said, 'and the calmer and happier time is yours, from this moment.'

'Mine?' she repeated. 'What do you mean?'

'Say the word,' I replied, 'and you and your child have a home and a future before you.'

She looked at me half bewildered, half angry.

'Do you offer me your protection?' she asked.

'I offer you a husband's protection,' I answered. 'I ask you to be my wife.'

She advanced a step nearer to me, with her eyes riveted on my face.

'You are evidently ignorant of what has really happened,' she said. 'And yet, God knows, the child spoke plainly enough!'

'The child only told me,' I rejoined, 'what I had heard already, on my way here.'

'All of it?'

'All of it.'

'And you are still willing to marry me?'

'I can imagine no greater happiness than to make you my wife.'

'Knowing what you know now?'

'Knowing what I know now, I ask you confidently to give me your hand. Whatever claim that man may once have had, as the father of your child, he has now forfeited it by his infamous desertion of you. In every sense of the word, my darling, you are a free woman. We have had sorrow enough in our lives. Happiness is at last within our reach. Come to me – and say Yes.'

I tried to take her in my arms. She drew back as if I had frightened her.

'Never!' she said firmly.

I whispered my next words, so that the child in the inner room might not hear us.

'You once said you loved me!'

'I do love you!'

'As dearly as ever?'

'*More* dearly than ever!'

'Kiss me!'

She yielded mechanically. She kissed me – with cold lips, with big tears in her eyes.

'You don't love me!' I burst out angrily. 'You kiss me as if it was a duty. Your lips are cold – your heart is cold. You don't love me!'

She looked at me sadly, with a patient smile.

'One of us must remember the difference between your position and mine,' she said. 'You are a man of stainless honour, who holds an undisputed rank in the world. And what am I? I am the deserted mistress of a thief. One of us must remember that. You have generously forgotten it. I must bear it in mind. I dare say I am cold. Suffering has that effect on me – and, I own it, I am suffering now.'

I was too passionately in love with her to feel the sympathy on which she evidently counted, in saying those words. A man can respect a woman's scruples when they appeal to him mutely in her looks or in her tears. But the formal expression of them in words only irritates or annoys him.

'Whose fault is it if you suffer?' I retorted coldly. 'I ask you to make my life a happy one, and your life a happy one. You are a cruelly-wronged woman — but you are not a degraded woman. You are worthy to be my wife; and I am ready to declare it publicly. Come back with me to England. My boat is waiting for you.'

She dropped into a chair; her hands fell helplessly into her lap.

'How cruel!' she murmured; 'how cruel to tempt me!' She waited a little, and recovered her fatal firmness. 'No!' she said, 'if I die in doing it, I can still refuse to disgrace you. Leave me, Mr Germaine. You can show me that one kindness more. For God's sake, leave me!'

I made a last appeal to her tenderness.

'Do you know what my life is, if I live without you?' I asked. 'My mother is dead. There is not a living creature left in the world whom I love, but you. And you ask me to leave you! Where am I to go to? what am I to do? You talk of cruelty! Is there no cruelty in sacrificing the happiness of my life to a miserable scruple of delicacy, to an unreasoning fear of the opinion of the world? I love you — and you love me. There is no other consideration worth a straw. Come back with me to England! come back and be my wife!'

She dropped on her knees, and, taking my hand, put it silently to her lips. I tried to raise her. It was useless: she steadily resisted me.

'Does this mean No?' I asked.

'It means,' she said, in faint broken tones, 'that I prize your honour beyond my happiness. If I marry you, your career is destroyed by your wife — and the day will come when you will tell me so. I can suffer — I can die — but I can *not* face such a prospect as that. Forgive me, and forget me. I can say no more!'

She let go of my hand, and sank on the floor. The utter despair of that action told me, far more eloquently than the words which she had just spoken, that her resolution was immovable. She had deliberately separated herself from me; her own act had parted us for ever.

CHAPTER XXXIV

THE TWO DESTINIES

I made no movement to leave the room; I let no sign of sorrow escape me. My heart was hardened against the woman who had so obstinately rejected me. I stood looking down at her with a merciless anger, the bare remembrance of which fills me at this day with a horror of myself. There is but one excuse for me. The shock of that last overthrow of the only hope that held me to life was more than my reason could endure. On that dreadful night (whatever I may have been at other times), I myself believe it – I was a maddened man.

I was the first to break the silence.

'Get up,' I said coldly.

She lifted her face from the floor, and looked at me doubting whether she had heard aright.

'Put on your hat and cloak,' I resumed. 'I must ask you to go back with me as far as the boat.'

She rose slowly. Her eyes rested on my face with a dull bewildered look.

'Why am I to go with you to the boat?' she asked.

The child heard her. The child ran up to us with her little hat in one hand, and the key of the cabin in the other.

'I'm ready!' she said. 'I will open the cabin door.'

Her mother signed to her to go back to the bedchamber. She went back as far as the door which led into the courtyard, and waited there listening. I turned coldly to Mrs Van Brandt, and answered the question which she had addressed to me.

'You are left,' I said, 'without the means of getting away from this place. In two hours more, the tide will be in my favour, and I shall sail at once on the return voyage. We part, this time, never to meet again. Before I go, I am resolved to leave you properly provided for. My money is in my travelling-bag in the cabin. For that reason, I am obliged to ask you to go with me as far as the boat.'

'I thank you gratefully for your kindness,' she said. 'I don't stand in such serious need of help as you suppose.'

'It is useless to attempt to deceive me,' I proceeded. 'I have spoken with the head-partner of the house of Van Brandt, at Amsterdam; and I know exactly what your position is. Your pride must bend low enough to take from my hands the means of subsistence for yourself and your child. If I had died in England——'

I stopped. The unexpressed idea in my mind was to tell her that she would inherit a legacy under my Will, and that she might quite as becomingly take money from me in my lifetime as take it from my executors after my death. In forming this thought into words, the associations which it called naturally into being, revived in me the memory of my contemplated suicide in the lake. Mingling with the remembrances thus aroused, there rose in me, unbidden, a Temptation so unutterably vile, and yet so irresistible in the state of my mind at the moment, that it shook me to the soul. 'You have nothing to live for, now that she has refused to be yours,' the fiend in me whispered. 'Take your leap into the next world – and make the woman whom you love take it with you!' While I was still looking at her – while the last words I had spoken to her faltered on my lips – the horrible facilities for the perpetration of the double crime revealed themselves enticingly to my view. My boat was moored in the one part of the decaying harbour in which deep water still lay at the foot of the quay. I had only to induce her to follow me when I stepped on deck, to seize her in my arms, and to jump overboard with her before she could utter a cry for help. My drowsy sailors, as I knew by experience, were hard to wake and slow to move even when they were roused at last. We should both be drowned before the youngest and the quickest of them could get up from his bed and make his way to the deck. Yes! We should both be struck together out of the ranks of the living, at one and the same moment! And why not? She, who had again and again refused to be my wife – did she deserve that I should leave her free to go back perhaps for the second time to Van Brandt? On the evening when I had saved her from the waters of the Scotch river, I had made myself master of her fate. She had tried to destroy herself by drowning – she should drown now, in the arms of the man who had once thrown himself between her and death!

Self-abandoned to such atrocious reasoning as this, I stood face to face with her, and returned deliberately to my unfinished sentence.

'If I had died in England, you would have been provided for by my Will. What you would have taken from me then, you may take from me now. Come to the boat.'

A change passed over her face as I spoke; a vague doubt of me began to show itself in her eyes. She drew back a little, without making any reply.

'Come to the boat!' I reiterated.

'It is too late.' With that answer she looked across the room at the child, still waiting by the door. 'Come, Elfie!' she said, calling to the little creature by one of her favourite nick-names. 'Come to bed.'

I too looked at Elfie. Might she not (I asked myself) be made the innocent means of forcing her mother to leave the house? Trusting to the child's fearless character and her eagerness to see the boat, I suddenly opened the door. As I had anticipated, she instantly ran out. The second door, leading into the square, I had not closed when I entered the court-yard. In another moment, Elfie was out in the square, triumphing in her freedom. The shrill little voice broke the deathlike stillness of the place and hour, calling to me again and again to take her to the boat.

I turned to Mrs Van Brandt. The stratagem had succeeded. Elfie's mother could hardly refuse to follow when Elfie led the way.

'Will you go with us?' I asked. 'Or must I send the money back by the child?'

Her eyes rested on me for a moment with a deepening expression of distrust – then looked away again. She began to turn pale. 'You are not like yourself to-night,' she said. Without a word more, she took her hat and cloak, and went out before me into the square. I followed her, closing the doors behind me. She made an attempt to induce the child to approach her. 'Come, darling,' she said enticingly, 'come, and take my hand.'

But Elfie was not to be caught: she took to her heels, and answered from a safe distance. 'No,' said the child, 'you will take me back and put me to bed.' She retreated a little farther, and held up the key. 'I shall go first,' she cried, 'and open the door!'

She trotted off in the direction of the harbour, and waited for us at the corner of the street. Her mother suddenly turned, and looked close at me under the light of the stars.

'Are the sailors on board the boat?' she asked.

The question startled me. Had she any suspicion of my purpose? Had my face warned her of lurking danger, if she went to the boat? It was impossible! The more likely motive for her enquiry was to find a new excuse for not accompanying me to the harbour. If I told her that the men were on board, she might say, 'Why not employ one of your sailors to bring the money to me at the house?' I anticipated the suggestion in making my reply.

'They may be honest men,' I said, watching her carefully. 'But I don't know them well enough to trust them with money.'

To my surprise, she watched me just as carefully on her side, and deliberately repeated her question.

'Are the sailors on board the boat?'

I thought it wise to yield. I answered 'Yes,' and paused to see what would follow. My reply seemed to rouse her resolution. After a moment's consideration, she turned towards the place at which the child was waiting for us. 'Let us go, as you insist on it,' she said quietly. I made no further remark. Side by side, in silence, we followed Elfie on our way to the boat.

Not a human creature passed us in the streets; not a light glimmered on us from the grim black houses. Twice, the child stopped, and (still keeping slily out of her mother's reach) ran back to me, wondering at my silence. 'Why don't you speak?' she asked. 'Have you and mamma quarrelled?'

I was incapable of answering her. I could think of nothing but my contemplated crime. Neither fear nor remorse troubled me. Every better instinct, every nobler feeling that I had once possessed, seemed to be dead and gone. Not even a thought of the child's future troubled my mind. I had no power of looking on farther than the fatal leap from the boat: beyond that, there was an utter blank. For the time being – I can only repeat it – my moral sense was obscured, my mental faculties were thrown completely off their balance. The animal part of me lived and moved as usual; the viler animal instincts in me plotted and planned – and that was all. Nobody, looking at me, would have seen anything but a dull quietude in my face, an immovable composure in my manner. And yet, no madman was ever fitter for restraint, or less responsible morally for his own actions, than I was at that moment.

The night air blew more freshly on our faces. Still led by the child, we had passed through the last street – we were out on the empty open space which was the landward boundary of the harbour. In a minute more, we stood on the quay, within a step of the gunwale of the boat.

I noticed a change in the appearance of the harbour since I had seen it last. Some fishing boats had come in during my absence. They were moored, some immediately astern and some immediately ahead of my own vessel. I looked anxiously to see if any of the fishermen were on board and stirring. Not a living being appeared anywhere. The men were on shore with their wives and their families.

Elfie held out her arms, to be lifted on board my boat. Mrs Van Brandt stepped between us as I stooped to take her up.

'We will wait here,' she said, 'while you go into the cabin and get the money.'

Those words placed it beyond all doubt that she had her suspicions of me – suspicions, probably, which led her to fear, not for her life, but for her freedom. She might dread being kept a prisoner in the boat, and being carried away by me against her will. More than this, she could not thus far possibly apprehend. The child saved me the trouble of making any remonstrance. She was determined to go with me. 'I must see the cabin!' she cried, holding up the key. 'I must open the door myself!'

She twisted herself out of her mother's hands, and ran round to the other side of me. I lifted her over the gunwale of the boat in an instant. Before I could turn round, her mother had followed her, and was standing on the deck.

The cabin-door, in the position which she now occupied, was on her left hand. The child was close behind her. I was on her right. Before us was the open deck, and the low gunwale of the boat overlooking the deep water. In a moment we might step across; in a moment we might take the fatal plunge. The bare thought of it brought the mad wickedness in me to its climax. I became suddenly incapable of restraining myself. I threw my arm round her waist with a loud laugh. 'Come!' I said, trying to drag her across the deck. 'Come, and look at the water!'

She released herself, by a sudden effort of strength that astonished me. With a faint cry of horror, she turned to take the child by the hand and get back to the quay. I placed myself between her and the side of the boat, and cut off her retreat in that way. Still laughing, I asked what she was frightened about. She drew back, and snatched the key of the cabin-door out of the child's hand. The cabin behind her was the one place of refuge now left to which she could escape from the deck of the boat. In the terror of the moment, she never hesitated. She unlocked the door, and hurried down the two or three steps which led into the cabin, taking the child with her. I followed them; conscious that I had betrayed myself – yet still obstinately, stupidly, madly bent on carrying out my purpose. 'I have only to behave quietly,' I thought to myself; 'and I shall persuade her to go on deck again.'

My lamp was burning as I had left it; my travelling bag was on the table. Still holding the child, she stood pale as death, waiting for me. Elfie's wondering eyes rested enquiringly on my face as I approached. She looked half inclined to cry: the suddenness of the mother's action had frightened the child. I did my best to compose her, before I spoke to her mother. I pointed out the different objects which were likely to interest her in the cabin. 'Go and look at them,' I said. 'Go and amuse yourself, Elfie.'

The child still hesitated. 'Are you angry with me?' she asked.

'No! no!'

'Are you angry with mamma?'

'Certainly not!' I turned to Mrs Van Brandt. 'Tell Elfie if I am angry with you,' I said.

She was perfectly aware, in her critical position, of the necessity of humouring me. Between us, we succeeded in composing the child. She turned away to examine in high delight the new and strange objects which surrounded her. Meanwhile, her mother and I stood together, looking at each other by the light of the lamp, with an assumed composure which hid our true faces like a mask. In that horrible situation, the grotesque and the terrible, always together in this strange life of ours, came together now. On either side of us the one sound that broke the sinister and threatening silence, was the lumpish snoring of the sleeping captain and crew.

She was the first to speak.

'If you wish to give me the money,' she said, trying to propitiate me in that way, 'I am ready to take it now.'

I unlocked my travelling bag. As I looked into it for the leather case which held my money, my overpowering desire to get her on deck again, my mad impatience to commit the fatal act, became once more too strong to be controlled.

'We shall be cooler on deck,' I said. 'Let us take the bag up there.'

She showed wonderful courage. I could almost see the cry for help rising to her lips. She repressed it; she had still presence of mind enough to foresee what might happen before she could rouse the sleeping men.

'We have a light here to count the money by,' she answered. 'I don't feel at all too warm in the cabin. Let us stay here a little longer. See how Elfie is amusing herself!'

Her eyes rested on me as she spoke. Something in the expression of them quieted me for the time. I was able to pause and think. I might take her on deck by main force, before the men could interfere. But her cries would rouse them; they would hear the splash in the water; and they might be quick enough to rescue us. It would be wiser to wait a little, and trust to my cunning to delude her into leaving the cabin of her own accord. I put the bag back on the table, and began to search for the leather money-case. My hands were strangely clumsy and helpless. I could only find the case, after scattering half the contents of the bag on the table. The child was near me at the time, and noticed what I was doing.

'Oh, how awkward you are!' she burst out in her frankly fearless way. 'Let me put your bag tidy. Do, please!'

I granted the request impatiently. Elfie's restless desire to be always doing something (instead of amusing me as usual) irritated me now. The interest that I had once felt in the charming little creature was all gone. An innocent love was a feeling that was stifled in the poisoned atmosphere of my mind, that night.

The money I had with me was mostly composed of notes of the Bank of England. I set aside the sum that would probably be required to take a traveller back to London; and I put all that remained into the hands of Mrs Van Brandt. Could she still suspect me of concealing a design on her life, after that?

'I can communicate with you in the future,' I said, 'through Messrs Van Brandt of Amsterdam.'

She took the money mechanically. Her hand trembled; her eyes met mine with a look of piteous entreaty. She tried to revive my old tenderness for her – she made a last appeal to my forbearance and consideration.

'We may part friends,' she said, in low trembling tones. 'And as friends we may meet again, when time has taught you to think forgivingly of what has passed between us to-night!'

She offered me her hand. I looked at her without taking it. Her motive was plain. Still suspecting me, she had tried her last chance of getting safely on shore!

'The less we say of the past the better,' I answered with ironical politeness. 'It is getting late. And you will agree with me that Elfie ought to be in her bed.' I looked round at the child, still busy with both hands in my bag, trying to put it in order. 'Be quick, Elfie!' I said, 'your mamma is going away.' I opened the cabin door, and offered my arm to Mrs Van Brandt. 'This boat is my house, for the time being,' I resumed. 'When ladies take leave of me after a visit, I escort them to the deck. Pray take my arm!'

She started back. For the second time, she was on the point of crying for help – and for the second time she kept that last desperate alternative in reserve.

'I haven't seen your cabin yet,' she said; her eyes wild with fear, a forced smile on her lips, as she spoke. 'There are several little things here that interest me. I want another minute or two to look at them.'

She turned away to get nearer to the child, under pretence of looking round the cabin. I stood on guard before the open door, watching her. She made a second pretence – she noisily overthrew a chair, as if by accident, and then waited to discover whether her trick had succeeded in waking the men. The heavy snoring went on; not a sound of a person moving was audible on either side of us.

'My men are heavy sleepers!' I said, smiling significantly. 'Don't be alarmed! you have not disturbed them. Nothing wakes these Dutch sailors when they are once safe in port.'

She made no reply. My patience was exhausted. I left the door, and advanced towards her. She retreated in speechless terror, passing behind the table, to the end of the cabin. I followed her until she had reached the extremity of the room, and could get no farther. She met the look I fixed on her – she shrank into a corner and called for help. In the deadly terror that possessed her she lost the use of her voice. A low hoarse moaning, hardly louder than a whisper, was all that passed her lips. Already, in imagination, I stood with her on the gunwale, I felt the cold contact of the water – when I was startled by a cry behind me. I turned round. The cry had come from Elfie. She had apparently just discovered some new object in the bag; she was holding it up in admiration, high above her head. 'Mamma! mamma!' the child cried excitedly, 'look at this pretty thing! Oh, do, do, do ask him if I may have it!'

Her mother ran to her, eager to seize the poorest excuse for getting away from me. I followed; I stretched out my hands to seize her. She suddenly turned round on me, a woman transformed! A bright flush was on her face; an eager wonder sparkled in her eyes. Snatching Elfie's coveted object out of the child's hand, she held it up before me. I saw it under the lamp-light. It was my little forgotten keepsake – the Green Flag.

'How came you by this?' she asked, in breathless anticipation of my reply. Not the slightest trace was left in her face of the terror that had convulsed it barely a minute since! 'How came you by this?' she repeated, seizing me by the arm and shaking me, in the ungovernable impatience that possessed her.

My head turned giddy; my heart beat furiously under the conflict of emotions that she had roused in me. My eyes were riveted on the green flag. The words that I wanted to speak were words that refused to come to me. I answered mechanically, 'I have had it since I was a boy.'

She dropped her hold on me, and lifted her hands with a gesture of ecstatic gratitude. A lovely angelic brightness flowed like light from heaven over her face. For one moment, she stood enraptured. The next, she clasped me passionately to her bosom, and whispered in my ear, 'I am Mary Dermody – I made it for You!'

The shock of discovery, following so closely on all that I had suffered before it, was too much for me. I sank, and fainted in her arms.

When I came to myself, I was lying on my bed in the cabin. Elfie was playing with the green flag; and Mary was sitting by me with my hand in hers. One long look of love passed silently from her eyes to mine – from mine to hers. In that look, the kindred spirits were united again; the Two Destinies were fulfilled.

THE FINALE

THE WIFE WRITES, AND CLOSES THE STORY

The prelude to 'The Two Destinies' began with a little narrative, which you may have forgotten by this time.

The narrative was written by myself – a citizen of The United States, visiting England with his wife. It described a dinner-party, at which we were present, given by Mr and Mrs Germaine in celebration of their marriage; and it mentioned the circumstances under which we were entrusted with the Story which has just come to an end in these pages. Having read the manuscript, it was left to us (as you may now remember) to decide whether we should continue our friendly intercourse with Mr and Mrs Germaine, or not.

At three o'clock, P.M. we closed the last leaf of the story. Five minutes later I sealed it up in its cover, my wife put her bonnet on – and there we were, bound straight for Mr Germaine's house, when the servant brought a letter into the room addressed to my wife.

She opened it – looked at the signature – and discovered that it was 'Mary Germaine.' Seeing this, we sat down, side by side, to read the letter before we did anything else.

On reflection, it strikes me that you may do well to read it too. Mrs Germaine is surely, by this time, a person in whom you feel some interest. And she is, on that account as I think, the fittest person to close the Story. Here is her letter:

'Dear Madam – or, may I say, dear friend? – be prepared, if you please, for a little surprise. When you read these lines, we shall have left London on our way to the Continent.

'After you went away last night, my husband decided on taking this journey. Seeing how keenly he felt the insult offered to me by the ladies whom we had asked to our table, I willingly agreed to our sudden departure. When Mr Germaine is far away from his false friends, my experience of him tells me that he will recover his tranquillity. That is enough for me.

'My little daughter goes with us of course. Early this morning, I drove to the school in the suburbs at which she is being educated, and took her away with me. It is needless to say that she was delighted at the prospect of travelling. She shocked the school-mistress by waving her hat over her head, and crying "Hooray!" like a boy. The good lady was very careful to inform me that my daughter could not possibly have learnt to cry "Hooray," in *her* house.

'You have probably by this time read the narrative which I committed to your care. I hardly dare ask how I stand in your estimation now. Is it possible that I might have seen you and your good husband, if we had not left London so suddenly? As things are, I must tell you in writing, what I should infinitely have preferred saying to you, with your friendly hand in mine.

'Your knowledge of the world has, no doubt, already attributed the absence of the ladies at our dinner-table to some report affecting my character. You are quite right. While I was taking Elfie away from her school, my husband called on one of his friends who dined with us (Mr Waring), and insisted on an explanation. Mr Waring referred him to the woman who is known to you, by this time, as Mr Van Brandt's lawful wife. In her intervals of sobriety, she possesses some musical talent; Mrs Waring had met with her at a concert for a charity; and had been interested in the story of her "wrongs," as she called them. My name was of course mentioned. I was described as "a cast-off mistress of Van Brandt," who had persuaded Mr Germaine into disgracing himself by marrying her, and becoming the step-father of her child. Mrs Waring thereupon communicated what she had heard to other ladies who were her friends. The result you saw for yourselves when you dined at our house.

'I inform you of what has happened without making any comment. Mr Germaine's narrative has already told you that I foresaw the deplorable consequences which might follow our marriage, and that I over and over again (God knows at what cost of misery to myself), refused to be his wife. It was only when my poor little green flag had revealed us to each other, that I lost all control over myself. The old time on the banks of the lake came back to me; my heart hungered for its darling of happier days; and I said Yes, when I ought, as you may think, to have still said No. Will you take poor old Dame Dermody's view of it – and believe that the kindred spirits once re-united, could be parted no more? Or will you take my view, which is simpler still? I do love him so dearly; and he is so fond of me!

'In the meantime, our departure from England seems to be the wisest course that we can adopt. As long as this woman lives, she will say again of me, what she has said already, whenever she can find the opportunity. My child might hear the reports about her mother, and might be injured by them when she gets older. We propose to take up our abode, for a time at least, in the neighbourhood of Naples. Here, or farther away yet, we may hope to live without annoyance, among a people whose social law is the law of mercy. Whatever may happen, we have always one last consolation to sustain us – we have love.

'You talked of travelling on the Continent, when you dined with us. If you should wander our way, the English consul at Naples is a friend of my husband's, and he will have our address. I wonder whether we shall ever meet again? It does seem hard to charge the misfortunes of my life on me, as if they were my faults.

'Speaking of my misfortunes, I may say before I close this letter, that the man to whom I owe them, is never likely to cross my path again. The Van Brandts of Amsterdam have received certain information that he is now on his way to New Zealand. They are determined to prosecute him, if he returns. He is little likely to give them the opportunity.

'The travelling-carriage is at the door – I must say good-bye. My husband sends to you both his kindest regards and best wishes. His manuscript will be quite safe (when you leave London) if you send it to his bankers at the address enclosed. Think of me sometimes – and think of me kindly. I appeal confidently to *your* kindness, for I don't forget that you kissed me at parting. Your grateful friend (if you will let her be your friend),

'MARY GERMAINE'

We are rather impulsive people in the United States; and we decide on long journeys by sea or land, without making the slightest fuss about it. My wife and I looked at each other, when we had read Mrs Germaine's letter.

'London is dull,' I remarked – and waited to see what came of it.

My wife read my remark the right way directly.

'Suppose we try Naples?' she said.

That is all. Permit us to wish you good-bye. We are off to Naples.

THE FALLEN LEAVES

WILKIE COLLINS

Banished from the Christian Community at Tadmor, Illinois, after a scandalous liaison, Amelius Goldenheart is sent to England with a letter of introduction to John Farnaby of the City of London. On arrival, he makes his way to Farnaby's residence, but his reception is somewhat unwelcoming. While Farnaby tolerates him, his wife seeks from every new visitor the answer to the long ago disappearance of her child, stolen from her, while their niece, who lives with them, is kept away from him. Yet, after one glimpse of Regina he finds himself captivated.

Increasingly troubled, and drawn into the web of the Farnabys' own unhappiness, he wonders if yet again he is to be involved with one of the 'Fallen Leaves' – those who have toiled hard after happiness, but have gathered nothing but disappointment. Alone in London, and longing to further his relationship with the beautiful Regina, he confides in Rufus Dingwell, who he met and befriended on his passage over. But Rufus has his own opinion as to the wisdom of Amelius's love for Regina, and fears his friend may be let down once again. . . .

MAN AND WIFE

WILKIE COLLINS

The daughter of a woman unjustifiably cast aside by her mulish husband and facing social disgrace when he contrives to announce their marriage invalid on a point of ceremony, Anne Silvester is taken into the household of her mother's childhood friend, Lady Lundie. Blanche, Lady Lundie's sweet-natured daughter, becomes inseparable from Anne – as their mothers were many years before. When Anne falls in love with manipulative social climber Geoffrey Delamayn it seems as if she is about to relive her mother's mistakes. Manoeuvred into an intolerable situation by the heartless Geoffrey, whose interests lie only in himself as an aspiring athlete and in the acquisition of money, Anne flees – to find that her honourable actions avail her nothing. . . .

Two main themes occupy Wilkie Collins in this novel of social mores: the inequality of the marriage laws and the spread of brutality among 'gentlemen' who practise violent and self-aggrandizing sports. In what is perhaps his most outspoken work he offers a treatise on the social problems rife among his contemporaries and an exposé of the myths of social status.

THE NEW MAGDALEN

WILKIE COLLINS

Caught up in the midst of the war between Germany and France are two very different women: Grace Roseberry, en route to England and the care of a Lady Janet following her father's death; and Mercy Merrick who, unable to avoid the stigma of her past as a fallen woman and ex-convict, now pursues a role for herself as a nurse. As the guns fire around them, night falls. Then Grace is hit by a loose shell.

Seizing what may be her only chance to escape her past, Mercy travels to England assuming Grace's identity. But just as it seems that Mercy may at last have found both security and happiness, Lady Janet's nephew turns up, not only immediately disturbing and attracting her, but bringing with him a mysterious companion. . . .

In The New Magdalen, one of his later novels, Wilkie Collins explores contemporary attitudes to fallen women, while weaving a skilful tale from the twists of fate and fortune.

VANESSA

HUGH WALPOLE

'The most moving of all the four volumes . . . a beautiful love story.'
                                                    The Sunday Times

Vanessa had loved Benjie from the moment she had first seen him. Everyone said that he was no good, but disreputable and wild, but Vanessa had Benjie in her blood and she vowed never to betray him. But then her father dies in tragic circumstances, a distance comes between them, and it seems that she and Benjie will never be reunited. . . .

The last of the Herries Chronicles, this unforgettable novel takes the reader from the triumphant success of Judith's 100th birthday party, through the turmoil and terror of the Boer War to the disillusionment of the 1930s. Enriched by vivid descriptions of the wild Cumberland countryside which provides its setting, Vanessa is above all a tale of jealous passions, where the past is never dead and the spirit of Rogue Herries lives on.

THE FORTRESS

HUGH WALPOLE

'The canvas is huge, but something is happening; there is movement, colour, life, in every square inch of it. There is not one tired, listless page.'   J. B. Priestley

'It had been the wish of her whole life to flee from all the Herries but Walter Herries had challenged her and she had taken up the challenge.' Judith Paris, now nearing fifty, returns to the Lakes to confront the bitter feud between the two branches of the Herries family. Walter, now living in Westaways, and as powerful as he is determined, wants to own Fell House, which once belonged to his father, but which is now home to the defenceless Jennifer and her children. To this end he ensures that everything Jennifer plans to improve her situation meets with failure, and he begins to build the huge house known as The Fortress which will overshadow her land. His one weakness is his children, whom he loves with a fierce affection, but will they too be drawn into the web of love and loss?

This third volume of the Herries Chronicles, traces the rich and romantic history of an English Lake District family through fifty years – from the summer fair at Keswick to the coronation of Queen Victoria.